The VAGABOND'S LEGACY

a novel

Charles Bice

The Vagabond's Legacy
Charles Bice

ISBN: 978-0-578-02359-5

Cover design consultant: Jack McCook
Front cover photo by William Carlton
Author photo by Matthew Harrison

the vagabond's legacy

CHAPTER ONE ────────────────────────────────

"Duncan, do you realize somebody just drove off in your car?" Sarah Bugbee panted slightly after her dash across the cafeteria to the faculty table where Duncan and Erma chatted across lukewarm slabs of the Tuesday evening baked lasagna.

Erma had noticed Sarah running girlishly up the sidewalk toward the cafeteria and had said, "Here comes the president of the Duncan Flowers fan club."

"Oh, give her a break," was Duncan's response. "She's just young and energetic. You've got to admit it's refreshing to have a faculty secretary who knows how to smile."

"Well, that may be, but she seems to smile more at you than anybody else."

Sarah's announcement about his car sent Duncan hustling out to the parking lot, and sure enough the only thing in his usual parking spot was that slippery black stain that he parked on top of each morning. This was actually the first time he could observe the slick up close, and it was impressive. He considered it briefly and the thought occurred to him that this must be the main collecting pond for the quarts of oil he added to his haggard engine every few weeks. His neighbor Willie insisted that he needed a new gasket of some sort. This contemplation of cause and effect allowed Duncan momentarily to postpone confronting the disappearance of his reliable old Honda. It took yet another moment for him to realize that his grandfather's viola, stowed in its battered case and tossed onto the Honda's rear floorboard, was also gone.

Sarah reached Duncan's side at the vacant parking spot. Erma, a few steps behind, moved at a less excited velocity. For a moment the three stared into the inky blotch on the asphalt. Sarah spoke first, "Oh my God, Duncan. Someone really stole your car?"

"I guess so," Duncan said, somewhat dazed.

Erma continued to frown into the gummy stain. On the gritty, grey lot, Erma stood out in dramatic relief. She had frizzy red hair above a pale, oval face. Her luminous lipstick—today it was orange—accented the collection of bright plastic jewelry that decorated her ears, neck and wrists. The color pallet for today's theme derived from her billowing, tangerine-colored caftan. "Duncan, did your car make this mess?" said Erma.

"I guess so."

"I don't know whether to call Greenpeace or the cops." Erma's comment elicited no reaction from Duncan, although Sarah's eyebrows rose in bewilderment. Erma waved away the statement and said, "Never mind. Come on, let's go up to the office and phone the police."

The patrol car arrived at the school about half an hour later. Duncan sat in the front seat while the officer, named Dixon, dutifully completed the report and diagnosed the situation. "Based on your description of the vehicle, Mr. Flowers, I doubt they stole it to sell. They probably just wanted a car for some foolishness. I expect it'll turn up. They might not even notice your violin in the backseat."

"It's a viola."

"Oh. I thought you said a violin. We'll have to fix that." The officer squinted at his clipboard. He had it propped on top of the steering wheel where he scanned it methodically. His belly touched the bottom of the wheel. As he breathed laboriously, the combination of his stiff uniform, his leather gun belt and the vinyl seat created a sound like a ship's rigging straining on a rolling sea. Finally, he found the place. "Alright. So, it's a..."

"It's a viola."

"V-i-o-l-a." Dixon carefully edited his earlier entry on the report. "Alright. There we go. So, what's a viola exactly?"

"Well, it looks just like a violin, only a little bigger. It *is* a member of the violin family though. So is the cello and the big double bass."

"Mmhmm." Dixon seemed disappointed. He gingerly plucked out the pink copy of the report with his fleshy thumb and forefinger and handed it to Duncan along with his card. "Alright. You'll probably need the report for your insurance. And there's how to reach me. We'll let you know when we find anything."

It was eight o'clock by the time Erma dropped Duncan off at his rented two-bedroom brick house about a mile from River Road Academy. His little neighborhood was built mostly right after the Second World War as veterans made their way back to this part of Virginia to embark on family life and career. Every house on the block was some version of the same basic design. There were two floor plans, which were mirror images depending on whether the front door was on the right or on the left. Over time, the residents had worked hard to evolve the look of the neighborhood by painting, landscaping or, in some cases, building elaborate additions. Duncan rented one of the few uncorrupted by investment, embellishment or, for the most part, basic maintenance. By all appearances, the paint on the shutters and trim may have been applied during the Eisenhower administration.

The evening breeze still stung pitilessly, in defiance of the calendar's claim of April's arrival. It swarmed up Duncan's khaki trousered legs, permeated inside his olive green sport coat and rearranged his uncombed brown hair. Despite the sudden chill to his lanky frame, Duncan avoided running up the uneven cement sidewalk. On more than one occasion, usually when coming home from a bar after a few drinks, that crumbling unlit way proved perilous. One Friday night the previous autumn, returning with his date— he could never remember if her name was Stephanie or Stacy— he tripped on one of the root-buckled fragments, upending the two of them. What's-her-name was fortunate to land on her backside with a splash in the weedy bog that covered the part of the front yard that was not bare dirt. Duncan's trajectory left him prostrate on the walkway. He taught class for nearly a week after that with a big raspberry scrape on his left cheek, helping to solidify his reputation as the teacher who, even at forty, was more like one of the rambunctious students than a member of the faculty.

Now reaching the dark front stoop and beginning to fumble with his keys, he noticed a wash of light from behind his neighbor's house. That meant Willie Hamilton was at work in his garage. Duncan walked back and entered the door on the side.

"*Mister* Flowers. How is my favorite mathematician about town?" Willie intoned, looking up from contemplating the engine compartment of his latest project. His powerful, coffee-colored hands each held a pencil-like electrical probe connected by a wire to a meter box.

"Fine, Willie. How about you?"

"Oh, I've never been better. I'll tell you what; this old Ranchero has a short in it, and I aim to find it."

"I haven't seen one of those things in years."

"I got it from an old guy that's been coming to my barber shop for as long as I've owned the place. What's that, more than thirty years? He's had it up on blocks in his garage. Now he's moving into an assisted living." Willie continued applying the probes and consulting the meter. After a moment he said, "Well, I've had enough of this for tonight. How about a beer?"

After grabbing two cans from the 1950's vintage General Electric refrigerator in the corner, Willie set up a couple of folding lawn chairs. The two men sat and talked. Mostly Duncan talked and Willie listened. Duncan sat, perched on the edge of his chair with his elbows on his knees, describing the events of the afternoon. Willie leaned back, nodding sympathetically, his bull-like mass supported improbably by the flimsy aluminum frame beneath him. By nine o'clock, Duncan finished five beers to Willie's one.

"You know I got that Honda brand new the year I started teaching at River Road Academy. That was before I married Claudia even."

"Hondas are good cars," Willie said.

"You should see the oil stain in my parking space at the school. I guess with the gravel in front of my place a stain never showed up as bad."

"I've been telling you that you need a new head gasket."

"Well, I guess now I'm gonna need a new car," Duncan said. He did not feel like adding that he would also need a new viola. That was something he couldn't really replace, and he was trying not to think about it.

"Well, my friend," Willie said after a moment of silence. "I better get on in the house before Mrs. Hamilton revokes my garage privileges."

Back in his own living room, Duncan tossed his sport coat onto the futon sofa and stared for a moment at the carelessly discarded garment. The pink police report protruded from its vest pocket. He considered how to spend the rest of this inauspicious, beer-buzzed evening. Normally, his inclination when in need of comfort was to play his viola. Actually, his first reflex typically was to break out his pot pipe, but recently he was trying to redirect his old inclination into more productive activities. Playing the viola was always calming and satisfying. Now he had no viola. If ever there was a justification to fire up the bong, this was it.

He pulled down the attic stairs from the ceiling in the hallway behind the living room and clambered up into the hushed space above. He stored a variety of seldom-used items up here: suitcases, broken furniture that someday somebody might fix, holiday decorations, unused since his divorce from Claudia, and all of his illicit possessions. He kept these last items in one box in case he ever had to destroy them on short notice. He had dozens of porn magazines and videocassettes, long obsolete with the advent of the Internet. He also had a stack of nude photos he took of Claudia during their trip to Cancun. They were always near the top of the box, never obsolete. Other items included a switchblade knife he got in Mexico, a diary that he wrote in high school and, of course, Herr Doktor Puffmeister, his bong. The frosted blue water pipe had been his friend and confidant since inheriting it from Bakieboy Whitman at the fraternity house some twenty years before.

Bakieboy was graduating and taking a job at an investment bank in New York, planning to start a new and lucrative chapter in his life. He would be called Richard and he would not need Dr. Puffmeister. Duncan was humbled to be selected as the doctor's new protégé. Together, the two would graciously spread good vibrations among the denizens of the fraternity house. Duncan's room, at the very top of the house, was called the Crow's Nest and came to be the refuge to which the brethren could repair at any hour of the clock to consult with the doctor.

Returning to the living room with the bong and the snuff tin that held his meager stash of pot, Duncan had a sudden flashback to the Crow's Nest. It occurred to him that his present dwelling was not entirely dissimilar to his old abode. Although the futon was not the same one—thank God— it might have passed for it. The framed Matisse print over the mantelpiece had graced the wall above his old Crow's Nest bed that consisted of a mattress supported by a sheet of plywood and elevated by cinder blocks. He paid fifty bucks for the print at the campus arts fair, a major investment at the time. The dusty books on the shelves had been with him for the most part since college, a mixture of classic literature and math textbooks. But the main similarity was the general state of disarrangement. The furniture was a scratched and frayed collection of cast-offs that he had accumulated without regard to any decorative theme. Cheap plastic blinds hung in the windows, but no curtains. The worn, undersized Oriental rug in the middle of the floor undulated at the edges like cooked bacon. To cap off the effect, the whole room was covered in a patina of grime and lightly perfumed with mildew and cigarette smoke.

He left the items on the coffee table, shoving aside old newspapers and a running shoe, and went to the kitchen to get water for his pipe. He returned with a white plastic cup emblazoned with *River Road Ravens* in red above an image in black of an anthropomorphic Raven pointing menacingly at the viewer. Duncan dropped heavily onto the futon and settled securely into the well-worn crater on the left side, nearest the television.

"Guten Abend, herr doktor. Did you think I had abandoned you?" Duncan poured the water into the bong and rummaged through the clutter on the coffee table for a lighter. His practiced fingers deftly packed the pipe and ignited its mesmerizing fuel. Now he could relax in anticipation of the old familiar sensations. The beers already made his body feel loose and rubbery. His eyes fixed on the Matisse print directly across from him, depicting five nudes with hands clasped, dancing in a ring against a mystical blue background. The fluid and flowing figures seemed to revolve effortlessly with an air of innocence and contentment. Yet the ring was not yet complete. Two of the dancers still extended their hands toward one another to close the circle. Duncan felt light and peaceful. He felt drawn to the dance, to complete the ring. As his thoughts drifted out of his body, they took him not into the dance but to Claudia.

When they met eleven years ago, Duncan was twenty-nine and in his sixth year of teaching math at River Road Academy. He was leading what he felt to be an idyllic life that was more or less a happy continuation of university. His insouciant charm and keen intelligence allowed him to skate through serious work with little effort and to indulge in all that the local singles scene had to offer. There was even a dalliance with a fellow member of the high school's faculty, music teacher Erma Tomkins. It was she who later introduced Duncan to Claudia. The two women met while attending a chamber music performance. From the moment Duncan picked up Claudia at her apartment, he knew this was someone very different from his usual recreational partners, and very probably out of his league. He took her to the Café Provençale, his standard opening parry. It trafficked mostly in sandwiches and salads, which meant it would not set him back too much, yet the French name and continental décor tended to attract an urbane crowd.

"Erma tells me that you play the viola," Claudia said once the two were settled into their wrought iron, art nouveau chairs. The question could have easily been a throwaway icebreaker, yet Claudia seemed genuinely excited by the prospect. Nobody ever got excited about the viola. Duncan would always remember the image of her leaning forward on the other side of that round tabletop. Though they were roughly the same age, she appeared to be much younger. She was petite, with the unabashed smile and porcelain complexion of a young girl. These glowed within the frame of her wavy black hair. But it was her gray-eyed gaze, telling of an underlying seriousness and tenacity, that captivated him.

"Yes, I do play. That is when I have time. I started when I was a kid, but you know how it is when you get busy with work and everything." For some reason, his palms had begun to sweat. "And I understand you play the cello. I love the cello," Duncan said.

"The cello is my therapy. It's what keeps me sane in law school." She continued to scan his face with those clinical eyes above her childlike smile. "So what's good on the menu?"

During the following week, before Duncan escorted Claudia to the spring symphony concert he read about in the newspaper, he decided he would brush up on his musical skills. He pulled his grandfather's old viola out of the closet and took it to Duval Violins for a new set of strings. He chatted with the shop's owner, Simone Duval, while she worked on his instrument. "This is a nice old viola," she observed.

"It's just a hand-me-down from my grandfather. It's not worth much but it's been good to me."

"An instrument can be like an old friend."

"I'm getting reacquainted with my old friend," he said. "I've just met someone who has inspired me to get back into playing. I may just try to serenade her." He blushed, surprised by his candor.

Simone glanced up briefly from her work and smiled. "Now that sounds romantic. Good for you."

Rather than watching television in the evenings, he practiced his student repertoire. He showed promise as a young musician, playing in the high school orchestra and even entering the youth concerto competition where he played the first two movements of Telemann's viola concerto in G major. Coming back to it, he wasn't as rusty as he expected. The viola seemed almost to remember the pieces for him. He decided that it was time for Dr. Puffmeister to take a sabbatical, emptying out its rancid contents and placing it unceremoniously in the porn box, which at that time resided in the top of his bedroom closet.

The couple continued to see each other, and within a year they consolidated households in Claudia's apartment. His old viola hung readily accessible on the wall just above the stand that held her cello. In the evening, he would often help her study for her law courses. One night she looked at him in mock exasperation across the kitchen table that served as her de facto desk. "How is it that I work my tail off learning this stuff and you remember it better than I do?" she said.

"I can't help it. Once I've read something once, I remember it."

"That's a pretty neat trick, but it makes us mere mortals feel insecure," she said. She came around the table and sat in his lap, putting her arms around his neck. She was wearing a Westham Law t-shirt and nothing else. Her smooth complexion glowed with a faint flush.

"I certainly don't want to make mere mortals feel insecure. For the most part I try to make them feel happy with their lot," he said. Claudia repositioned herself astride him.

"Well, I have to admit, you do make me feel pretty happy."

CHAPTER TWO ———————————————————————

Duncan and Claudia lived together for two years before marrying. He broached the subject very early in the relationship, but she was adamant that she would complete her law degree and pass the bar before she would add marriage to her to-do list. The time flew by. During Claudia's second and third years of law school, each would trek off in the morning, him to teach high school math and her to study law. In the evenings, he might grade papers or help her study, or the two of them might work on one of the cello and viola duets that Simone Duval ordered for Duncan through her shop.

During the summers, Claudia clerked at the local law firm of Brice & McMillan. She had other more prestigious opportunities in DC and down in Atlanta, but declined. Duncan signed-up for a full load of teaching summer school classes and even began teaching beginning viola to some of the students in the high school strings program.

At the end of each summer, the couple took a trip. First they made a bed and breakfast tour of New England. The next year, Duncan chose the destination, and they went to Cancun. This trip was an occasion for celebration. Claudia had graduated and had accepted an offer from Brice & McMillan. She had also sat for the Virginia bar exam in July after an intensive schedule of test preparation. The firm encouraged her to take an end-of-summer break to unwind.

For the Cancun trip, Duncan envisioned a week of relaxing in the sun and sipping exotic drinks. For Claudia, travel was about seeing the sights, so they spent all but one day visiting what seemed to Duncan like every Mayan ruin within a one hundred mile radius of the resort. He did not really mind. She made it all an adventure, and her wonder and curiosity were infectious. Also, getting to watch her trot playfully around the tropical sites in short-shorts and a skimpy tank top kept his motivation level high. On the final full day of the trip, the one she conceded for "doing nothing," they strolled down the beach and took a swim in the lazy sea that dozed beneath the bright, seamless sky.

"I now know more about the ancient Mayan's than I know about my own family," Duncan said, squeezing Claudia's hand playfully beneath the surface.

"Thanks for indulging me. This trip has been just what I needed."

"Well, you earned a break." Duncan turned from the horizon and looked into those thoughtful eyes that had first transfixed him. "You've achieved the two big things on your to-do list."

Claudia smiled shyly. "I don't even know yet if I passed the bar."

Duncan put his hands on her waist. "You and I both know you passed. When you put your mind to something, you make it happen."

Her smile became placid and she put her arms around his neck. "You were beside me every step of the way."

"Claudia, I want more than anything to be with you every step of the way for the rest of our lives."

The following June 26, the two were married. For a honeymoon, they rented a villa in Aix-en-Provence. Duncan chose the destination in honor of their first date at the Café Provençale. Claudia loved all things French and always claimed that it was his selection of the café that first piqued her fancy for him. Having arranged the villa, he knew he could leave the rest to Claudia. She organized a historical and gastronomical journey through two thousand years of Mediterranean culture. Each day they would tramp relentlessly through villages, cathedrals and Roman landmarks, and each evening they would sample the best wines and dishes the region had to offer. After returning home from France, the whirlwind summer was made complete when they purchased and moved into a two-bedroom row house in the museum district. The newlywed's new home was perfectly situated between her law firm downtown and River Road Academy out in the suburbs. Each morning, she would head east in her little BMW and he would putter to the west in his Honda.

Now that Claudia was practicing law, fresh from being accepted to the bar, their lifestyle settled into a routine. No longer were evenings focused on studies. In Claudia's case, the evening was the time for her to decompress after a ten- or twelve-hour day. The pre-bedtime pattern generally consisted of a microwave meal followed by a generous dose of prime time television. They occasionally pulled out their instruments, but music became far less of a priority than it had been for them before marriage. This sedentary mode suited Duncan perfectly; it was essentially his default lifestyle anyway.

Occasionally, Claudia would prod Duncan to play a greater role in the household chores, given that he generally got home well before she did each day. This would spur him for a time, but not for long. It was not that he was unwilling to pull his weight; he simply saw little that needed doing. He considered dusting, vacuuming and ironing to be unrewarding and nearly pointless tasks. He did not mind doing laundry or running the dishwasher because of the useful results: fresh clothes and clean dishes. Putting away the clothes and clean dishes was another matter. Stowing things that you were just going to drag out again made about as much sense as making a bed in the morning only to muss it up when you slept in it again that night.

The following summer, Duncan signed on to teach just one afternoon summer school class plus a couple of time slots for beginning violists. Depending on the day, he had to be in either at eleven in the morning or one in the afternoon. He was always finished by four o'clock.

"So, are you enjoying your summer vacation," Claudia asked one evening as she gathered up their dinner plates. His was the oven-roasted beef while she dined on grilled chicken Caesar.

Duncan loved that they could each choose independently, like in a restaurant, and if Claudia would only allow them to eat out of the microwave dishes that came in the packaging, there would be almost no clean-up.

"Being able to take it easy in the summer is what first attracted me to teaching," Duncan said. He aimed the remote control at the television and squinted one eye as if a perfect bulls-eye were necessary to turn it on.

"Do you have any plans to use your spare time for any other endeavors?"

"I'm teaching math. I'm teaching viola. What else should I be doing?" He flipped the channels distractedly.

"You teach full-time during nine months of the year. I was just asking if you had thought about ways to make the most out of the summer months."

"Claudia," Duncan said impatiently. "I'm not like you. I don't need to *make the most* out of everything."

"Okay. That's fine, but I don't have time to work from seven in the morning until seven at night and still buy the groceries and keep this house looking presentable."

"Presentable? To whom? Our place looks fine. What are you so up tight about?"

"Up tight? I'll tell you what I'm *up tight* about. You don't seem to want to put out any effort around the house. This is supposed to be a partnership, but I'm the one doing all the work."

"What work? You invent work and then drive yourself crazy trying to get it all done. I'm not getting sucked into that cycle because it never ends."

"Look at this room. It looks like a fraternity house. There are three days worth of newspapers on the coffee table, not to mention the empty beer cans. Your sweatshirt has been draped over that chair for a week and I can write my name in the dust on the mantelpiece."

"So what? Why get worked up over a few imperfections. Life's too short," Duncan said. Claudia didn't' respond. She stood over him, hands on hips, glowering. Duncan feigned interest in the commercial for a pill designed to deliver on-demand erections. Claudia did not move and her glare was undiminished. Finally, Duncan got up from the sofa. "Fine. Okay. I'm straightening things up."

The two continued in the margins of discontentment throughout the summer, with the occasional flare-up acting to prompt temporary, superficial remediation. Duncan stopped by Duval Violins one afternoon to browse the sheet music. Neither he nor Claudia had picked up their instruments in months. Simone Duval stood behind the counter writing something on a yellow legal pad. "Well hello, stranger," Simone said with a smile. "I was beginning to think my favorite violist had skipped town."

"Hi, Simone. Yeah, I've been out of circulation for a while. I thought it was high time I peeked in."

"I'm glad you did. Are you after anything in particular or just peeking?"

"I don't know. I was thinking about getting some more sheet music that Claudia and I could play together." And then he added, "We haven't been very good playmates recently." He felt a warm flush crawling under his scalp alerting him that once again he was blurting out more than he intended to share. What kind of dolt discusses marital problems in a violin shop?

Simone tilted her head almost imperceptibly and put her pen down on the pad. She tapped her forefinger on her chin in contemplation. "Let me think. I'm pretty sure you already have the most interesting duet pieces, " she said. After a moment, her eyes widened and she drew in a breath. "Have the two of you ever played in an orchestra?"

"Not since high school for me. I'd say the same is true for Claudia. Why?"

"Are you familiar with the Church Hill Philharmonic?" she asked.

"I suppose I've heard of them, but that's about it."

"They are a community symphony orchestra consisting of amateur musicians, mostly folks with full-time jobs, who love to play. They rehearse one evening a week and put on four concerts each year. I'd get involved myself except that running the shop keeps me tied down. But I get their newsletter and I noticed that they are getting ready to hold annual auditions. You and Claudia might be interested. It's a fun group of people."

On his way home, Duncan poked at the idea. He read the newsletter that Simone gave him. She assured him that he and Claudia would be more than capable of meeting the musical requirements of the orchestra. She said that Dr. van Winkle, the conductor, had a reputation for making the Philharmonic entertaining for players and audiences alike. By the time Claudia arrived home, Duncan decided that he loved the idea. The excitement even incited him to fold and put away the mounds of clean laundry that had accumulated over the preceding couple of weeks. Two days before, Claudia complained that their two laundry baskets were full of clean clothes and there was no longer any receptacle for clothes coming out of the dryer. Duncan's solution was to go out and purchase a third, extra large laundry basket to substantially increase their clean-laundry storage capacity. Apparently, this did not please Claudia because she only stood, arms akimbo, glaring at the new, barrel-sized, plastic basket, perched by Duncan atop the other two full baskets and crowning what was poised to become a massive pyramid of wrinkled clothing. She did not speak to him for the rest of the evening, that is the previous evening. For all he knew she was still disgruntled because, as usual in summer, he was sound asleep when she rose and left for work that morning.

"Hi, baby," he said when she walked in from her commute. "I've got a surprise for you."

Claudia was about to hang her car keys on the hook by the door, but paused with them suspended at arm's length. The last time Duncan announced a surprise, he had signed them up for twenty-eight additional cable television channels. A side effect of him being at home much of the time in the summer was that he was subject to whatever telemarketing pitch came over the phone during the day. He parroted impeccably what must have been the marketer's spiel. They would be paying the cost of two premium channels and getting twenty-six more absolutely free. One of those bonus channels was adult-only *Romp*. She suspected that Duncan filled much of his alone time ogling the wet, bronzed, silicon-enhanced women who were the exclusive focus of the network's programming. To Duncan's current announcement of a surprise, she withheld the sarcastic response that begged for release. Instead, she just stared blankly at him and said, "Okay."

"First, I folded and put away all the clothes. But that's not my surprise."

Claudia exhaled. Her shoulders deflated slightly below their suit jacket casing, and she hung her keys on the hook. "Thank you. That's a big help." She smiled in spite of herself. "What's the surprise?"

"I know things haven't been so hot between us recently and it occurred to me that at least part of it might be that we don't do some of the stuff together that we used to enjoy."

"Okay," she said.

He told her about the Philharmonic and about how it could be a great way for them to rekindle their musical passion while making some new friends in the bargain. "We each have our friends from work, but we don't really have friends that we've met as a couple. Music is kind of our shared thing. I thought maybe we could give it a try."

"Duncan, I don't know. It sounds like fun, but I just don't have a lot of time," she said. "But that shouldn't keep you from doing it."

"I want you to do it with me. I want us to do it together," he said. "It's just two hours on Wednesday nights and one concert every three months. It would kind of be like *dating*."

Professor Theo van Winkle waved his arms frenetically in front of his face as if attempting to dispel a rotten odor. His untamed eyebrows hunkered down over an operatic grimace. Here in the last few minutes of rehearsal in the Holy Trinity Lutheran Church gymnasium, Theo was approaching his weekly crescendo of animation. What he lacked in height, he made up for in loudness and perspiration. Below his glistening white crown he had tugged at the surviving band of gray-brown hair until it stood out sideways. From behind, his head resembled an ostrich egg seated in a carelessly constructed nest. "How was that oomph? That wasn't oomph. Anybody can play loud." He gripped the edges of the metal lectern before him, lifting it and smacking it onto the floor three times. "*I – want – oomph.* Let's take it from the same place. And let's make Mrs. van Winkle feel the oomph." In response to the conductor's last comment, a septuagenarian lady who was knitting in the bleachers looked up and smiled beneficently at her baton-wielding paramour.

The Church Hill Philharmonic was several rehearsals into its preparation for the fall concert, Peter Tchaikovsky's symphony number four in F minor. Despite her initial misgivings about being too busy, Claudia enjoyed taking part at least as much as Duncan did. As the musicians packed up their instruments and stacked their chairs no more than seven high along the south wall, one of the violinists strode over into the cello section.

"How do you do? I'm Nils Nilsson, violin," said the sturdy man standing over Claudia, who was on her knees fiddling with the lower buckle of her cello case. He had the robust glow of someone who might well start each morning of the year with a brisk swim in the neighborhood fjord.

"Hello," she said. She stood and hazarded a semi-smile. "Nils is it? I'm Claudia."

"I'm very glad to know you, Claudia." He added conspiratorially, "Actually, my given name is Øystein, but Nils feels more- I don't know- to the point. And it's certainly easier to spell."

The two were conversing amiably when Duncan arrived, viola case in hand. "Sorry for the delay," he said. "One of the oboists tried to put an eighth chair on one of the stacks. The custodian guy, Hanes, had to intervene. It wasn't pretty."

Claudia introduced Duncan to Nils, who welcomed the couple to the Philharmonic. He said he had been with the Philharmonic for two years and found it to be a great counterbalance to his day job as head of The Nilsson Group, a real estate development company whose silver and burgundy placards stood in front of many of the town's high profile construction projects.

"So, the Nilsson building downtown – is that you?" Duncan asked. The steel and mirrored glass Nilsson Center had the distinction of being the tallest building in town. As with most marks of ostentation, few local residents were without an opinion on the Nilsson Center.

Nils seemed mildly disappointed that Duncan and his young wife did not recognize him immediately. He likely presumed the couple would have sighted him on the first night of fall rehearsals, after which they would have driven home asking themselves, *was that HIM?* "Yes, the Nilsson Center is one of my many projects, and it remains near and dear to my heart," he said. "And speaking of projects, I have another one in mind involving music. The Philharmonic is fine, but I'd like to be able to spread my musical wings a little bit. I am starting a string quartet, nothing time consuming, just a fun little vehicle to stand apart from the crowd. The church has space available immediately after orchestra rehearsal. I was thinking of rehearsing the quartet for maybe an hour each week. I'd be honored if you would consider joining me."

Duncan glanced over at Claudia, who seemed to be appraising the intentions of this curious newcomer. He turned back to Nils. "Wow, we're certainly honored. It would be a great opportunity to play in a quartet, but unfortunately our calendar is really tight. Just doing the Philharmonic has been a stretch." Duncan felt a surge of self-satisfaction at having headed off an encroachment that might spoil Claudia's tenuous commitment to the Philharmonic.

"I know this is very sudden," Nils said. "I'm afraid I can come on a bit strong. After last week's rehearsal I decided that I would like to be able to play in a more intimate arrangement. It came to me that I would start a quartet. Once I decide what I want to do, I go do it. That is one reason I'm so successful in business, but I imagine that approach could be off-putting in the realm of string quartets. Please accept my apologies, but please also say you'll think about my offer."

Duncan was about to put paid to the matter when Claudia said, "We can certainly think about it. Can we let you know at next week's rehearsal?"

"That's wonderful," Nils said. "So, I'm holding spots for the cello and the viola. That just leaves a second violin. If you need to reach me in the meantime, here's my card."

As the couple was leaving the church parking lot in Duncan's Honda, he turned to Claudia. "I had no idea you would want to add a string quartet on top of the Philharmonic."

"You're not interested in doing it?"

"Sure, I'm interested," he said. "But I thought you weren't looking to add more stuff to your calendar."

"I haven't decided what I want to do, but it doesn't hurt to think about it. Plus, it's not a completely new thing. It's more like a small extension of something we're already doing," she said. Claudia gently squeezed high up on Duncan's thigh. The Honda's engine surged for an instant after his reflexive nudge to the accelerator. "I've enjoyed getting back into playing. I'm glad you had the idea. I was missing it and didn't even realize it."

The next day, Duncan dropped in at Duval Violins. "Well hello, stranger," Simone said from her customary perch behind the counter. She now wore her hair pulled back in a ponytail. Duncan liked her hair this way, giving full advantage to her smooth olive complexion and compassionate brown-black eyes.

"Hi, Simone," Duncan said. "I took your advice."

"You're going to have to remind me of what my advice was. I haven't seen you in what, two months?"

"The Philharmonic. You suggested that Claudia and I join," he said. "Well, we did and it has been great. I wanted to thank you for turning us onto it."

"That's wonderful, Duncan," she said. "One of these days, I'll get a sane work schedule and try it myself."

"Funny you should mention that," Duncan said, beaming with satisfaction. From beside the cash register, he casually picked up one of Simone's business cards, which identified her as *Owner, Violin Instructor.* "I also came today in hopes of returning the favor." He told her about meeting Nilsson and about the string quartet. "If you would be interested, I'd love to call Nilsson and recommend that you take the open violin slot. The one-hour rehearsal would be from nine to ten. By then, your shop is closed with plenty of time to spare."

"I don't know, Duncan."

"Come on, it would be perfect. Claudia had the same reaction when I proposed the Philharmonic. Now she loves it and she's excited about the quartet. You said you wanted play," he insisted. After a few more minutes of debate and indecision, Simone agreed.

Driving home from visiting the violin shop, Duncan phoned the number on the card he received the night before. He connected with Nilsson's assistant, Norma. "Mr. Nilsson is in New York for the day. May I help you?"

"Please just relay to him that his cello and viola players are confirmed and we have a violinist lined up for him as well. His quartet is complete."

Nils phoned Duncan that evening to express his enthusiasm at having the couple join the quartet. After some discussion he also agreed that Simone should make a good fourth. He suggested that they kick off their group in January rather than starting the new endeavor in the late fall with the holiday season fast approaching.

On the second Wednesday of the new year, the Euterpe Quartet convened for its inaugural rehearsal in the library of the church. Mr. Hanes provided them with precise instructions on proper use of the room, including the furniture (leave it like you found it), lighting (off on departure) and thermostat (do not touch). He also left them with his pager number, although he assured them that he would not be far away and that at any moment he was liable to be passing in the corridor.

"I guess that kills our plans for a water balloon fight," said Duncan after Mr. Hanes left the four of them setting up their stands.

"A man like that is worth his weight in gold. I've got a few property managers who could take a lesson from Hanes," Nils said. "But, yes, now that we are unsupervised, we can have some fun." At this, an improbably warm smile overcame the all-business expression on his wind-burned, Nordic features. "Simone, I can't believe I never knew about your shop. I'll have to drop by sometime."

"Please do. It was my father's pride and joy. I took it over several years ago when he passed away. It's a labor of love." Simone said.

"And Duncan tells me you also give lessons," Claudia said, adjusting her cello's endpin.

"I have a few students, but with just me and an assistant running the shop, I don't have a lot of capacity myself. I make the rehearsal room available for a couple of instructors I work with. They get to use the space for free and it generates traffic in the shop."

The four spent most of that first rehearsal getting to know one another and discussing what pieces they might like to work on. Nils already had the sheet music for several Haydn quartets. They all agreed that they would give themselves a few months before worrying about performing. They were just beginning to sight read one of the quartets when Mr. Hanes appeared to enforce curfew.

As agreed, they met weekly after orchestra rehearsal. Duncan and Claudia each practiced their assigned parts for twenty or thirty minutes a day, but not together. Duncan generally practiced at school in the music room. He liked to have all his work done before leaving campus for the day, whether it was grading papers, preparing lessons or, recently, practicing the viola. Years ago he got into the habit of clearing his docket before sundown. At the time, it afforded him the freedom in the evening to moonlight as a frat boy emeritus. Now he was more likely to use the free time in the evening channel surfing the boundless ocean of options offered by his cable television service. Having his viola practice out of the way also meant the living room would be open in the evening for Claudia to work on her parts.

The Philharmonic and the Euterpe Quartet created a shared social outlet for the two, but there was not the rekindling of passion that Duncan anticipated. The new activities just became absorbed into the couple's routine. There also remained the recurring theme of how the household should be kept. Claudia insisted that two adults with no children should be able to keep a tidy house while Duncan protested that life was too short for such perfectionism.

By March, the quartet had rehearsed a variety of compositions, and settled on a Haydn and a Beethoven to be their calling card pieces. That first Wednesday in March, the other three players were already set up in their places when Nils strode in with an even greater air of cockiness than was usual. Though he was the fourth chair in the Philharmonic violin section, having moved up a slot when Thelma Westmoreland retired due to bursitis, he carried himself as if he were a virtuoso concertmaster.

"Hi, everybody. Sorry I'm late," Nils said. Rather than moving into his seat, he squared up in front of the group and assumed an air of significance. Duncan glanced furtively at Simone. The two of them were amassing a collection of Nils anecdotes and he was sure she would be mentally preparing to add the forthcoming routine to the stockpile. They placed the anecdotes in two categories: *Maestro Nils* and *Magnate Nils*. In the former category were the stories relating to the quartet and the Philharmonic, like sending each member of the orchestra a holiday card with a signed photo of himself posing in white tie and tails with his violin. The caption read *Best Wishes from Nils Nilsson, Leader of the Euterpe Quartet.* The card created quite a buzz since, besides being obnoxious, at the time the quartet had not even kicked off. In the magnate category were the various stories Nils would relate about his business dealings. Duncan and Simone would occasionally try to predict how many times Nils would use the words *million* or *billion* during an evening, inevitably as monetary quantifiers. That would include variations like *multi-million* or *quarter billion*. Duncan initially sought to include Claudia in what he felt was harmless kidding about their bumptious leader, whom he actually liked, but she scolded him for acting childishly. He therefore saved his observations to share with Simone when he would drop by her shop.

Now either Maestro Nils or Magnate Nils stood confidently before the group, hands behind his back. "As leader of the quartet, I have been working behind the scenes to find the right opportunity for us to make our debut," he said. "In that regard, I have invited a very special guest to join us this evening and to say a few words. Without further adieu, let's welcome him now." Nils turned a little and inclined his head toward the library door, standing slightly ajar. The gesture of his upturned palm would have to suffice for pageantry. Duncan sensed that Nils might have appreciated having a spotlight available for the occasion, but sadly the library was underequipped.

After a moment, Theo van Winkle's voice squeezed into the room as a hollow echo from the linoleum-paved corridor without. "Nils, let me know when you want me to come in."

"Now, Dr. van Winkle," Nils said evenly. "Now is perfect."

As Theo entered the library, appearing mildly disoriented, Duncan good-naturedly played a whimsical arpeggio. Theo, unlike Nils, seemed genuinely tickled by the humorous fanfare. Duncan could tell by the way that Claudia cleared her throat behind him that she was not pleased. "Hello, friends," Theo said settling into one of the winged back chairs. "Nils invited me to sit in for part of your rehearsal. He tells me that your quartet is shaping up nicely. Something we might consider is having you play a piece to open one of the Philharmonic concerts." Reading the terrified looks on the faces of Nils's three collaborators, Theo leaned forward with an avuncular grin and rubbed his knees jovially. "Don't worry, I'm not talking about next week's concert. I'm thinking toward the June concert. I've had occasion to catch a few snippets of your labors drifting down the hallways each Wednesday night. You seem to be coming right along. Now, the June concert is a shorter than normal program. I think a nice piece of chamber music would fill out the evening wonderfully."

"I thought that when we eventually performed, it would be at something small," Simone said apprehensively. "A concert hall setting is a bit intimidating."

"Simone, I promise you," said Nils. "This is the perfect opportunity for us to launch our offering."

"Our what?" Duncan asked.

Before Nils could respond, Theo interceded with amusement. "I remember the first time I played in a quartet in front of a large audience. I was scared to death. I was used to being background music at weddings and business receptions, affairs where most people couldn't tell you afterward if there even *was* any music. Anyway, our quartet had been invited to play ahead of the Philadelphia Symphony. I was a viola player. Did you know that? I still dabble at it. Anyway, before going on stage, I was so nervous that I broke out in hives. I was clawing so violently at my neck that it looked like raw hamburger by the time we took the stage. But you know what, as soon as we set into the first measure, the whole concert hall seemed to dissolve and it was just the four of us playing the piece that we knew so well. We might as well have been playing in ... the library of Holy Trinity Lutheran Church."

Theo stayed for about half of the session, providing a few pieces of advice. He suggested that they should perform the first and fourth movements of the Haydn piece they were rehearsing. "I like what I hear. I'd love to have you play in June," he said. "Just let me know soon so we can update the program. Now, I've got to run. I don't want Mr. Hanes to try and fold up Mrs. van Winkle in the bleachers. She would skewer him with a knitting needle for sure."

CHAPTER FOUR ———————————————————

Late June and the night of the summer concert of the Church Hill Philharmonic arrived. The concert was billed as "An Evening with Saint-Saëns." A subheading declared, "Chamber Music Prelude Performed by the Euterpe Quartet." They would play one of Haydn's Russian quartets known as *The Bird*. The Philharmonic had no home concert hall. They migrated among several local venues depending on competing demands for space. Most frequently they played in the auditorium of William Mayo High School, where Theo headed the music program.

The June concert tended to be the best attended each year and this night was proving to be no exception. Some of the draw had to be attributable to the efforts of Nils, who frequently reminded his fellow players that PR was half the game whether you are developing a shopping mall or launching a quartet. This was one of many aphorisms that Duncan and Simone would be forced to cross-classify under both *Maestro Nils* and *Magnate Nils*. Nils contacted a few local journalists to create some buzz around the performance, and Duncan commented to Claudia that Nils must have been dreaming to think their performance would qualify as news. On the morning of the concert, as the couple ate bagels at their kitchen table, Claudia only smiled when a profile of Nils popped up on the channel five morning show. It lasted only about thirty seconds. Nils was interviewed standing next to one of the silver and burgundy Nilsson Group signs pronouncing banalities such as "real estate is my pride and music is my passion." During a portion of his comments, among which he plugged the quartet's world premier, the image on the screen was replaced by video footage of him playing the violin in a sumptuous study walled with books and furnished with fine antiques. He wore a navy blue cashmere sweater with a bright yellow ascot bursting forth from the collar. Duncan grudgingly admitted that Nils knew how to make things happen.

Duncan chose not to draw Claudia's attention to the article that he turned to moments later in the Leisure section of the paper. Again, Nils was the feature. The effusive piece represented him as a renaissance man who constructed great buildings, leaving open the possibility that he did so his own bare hands, and yet also played the most refined of classical instruments: the violin. He was a third generation American who emerged from modest origins to great success. He was humbled at having the opportunity to benefit his fellow man by providing him with shelter—usually in the form of Class A office space—and by offering him beautiful music by leading the Euterpe Quartet.

Waiting for the evening's performances to begin, the musicians of the Church Hill Philharmonic prepared themselves in the band room adjacent to the auditorium. Theo was relatively permissive about what members wore as long as it was some version of a black suit, white shirt and black tie for the men and a black dress or suit for the women. For those women wearing dresses shorter than calf length, black hose or stockings were required. This still left a lot of room for variety. The men could have passed variously for waiters, magicians, funeral directors or bridegrooms. Among the women, the outfits ranged from frumpy to corporate to Duncan's personal favorite, worn with pride by flutist Holly Asplund, the leather mini-skirt with fishnet stockings.

Nils gathered the quartet in the back of the band room. He wore a neatly tailored tailcoat, accented with glistening silver studs and cuff links. He took the liberty to skirt Theo's monochromatic dress code by donning a bright red carnation beside his satin lapel. "This is it, team. All we have to do is execute," he said. Nils had a way of sounding like a basketball coach or drill sergeant when he went into "leadership" mode.

"Have you seen the crowd? Theo was saying that this is the biggest turnout he's had in years," Claudia said. "It looks like your PR blitz may have boosted the audience."

"PR is half the game," Nils said.

"How long before we're supposed to go on? I think I have to use the restroom." Duncan said.

"You just went," said Claudia.

"I can't help it," Duncan said. "My stomach is doing flip-flops."

"I know what you mean," said Simone. "I've got a major case of butterflies."

At that moment a young woman carrying a clipboard and wearing a headset approached and informed the four that it was time to move to the stage where they stood in the wing while Theo gave the audience a short tutorial on Camille Saint-Saëns and on the pieces that the Philharmonic would play for them. "But before we transport you to Paris at the end of the nineteenth century, I would like us to pass through Vienna at the end of the eighteenth century," he said. "We will visit the classical period that set the stage for the romantic era and for the work of Saint-Saëns. Tonight, the Euterpe Quartet will play for you the first and fourth movements of Haydn's quartet number thirty-two in C-major, *The Bird*." Theo turned beaming and extended his arm toward the waiting cluster. By the time the woman with the headset prodded Duncan to get the group moving, Nils was already striding halfway to center stage, waving jauntily to the applauding spectators.

The performance lasted less than ten minutes. As foretold by Theo, Duncan's sick sensation quickly faded. At the end of the first movement he felt a thrill akin to making it through a terrifying roller coaster ride and wanting to stay aboard for another go. The fourth movement flew by so quickly that he wished they were playing the entire piece. Not since eighth grade when he played his grandfather's viola in front of the entire school did he feel this way. Mrs. Boykin, the music teacher at Grove Avenue Middle School, tapped Duncan to play a solo piece at the fall assembly. With her piano accompaniment, he played the allegro from Telemann's viola concerto in G-major from his Suzuki book, the one he would later perfect for the youth concerto competition. He was the only student Mrs. Boykin selected for an individual performance. Just as with tonight, he had felt a warm wave of invincibility and possibility expanding in his chest. And it did not fade completely for sometime afterward. Classmates who kidded him about the viola case that he carried up and down the hallways like a scarlet letter *D*, for dork, suddenly held him in high esteem and even envy. For a week or two at least, Duncan Flowers was a kid destined for great things.

After the Philharmonic concert, the four left the auditorium together, invigorated by the plaudits offered them in the band room by their fellow musicians. Nils declared that this milestone called for a celebration and that they should accompany him to Girardi's for a late dinner and a nightcap. Girardi's was the upscale Italian restaurant in the mezzanine of the Nilsson Center downtown. All were glowing in enthusiastic agreement when they came upon the scene in the parking lot of a catering truck with its rear end crushing the hood of Simone's Ford Taurus. It looked like an elephant relaxing on a beach chair.

Standing next to the impact site was a scarecrow of a man, motionless, with his arms raised as if reacting to an unseen bandit's shout of "freeze and put your hands on your head." He made no sign of hearing the group's approach, despite the rumble of Simone's cello case bumping on its little luggage wheels across the uneven asphalt. The four reached the spot before the man gave any sign of animation. "Oh my God. Oh my God. I can't believe this is happening," he said. "Is this your car?" As he spoke, his Adam's apple hopped up and down as if it were struggling for a way out.

"It's mine," Simone said, staring forlornly at the boxy van still sitting on her car's hood.

"I'm so sorry," he said. "I'm so fired. This is my second wreck since I got this job in January.

They agreed that they should get a police report for the insurance claim and that the driver should pull his truck forward so they could assess whether Simone's car was drivable. Simone covered her ears and looked away as the loading platform on the back of the van scraped its way off of her car. When the van was clear, the front end of the Taurus popped up feistily as if to declare that having its nose rammed into the pavement was nothing. Duncan got in and turned over the engine, which started right up, but he also established that the headlights did not work, having been smashed to bits. Not only would they need a police report, but they would also need a tow truck since by now twilight was quickly fading into night.

The collision threw a wet blanket on the idea of a celebration. "I guess we should postpone dinner," Duncan said. "Once the tow truck gets here, one of us can run Simone home."

"I'd be glad to, but I'm driving my Porsche," said Nils. "I'm afraid it didn't come with a cello compartment."

"No problem. Simone can ride with Claudia and me," said Duncan. "The Honda can swing it. Actually, Nils, we can wait with Simone if you want to head on."

"Well, I feel guilty being so useless. I'll tell you what. Why don't I at least run Claudia home?" said Nils. "Claudia, there's no sense in all three of you waiting around."

Claudia hesitated for a moment and then said, "Simone, would you mind if I went ahead? I think I feel a headache coming on, and if I get home and take a couple of aspirin I can probably nip it in the bud."

"Of course I don't mind," said Simone. "I really appreciate you all being so helpful."

While Nils and Claudia buzzed out of the parking lot in his silver roadster, Duncan fitted Simone's cello into the back seat of the Honda. The two sat down on a bench to wait. The driver of the van sequestered himself in his vehicle, assuming anew the forward stare with hands on head. His lips formed words addressed toward the steering wheel in front of him.

"Wow, what an evening!" Duncan said. He could tell Simone was downcast about her car. "Don't worry about the car. It looks a lot worse than it is. All that mangled stuff on the front just pops off. You'll be good as new."

"Do you think so?" Simone said, unconvinced.

"I'm sure of it," he said. "My neighbor, Willie, works on cars in his spare time. He says cars are like Legos nowadays. And the catering company's insurance will take care of the repairs. It's the same caterer that runs the dining hall at River Road Academy. They'll have top notch coverage."

"I know you're right," she said. "It's just such a bummer, especially on the night of our concert."

"You mean our *world premier* concert," he said wagging a finger at her facetiously. "Don't forget to use the proper PR terminology."

"Of course. You're right," she said, laughing. "PR *is* half the game."

It was nearly ten o'clock by the time Simone got the police report, and the wrecker departed with her Taurus in tow. Duncan could not help but feel sympathy for Mr. Scarecrow, who by now had received an earful from his boss and seemed to be considering the option of just walking away from the site and leaving his troubles behind with the truck. As Duncan swung his Honda out of the school parking lot, he caught a glimpse in the rear view mirror of the driver reluctantly mounting into the cab of his van.

"You're welcome to come in for a cup of tea," Simone said when they pulled up at her house. "It's the least I can offer you after spending your evening hanging out in a parking lot waiting for my car to get towed." Her house doubled as her shop. Her father modified the small, 1930's-era wood frame residence when he started the business over thirty years before. He converted the ground floor into a showroom, a workshop and a small rehearsal room. The upstairs became an apartment with a separate entrance on the side. When he ran the shop, he rented out the apartment, but it became Simone's place when she returned from college to work in the shop full time. He died of a heart attack not long after that, and she took over the shop and continued to live upstairs.

"Why not; a cup of tea sounds good," he said. "Actually, I've been meaning to have you take a look at my viola. I think my bridge may be starting to warp."

"Absolutely," she said. "Bring it up."

While the teapot heated on the stove, Simone examined Duncan's viola. "You told me you got this viola from—was it your grandfather?" she said.

"Yes, he was quite a rascal in his day," Duncan said. "Or that's the impression I've formed. He kind of lived like a tumbleweed, rolling from one adventure to another. At least the rolling part seems to be true, I don't know about the adventures. He could sure spin a yarn though. He'd talk of piloting a hot air balloon at carnivals in Mississippi and then driving cattle in Wyoming, and next he's talking about having breakfast at the Hollywood Roosevelt Hotel with Errol Flynn. He came to live with my family for a couple of years before he died. I guess I was about seven when he came. One day he gave me this viola. I don't think he really knew much about it. I'm sure it was just one of the oddities that he came across in his meanderings and for whatever reason he held onto it. He said he got it back in the thirties as a gift from a friend who didn't have any family."

"He sounds like an interesting man," she said.

"He was definitely interesting."

"And he left you a mysterious old viola."

"There's no label in it, so I don't know where it came from. He probably won it in a card game or maybe he traded a farm animal for it. Who knows? If it could talk, I wouldn't ask it where it came from though, I would ask it to tell me the real story of what my grandfather did for all the years he kicked around the country."

The pot on the stove started to whistle. Simone set the instrument down carefully on the coffee table in front of the sofa where they were sitting and went to pour the tea. "You were right," Simone called from the kitchen. "That bridge is starting to bend a little. If you'd like to leave it with me I can put a new one on for you, no charge." She emerged carrying two mugs and sat next to Duncan.

The two sat for a moment, wordlessly considering the depths of their respective Earl Grey's. Finally, Simone said, "The Philharmonic sounded great tonight. Are you and Claudia still enjoying it?"

"I suppose so," he said. "The truth is, things have stayed kind of bumpy between us for a while. I thought playing in the Philharmonic would make things better. It hasn't hurt, but it hasn't helped."

"I'm really sorry to hear that, Duncan," Simone said sympathetically. She turned to face him and rested her head lazily on the back of the sofa.

"Yeah," he said absently. He squirmed in his seat, crossing and then uncrossing his legs. Having returned to his original position, his gaze wandered across the items on the coffee table: a miniature bronze bust of Beethoven, a couple of atlas-sized, hardbound picture books on American antiques and, perched atop the books, his viola. Finally, he turned to Simone. "The quartet has been great fun. I'm glad I twisted your arm to get you to join."

Simone laughed. "You didn't twist it that hard. Who could turn down an opportunity to play violin with Maestro the Magnificent Magnate?"

"You know you're a better violinist than he is," said Duncan.

"You're sweet," she said. "I don't know about that, but I know that he's the better impresario."

Duncan took Simone's mug and placed it along with his on the little side table next to his end of the sofa. She didn't object to the confiscation. When he turned back to face her, she met his gaze with unclouded brown-black eyes. He wanted to reach out and touch her face, but he was aware that his palms were sweating. She seemed to be waiting to see what he would do. He leaned over and pressed his lips to hers. The next thing he knew they were tumbled over on the sofa. He was on top of her, still kissing her. His right hand was taking advantage of the diversion to make its way up her black silk blouse. At first, Simone was tolerant of Duncan's advance, but when it became an onslaught, she began to resist.

"Duncan, stop. Please stop. We can't do this."

He came to himself as if awakening from a hypnotic spell. He propped himself up and glanced about him. He perceived to his apparent surprise the adventures of his sweaty right hand. "Oh my God, Simone. What am I doing?" He sprung up from the sofa and backed into the coffee table, toppling it over onto the carpet. The dull crash of wooden table and tumbling books culminated with a loud knock and the reverberating twang of a C-string.

When the pair completed the excavation of the viola from the wreckage, Simone gave it a careful examination while Duncan righted the coffee table and replaced Beethoven and his literary companions. "Simone, I'm such an idiot. I don't know what got into me."

She continued to inspect the instrument, but smiled. "You're not an idiot," she said. "I like you a lot, Duncan. I think we both got a little carried away. That shouldn't keep us from being great friends."

"Really? I'm glad," he said. You must know that I'm not usually so violent. Kicking over coffee tables tends to be the exception rather than the rule."

"Well, you must have kicked it just right because your viola is virtually unscathed," she said.

"Virtually?" Duncan winced.

Simone pointed to a fresh gouge at the very top of the scroll, above the tuning pegs. "It looks like Ludwig gave your viola a head butt on the way down."

"'Tis merely a flesh wound," he said. "I suppose Beethoven was a little jealous that we chose to play the Haydn tonight."

When Duncan arrived home a little after eleven, he found the house dark except for the porch light. He assumed Claudia was in bed, nursing her headache. Trudging up the sidewalk, he could feel his chest constricting in anticipation of getting into bed with Claudia after acting like such a lout with Simone. He made his way inside and decided to have a beer in the kitchen to calm his nerves. He did not feel like sleeping, but he felt he should go up soon to join his wife. Sitting at the kitchen table, he fumbled in his jacket pocket and pulled out the program from the evening's performances. He stared absently at the familiar cover image that the Philharmonic used for all of its programs. It featured the orchestra's trademark cartoonish silhouette of a conductor with arms raised high and baton poised as if to signal a gigantic crescendo.

His eyes focused on the date of the performance. Duncan's brow crinkled slightly and he pushed out his lower lip as if trying to do arithmetic in his head. Something about the date bothered him, but he did not know what. Then he knew. His mouth dropped open in disbelief. "June 26! I can't believe I forgot our anniversary." He jumped up from the chair as if to run out of the room, but remained nailed in place, breathing heavily, his mind racing. He felt he should do something, but what does one do when he remembers his second wedding anniversary minutes before it expires? He noticed that the message light on the answering machine was blinking. Although the blinking light did not offer much promise of extricating him from his predicament, it did offer a brief distraction, like a last cigarette for the condemned.

He pressed the message button and heard Claudia's voice. "Hi, Duncan, Nils and I are going to pick up some Chinese food. Since his place is near the restaurant, we're just going to take it over there. You should come on over when you get this message. I tried information to call Simone's, but her home number isn't listed. They only had the number for her shop. Maybe you can phone her to see if she wants to come to." Claudia gave Nils's address and the message ended with the robot-like voice that always said, "End of new messages. To review old messages, press play."

The last thing Duncan wanted to do was to drive over to snobbish Tudor Forest, but he had to go. Claudia would be expecting him, if for no other reason than for a ride home, and he dared not compound his stupendous offense of forgetting their anniversary. Inviting Simone at this hour, and after what happened at her apartment, was out of the question.

Duncan had never been to Nils's house, but he assumed it would be in keeping with the other estates in the Tudor Forest fiefdom. It was probably a walled castle surrounded by a moat, Duncan thought. In fact, there was no moat, but Duncan did have to navigate his Honda between two colossal granite pillars at the entrance to the winding cobblestone drive. Nils acquired this mansion after his high-profile divorce several years before. When most men would have downsized, he apparently decided to demonstrate that the split had done nothing to diminish him. As Duncan pulled up beside Nils's silver sports car, he glanced at his watch. It was nearly midnight. He should have phoned. Claudia would be wondering what the hell was keeping him.

Duncan approached the rough-hewn, dark-stained front door, bracketed on either side by narrow, full-length windows. As he was about to press the doorbell button, ensconced in an ornate, polished brass setting, he caught a glimpse of Nils through the window. The thick, hand-blown glass made the scene inside look woozy. The hallway leading back from the front foyer opened into what must have been a large living room. Nils was seated on a small couch facing away from the front door. He was either relaxing or sleeping because his head was reclining against the back cushion with his face inclined toward the ceiling. His arms were extended along the back of the couch. His broad wingspan allowed his hands to drape loosely over the ends of the sofa.

Seeing that Nils was obviously alone and retired for the evening, Duncan hesitated. He had screwed up. He definitely should have phoned. Claudia probably tried to call him after he left, assumed he was missing in action and borrowed a car from Nils's inevitable fleet to drive home. Could Duncan be a bigger idiot? He glanced back in at the back of Nils's head. The Maestro was stirring now, actually quite vigorously. His head was lolling about like he might be gagging on something. Perhaps Nils was having some kind of dream. Or it might be a seizure. Duncan wondered if he should do something. But now Nils sat up and hunched forward. Whatever was tormenting him, it was over. Just then Claudia appeared, bare breasted and laughing, slithering up Nils's chest and kneeling astride him.

It was another two hours before Claudia made it home. Duncan could hear Nils's roadster humming away up the street as his wife entered the front door. "Duncan, you're still up?" she said. "Didn't you get my message?" She did not seem the least bit agitated.

"I got it, but it was so late," he said.

"Was there a problem dealing with Simone's car?" she said.

"No. We got it taken care of, but I stopped by her house afterward and we were chatting.

"Oh," she said. "Well, you missed some good Chinese. What did you chat about?"

"Well, she took a look at the bridge on my viola." He paused. "And then I tried to kiss her."

"You did what? What do you mean you tried to kiss her?"

"I just suddenly wanted to kiss her and next thing I knew, I had kissed her."

"So you did more than try."

"I guess I did, but she didn't know it was coming. I felt terrible."

She glared at him. He felt her anger, but he also saw a hint of triumph in her clinical, gray eyes. "Duncan, it's late," she said evenly. "My headache is getting worse and I'm going to bed. We can deal with your little adventure tomorrow."

"That's fine," he said. "Before you go, I wondered if you didn't have any adventures to tell me about." At first, Claudia demurred, but it did not take long before all the cards were on the table, and Duncan got more than he bargained for. He learned that his wife and the Maestro had been passionately involved since the quartet began. Claudia knew she wanted Nils from that first introduction at the Philharmonic. She did not plan to have the conversation yet, but while they were on the topic, she wanted a divorce.

As Claudia walked out of the room, leaving Duncan to occupy the sofa, he said, "Claudia, there's just one more thing."

"What's that?"

"Happy anniversary."

CHAPTER FIVE ———————————————————

The same evening the thief stole Duncan's car and viola, Simone Duval was working in her violin shop, standing behind the counter reviewing the packing list from a batch of new instruments delivered that afternoon. It was nearly seven and time to close up for the day. The cluster of tiny Christmas bells on the entrance door tinkled as Alejandro Alvarez slid in like an obsequious adolescent late for detention. Simone found herself more and more immune to his Latin charms. When they met, he was irresistible. He had reminded Simone of her father, whose family came from the French Mediterranean, near Spain. Alex's predecessors were Cuban.

Both men, though not tall, were powerfully built with dense, unyielding shoulders and intelligent hands that could create or crush, depending on the requirement. Similarly, both men had rugged, ruddy complexions handed down through generations and marinated in the toil carried out by those brawny shoulders and hands. Here was where Simone was beginning to recognize a breakdown in the comparison, where Alex was starting to appear as a cheap imitation of what she thought she was getting. He had certainly done his share of toil, but recently it was as if he had decided that work in any form was overrated and he was ready to move beyond it.

Simone and Alex met at the town's annual Apple Festival that is held one weekend each autumn in the shopping district a few blocks from Duval Violins. She paid a couple of hundred dollars each year to be a member of the merchant's association, which got her shop listed in various publications including those promoting the Apple Festival. On the Sunday of the festival, she had set up a booth advertizing her shop. She gave away key chains with miniature violins bearing the shop's name, phone number and web address. There was also a fish bowl where visitors could drop in a ticket for a chance to win a student violin. She figured that was a pretty good trade to be able to add a couple of hundred potential customers to her mailing list.

Simone noticed Alex well before he happened up to her booth. He wore a flannel shirt with the sleeves turned up and worn blue jeans that hugged his solid thighs. Frayed cuffs gathered at the ankles of his scuffed western boots. This man with a rakish black swath of hair swept across his forehead became a distraction to her on that afternoon from the moment her glance was drawn magnetically to him. She even considered leaving her station in hopes of orchestrating an encounter with him. The booth could survive without constant supervision. And then he was there, standing at the booth. He was asking her questions and she was laughing, probably blushing, and answering them. Later she would have no idea what was said.

As they had begun dating, Alex expressed a passion for working with his hands and especially with wood. He had gained skills in technical college and worked for a cabinetmaker for several years until he got laid off. Since then he was earning a living as a trim carpenter, but was looking to get back into something where he could do more intricate work. Making musical instruments had crossed his mind. That is what pulled him to Simone's booth. He said he had no idea he would find a beautiful woman there. He said he had expected he might meet a stooped, old man with spectacles, "like Pinocchio's dad."

Simone could hardly believe the good fortune placed before her. She was dating the most gorgeous man she had ever seen, and he wanted to learn about working on violins. Owning and running the shop since her father's death had left Simone with little spare time for anything, and she could not do it without help. To take care of basic repairs and to mind the shop when she was out, she always employed an assistant, identified in her want ads as a *music shop technician*. She usually hired recent college grads and they rarely stayed long in the low-paying job, but she liked working with young, energetic, educated people. It just meant that every year or so, she was back in the marketplace.

The arrival of Alex opened up whole new avenues for Simone, although some of those avenues were dubiously devoid of speed limits. After they had dated for a couple of months and the initial explosive passion of new romance moderated into mere burning passion, Alex began to talk of a desire to go back to school to become certified as a luthier. He had built up to this idea after spending many hours, especially on Saturdays, hanging about the shop and becoming a sort of supplemental assistant to make himself useful while waiting for the shop to close in the early afternoon. Without a certified luthier, Simone did not handle major repairs in her shop. She or her technician would do the basics like replacing bridges, re-setting sound posts or replacing strings. Complex jobs that might require opening up the body she sent out.

Simone had long weighed the idea of having a certified luthier in house, not only to repair instruments, but also to make them. Given that her shop did nicely under the existing set-up, she had never acted on the idea, but it remained an enticing vision. Now, here was Alex, the man of her dreams with the potential to make everything glow in her life. She no longer remembered who originated the idea, but three months after they met, Alex moved in with her and took the position of technician that opened when the previous incumbent left in early January for divinity school. Simone paid Alex the standard rate, but he lived rent free with her in the apartment that she fully owned. She looked forward to him enrolling in the violin making certification program offered at Patrick Henry Community College in the evenings beginning in the fall.

But now Simone wondered how she had allowed herself to get swept up in a relationship with Alex. During the more than a year of living and working together, things had not played out at all as she had hoped. The violin making training never came to be, and she wondered whether Alex thought of her as a girlfriend or just a meal ticket. "Alex, where have you been?" she said. "How long can it take to get your oil changed? We got the new shipment in and I needed you to unpack it and set up the instruments."

"I know," he said. "It was crazy. There was only one car in front of me. I thought I would be right out of there. They must have given that lady a new transmission or something."

Or something. "Alex, working in this shop is a full time job," she said. "If you want this to be your livelihood, you've got to make it a priority."

Alex put on a theatrical pouty frown. "Don't be mad with me, baby," he said, slipping behind the counter and hugging Simone from behind. "I promise, you and the shop are my priority. I just got delayed."

Simone smiled reflexively, but it quickly melted as she raised her arms to disengage from his embrace. "Alex, please. I've asked you not to do that in the shop. It's not professional."

"But this is our home, baby."

"Our home, the *apartment*, is upstairs."

"Okay, okay. You are right," he said. He moved from behind the counter. "It is seven. Why don't I take you out to dinner? If you want to go get ready, I will tidy up the workshop and lock up. What do you say?"

Alex had not yet dissolved Simone's annoyance, but she could feel it fading. "Alright," she said. "I'll go get ready. Don't forget to set the alarm."

"I got it covered," he said with a smile. Simone was trying not to look at him because she knew his smile would make her smile and that might give him the impression that his behavior was forgotten. But she also did not want him to realize that she was avoiding his gaze so she gave him a perfunctory glance. Of course, that was all it took. Alex laughed as she scurried, blushing, out of the shop.

Once she had gone and Alex could hear the sound of her footsteps in the apartment above, he pulled out his cell phone and dialed a number. After the party answered and he explained who he was, he got down to the business of his call. "I have come into possession of an extraordinary antique viola, one which I believe may have come from one of the great workshops of Cremona." He paused. "No, no. I understand you are probably getting calls everyday from someone who thinks he found a Stradivarius in his attic. I do not know if what I have is authentic, but it appears to be extremely old. It does not have any paperwork." He paused. "No, no. I understand. Anyway, it is not a Stradivarius. I found a label, not in the usual place, and it appears to be from the shop of Nicolò Amati from sometime in the 1660's." He paused, longer this time. "I can do that. No problem." He plucked a pen from the can next to the cash register and began to write on the legal pad that Simone kept there. "So, high resolution photographs. Front and back, side views. Close-ups of the scroll and peg box." He paused. "I do not have a way to photograph the label. It is nailed to the end block." He paused. "Yes, nailed. You can barely see it by squinting through the soundholes up toward the neck. I can send you what I copied down." He paused. "No, no. I understand you have to examine the viola directly. I will email you the photos and you can tell me if you think that would be worthwhile."

After hanging up, Alex folded the sheet from the legal pad and slid it into the pocket of his jeans. Glancing at his watch he flinched, realizing that Simone would be wondering what was keeping him. He had one more task to complete. He jogged quickly through the workshop to the rear entrance of the store. He opened it quietly, leaned out the door and pulled in three objects that had been left there. One looked like a violin case, only a little bigger. One was a can of spray paint. The last was a can of charcoal lighter fluid. He placed the paint and lighter fluid in the supply closet and found a secure sanctuary for the case in the rear of the cabinet below the workbench. He set the alarm at the front of the shop and went out, trotting breezily up the exterior stairs to the apartment.

After the pair returned that evening from their old standby dinner spot, Sidetracks, Alex told Simone that he would go down to the workshop to unpack and prepare the new instruments for display.

"You don't have to do it tonight, Alex," she said.

"I want to do it," he said. "I should have been there to do it this afternoon."

Gratified that Alex was seeing the error of his ways, Simone said, "Don't worry. You can just knock it out first thing in the morning."

"No. I feel bad about it," he said already moving to the door. "I will be back up before you know it."

In the close silence of the workshop, Alex extracted the case from the cabinet and placed it on the workbench. From his jacket pocket he pulled the small digital camera that Simone had given him for Christmas. After examining it for a moment to refresh his memory on how it worked, he scooted out to the front of the shop where he powered on the computer behind the counter. He returned to the workshop and set about his task with pride and precision. He had now reached an important milestone in advancing himself. Soon he would no longer be a helper, a laborer. He would not have to earn a living by the hour but by his ability simply to see the abundant treasures that those who toil do not take the time to look up and recognize.

It was over eight months ago, the previous July, when Alex realized that his plans had been all wrong, that he had been too narrow-minded. Moving from trim carpenter to luthier might be a step up the technical ladder, but that was all it was. It was another manual labor job. He could not deny that the possibility of obtaining a financial interest in the violin shop was also an attraction, but he had even come to see what a job that was for Simone, who was virtually chained behind the counter six days a week. This was a realization that came to him quite suddenly during a visit to the regional antiques show at the fair grounds.

One of the few interests Simone was able to maintain outside of the all-consuming violin shop was antiquing. It was rare that she had time to go out and explore, but the annual regional antique show at the fairgrounds was an event she never missed. When that Sunday morning in July arrived, they sat up in bed sipping coffee, as was the ritual on their one day away from violins. Alex looked for excuses not to accompany her to the show, but she insisted.

"Alex, we never seem to do anything together," she said. "This will be fun."

"We never do anything together? Don't we spend all week together in the shop?"

"You know what I mean. We should do some things besides just working."

"You know that is not all we do," he said sliding his free hand under the sheets to caress her warm, bare thigh.

"I'm not talking about that either," she said a bit impatiently. "This is something that is important to me and I just want us to share it."

That was that. Later at the fairgrounds, Alex trudged along with Simone like an ox led by a nose ring. After about an hour, Alex suggested that maybe they could split up and reconvene for lunch in the concession area. Simone took pity and decided to give him this reprieve. They set a time and went their separate ways. With no restrictions on his movements, Alex wandered about at a much faster pace than that enjoyed by Simone, who seemed determined to explore every booth at the show. He did find himself drawn into a display of civil war artifacts, including rifles, pistols, uniforms and camping implements. He even bought a three-ring, .58 caliber bullet for fifteen dollars.

After about half an hour, Alex came upon a stall displaying antique musical instruments. A brass plaque, set onto a wooden backing was propped on the table at the entrance. It declared simply, *Allegro Antiquities* with smaller text engraved below stating *Boston - London*. He found himself attracted to explore the offerings as much by the proprietor as by curiosity to learn about the antique counterparts to what he and Simone sold in the shop. Most of the sellers at the show looked rumpled and unkempt, sitting on lawn chairs as if overseeing a yard sale. They also generally exhibited an air of indifference or, in some cases, annoyance. They were the antithesis of sales people, or at least the sales people he was used to seeing in say a furniture store or car dealership. Perhaps that was the idea. In any case, the proprietor of the *Allegro Antiquities* stall stood apart from the rest.

The proprietor was speaking with a plump, sixtyish woman in a bright pink, velour tracksuit. She held a shadeless lamp, the body of which was in the form of a whimsical goose. Her interlocutor by contrast wore an elegantly tailored, double-breasted navy pinstripe suit set off by gold cufflinks, a snugly knotted burgundy tie and a flourish of white silk in his breast pocket. The woman was asking if he might have a Victorian era brass spittoon. Alex could not imagine that this man would have such a curio among his stringed instruments, and yet the proprietor treated the woman's inquiry with the utmost respect and consideration before declaring remorsefully that, alas, he had no such treasures to offer. Even as the woman departed with a grunt, the gentlemen exhibited no sign of chagrin. He merely smiled deferentially and turned to Alex.

"How do you do, sir? Welcome to Allegro Antiquities," the man said. Alex could not place his accent. It seemed not quite American, but not different enough to place it. Maybe it was just his manner of speaking, sort of theatrical.

"Hey," said Alex.

"Please feel free to have a wander around," the man said, indicating the collection on display with a sweep of his hand. "If you require any information, don't hesitate to ask. I'm James Dickerson."

Alex nodded and started to peruse the stringed instruments, some on stands, others suspended from overhead. There were violins, violas, cellos, guitars, and some others that Alex could not identify. Compared to the new instruments sold at Duval Violins, these were for the most part significantly more expensive. Alex came upon one six-stringed specimen that looked like an odd combination between a guitar and a cello. As he stood before it tugging on his chin in wonder, Dickerson stepped up casually.

"Are you a collector?" Dickerson said.

"No, not really. I have a violin shop," said Alex, indulging in a mild exaggeration.

"Do you have an interest in viols?" Dickerson said.

"This is the first time I have seen one up close," Alex said, not wanting to admit that he, supposedly a man of the trade, had no idea what he was looking at.

"Well, this is a fine example," said Dickerson in earnest. "The viol, or viola da gamba, was highly popular among cultivated circles during the renaissance. Today, there is quite a demand for them among collectors and among aficionados of early music."

"So, how do you play it?"

"It is held between the knees and bowed, like a cello, but you will notice that there is no end pin, a much later development. The player supports the instrument entirely with the legs."

"Three thousand dollars seems like a lot for an old instrument that hardly anybody knows how to play," said Alex.

Utterly unperturbed, Dickerson replied, "Actually, this instrument is not that old. It is a reproduction of a viol from the late sixteenth century made by Gasparo da Salò. I have dealt with da Salò originals and I can assure you that they fetch *many* times the price you see before you."

"So, where do you get an original?"

"They are typically held in private or public collections," Dickerson said. "But as with any market, there is always some level of activity depending on who has money and who needs it. As a qualified appraiser I often have the privilege of assisting with transactions that involve rare antique instruments."

Alex glanced around the stall and then out into the flea market beyond. "It seems like you would have better luck with the wine and cheese crowd than the Pepsi and chili dog crowd."

Dickerson smiled congenially. "Actually you might be surprised, Mr.-- "

"Alvarez."

"Mr. Alvarez. It's true that I don't do many events like this one, and I certainly don't bring my top end inventory, but there are a lot of amateur collectors out there. And then there are the gems that you come across that make it all worth it."

"What kind of gems?" said Alex.

"The trained expert can see treasures that others don't recognize. By knowing varnish textures and colors, tool marking patterns, wood qualities and subtle features like the turn of a scroll, I know at a glance when I am looking at a superb treasure or a counterfeit," Dickerson said. "Actually, you don't run into counterfeits so much as you run into imitations. I've seen countless instruments that present themselves as made by Stradivari. Factories churned them out by the thousand during the eighteenth and nineteenth centuries and sold them inexpensively. It was a novelty to own a *Strad*. I get calls every month from someone who has found a dusty old Strad in their grandmother's cedar closet or some such place."

"So, it sounds like the gems are rare among the junk," said Alex.

"Not so," said Dickerson rubbing his palms together. "*Strads* are rare, to be sure. Actually, I'd venture to say that there is no surviving Stradivarius that is unaccounted for. But gems are not rare. Allow me to show you." Dickerson strode across the stall and slid an instrument case from beneath the velvet cloth covering a folding table. He deftly removed a violin and held it to the light. "Do you see this violin? What do you think?" He handed the instrument to Alex.

"I don't know," he said. "We do not deal with antique violins."

"What do you think of the color?"

Alex considered the rich orange-red glow. He also noticed the price tag attached by a red string to one of the tuning pegs, $995. "The color is a little... richer than the ones I usually see."

"I bought this violin yesterday, right over there, for less than the price marked," said Dickerson, pointing toward the far corner of the expansive hangar that today masqueraded as an antiques bazaar and soon would host an array of livestock and farm implements for the state fair. "This was made in Trieste by Giovanni Dollenz around 1845. This is a superb violin. Its true market value is far higher than the vendor realized."

"So what is it worth?" said Alex.

"You're looking at a violin that will probably fetch over ten thousand dollars."

This anecdote was all it took for Alex to become fascinated by the world of fine antique instruments. He was intrigued by Dickerson's suave confidence and seemingly effortless ability to weave among the oblivious masses and reap the treasures lying unrecognized at their feet. This was what he wanted to do. He would not waste his time becoming a luthier, a fancier carpenter. He quizzed Dickerson on what he had done to become a dealer and an appraiser. There was of course formal training, but mainly he said experience was the best teacher. He had begun dealing with modest antiques and over time, with knowledge of the marketplace, he ratcheted his way up the scale, developing his reputation along the way.

On that occasion, Alex could not stay long since Simone would be waiting for him, and in any case Dickerson had to assist a customer interested in a "fiddle to nail up over his fireplace." But for Alex, a new course was set. By the time they got back to the apartment after the antique show, he decided that his plan was solidified and he sprang it on Simone. He told her of his encounter with Dickerson and of his sudden realization that he had been on the wrong track.

"I don't understand, Alex," she said. "I thought you wanted to become a luthier. It would be such a valuable skill for you and for the shop."

"I am tired of just being a worker all the time. A luthier is just another worker."

Simone had been trying to hide her disappointment. Now there was exasperation to suppress. "What are you talking about, Alex? What do you propose to do instead of work?"

"No, no, baby, you do not understand," he said. "I can help the shop more by offering antique instruments besides the new ones. There is so much more value in antiques than in new instruments if you know what you are doing."

"We don't know anything about antique instruments," Simone said evenly. "I've been going to antique shows for years and I still don't consider myself particularly knowledgeable."

"That is because you just go for fun. You have not tried to make a business out of it. This guy, Dickerson, basically made ten thousand dollars on a stroll through the place just by knowing what to look for," Alex said.

"Alex, please. You don't even know this guy." Her irritation was bubbling to the surface. "I can't believe you would suddenly change your life plans based on meeting a stranger for a few minutes at the fairgrounds."

"This is not a sudden change," he said, affronted. "For a long time I have been tired of just working in the back. I want to be more than that. Today I just happened to figure out a good way to do that. Or do you just like having me as the hired help?"

Simone sat stunned, her mouth agape. After a moment she said quietly, "I had no idea you felt that way."

They continued to talk for some time. Alex's charge had disarmed his own temper as much as hers. In the end, they agreed that Alex should not train to become a luthier if that was not his interest. Alex would continue doing the technician job. Simone would involve him more up front with sales and customer service. At the same time, Alex would begin learning about antique instruments and the market for them. He emailed Dickerson and got some suggestions on books and resources. He even invested several hundred dollars in a bulky, two-volume encyclopedia of violin makers that Dickerson said would serve as an invaluable reference for identifying obscure makers and the traits of their work. It also included photographs of many of the instruments and labels.

For perhaps two months following the encounter with Dickerson, Alex threw himself into his newly found passion. He poured over the books. For three Sunday's straight, it was he who pulled Simone to a variety of antique malls and flea markets. This was certainly a nice side effect of this fever of Alex's as far as Simone was concerned, except that he soon began to adopt an annoyingly supercilious manner when browsing the wares. He carried a little notebook around with him in which he wrote down observations. Often he would shake his head and make a smug little snort as he chronicled what he considered to be a particularly outlandish asking price.

One evening, Alex came up to the apartment from the shop, where he had been doing research on the Internet. "I think I have found our first deal," he said excitedly. "There is a cello on eBay, and they are asking only a fraction of what it is worth."

"What?" she said. She tried not to sound skeptical, although she assumed his assertion was about as credible as those letters that arrived in the mail congratulating her on winning a sweepstakes.

"They are selling a Carlo Landolfi from 1755 and asking only eight thousand for it."

"Oh, only eight thousand," she said smiling. "Does it come with free shipping?"

"This is serious. You have no idea," he said. Landolfi cellos go for over a hundred grand. Even the shabby ones go for way more than this one, and *it* is gorgeous. You should come and see it."

She followed Alex down to the shop to indulge his enthusiasm. She examined the variety of photos displayed on the site. Alex said, "Well, what do you think?"

"It is certainly a nice looking cello, but they make nice looking ones in Chinese factories," she said. "I don't really know what I'm looking at."

"Well I do," he said impatiently. "It comes with a certificate attributing it to Carlo Ferdinando Landolfi of Milan. The label inside is an exact version of the ones that he used. This is the real deal. The vendor just doesn't have a clue."

Simone looked back at the photos for a moment and then shrugged. "Well, you're the expert. Congratulations."

Alex beamed triumphantly. "So, shall we get it? It would be our first fine antique offering."

"You're the dealer," she said. "It's your deal. I can't invest in something I don't understand."

"What are you talking about, baby?" he said. "This is for the shop. It is for us. I thought you supported me."

Oh, I support you all right. "I do support you, but this is not what we discussed," she said. "You were going to purchase some inexpensive, underpriced antiques, clean them up and sell them in the store. You were going to 'ratchet yourself up' into the high-end market. That's all fine with me, but I never signed on to making investments like this."

Alex was livid. He could not believe that Simone would do such a thing to him. He knew she could afford to make this purchase and yet she refused despite his assurances. He suspected she was being pigheaded because she did not want him to rise above being her kept workman. She was even willing to walk away from tens of thousands of dollars in ready profit just to keep him down. He spent the next two days in a funk. He finally phoned Dickerson and asked him to take a look at the instrument online. Dickerson pulled up the vendor's website. "It might be worth eight thousand," he said. "I'd have to see it first hand since these photos aren't the best. "This is certainly in the style of Landolfi, but the purfling is a bit clumsy and the varnish doesn't have the yellow underglow that I would expect to see. Personally, I would never buy a fine instrument online, but a lot of people do. It's probably not a terrible deal, but you know what they say, *caveat emptor*."

After that, Alex's excitement about becoming a dealer with the Midas touch waned. He was no longer interested in trolling the flea markets or spending evenings comparing his notebook jottings to the entries in his encyclopedia. Nor did he lose his sense that Simone preferred that he remain just a manual helper. It did not matter that her instinct about the cello had been exactly right. If she really cared about his advancement, she would have supported him.

CHAPTER SIX ————————————————————

By the time Nils Nilsson appeared in the shop in late September, seven months before Alex's machinations involving late night photography, Alex was all but cured of his interest in antiques dealing. Simone was sitting on her stool behind the counter and Alex was re-stocking the sheet music rack when the jingling bells on the front door announced Nils's arrival. Simone was startled by his sudden appearance. It had been five years since the quartet disbanded after the one performance at William Mayo High School. She had not seen Nils or Claudia since, although Duncan re-appeared from time to time. Duncan had even phoned her on numerous nights when arriving home drunk and alone from some twenty-something venue he had visited. These calls had stopped after Alex moved in and grabbed the receiver one night, telling Duncan to find his own girlfriend.

"There is my old friend Simone," said Nils, gliding through the door, characteristically puffed up with his chin held high and his shoulders back. He might have been about to sing an aria.

For Simone, this surprise was accompanied by an involuntary image from the story Duncan had told her of his experience at Nils's mansion on the night of the concert. During one of his late night ramblings to her he had shared entirely too much information. "Well, this is a surprise, Nils," she said. "What brings you over our way?"

"I needed some rosin and I said to myself, I wonder if my friend Simone is still in the violin business. And here she is. I told you I would drop by sometime." Nils seemed very proud of himself, as if he had delivered on a sacred promise to slay a dragon or retrieve a magical amulet.

"Thanks for thinking of us," she said. "Nils, this is my colleague Alex Alvarez. Alex, this is Nils Nilsson." Simone gestured behind Nils to Alex who was fidgeting with the sheet music, rearranging what he had already arranged. Nils had completely blown by Alex, unaware of his presence.

Nils turned. The two men acknowledged one another with mildly polite nods and monosyllabic greetings. Alex had heard of Nils. Everybody had heard of the Nilsson Center, and there was the upcoming Nilsson Town Square, planned to be the largest outdoor shopping mall in the state. Simone had also once mentioned that she knew Nilsson several years before as part of the string quartet with that jackass Duncan who used to call her up in the middle of the night. She had asked Alex to have some compassion because Duncan's marriage broke up when his wife started sleeping with Nils.

Nils turned back to Simone. "Since I'm here, I should also tell you about my most recent endeavor."

"Yes, I saw an article in the paper," Simone said. "The editorial page loved that you would be taking over the municipal golf course project."

"Actually, that's not what I'm referring to," he said. "But the golf course *is* taking some of my attention. Do you know that the course closed five years ago for renovations and, after spending five million dollars, the city council has nothing to show for it but a swamp? I'm doing this deal for no fee. I'm just sick of driving by that eyesore and watching those nincompoops waste taxpayer money. Now the town will have a great municipal course within nine months. By the way, I made them the same offer two years and two million dollars ago."

Simone made a mental note not to lose track of the how many times Nils said *million*. "And on top of that big project you have time for others?" she said.

"It's actually not all that big. The key is working with the best in the business, not the cheapest tin-pot outfit with a bulldozer," he said. "But don't get me going about city

government. I want to tell you about my *musical* endeavors."
He drew out the last bit, leaning toward Simone across the
counter, as if in confidence, and illuminating his photogenic
grin.

"Okay," she said. "Are you still with the Philharmonic?"
Perhaps an oblique reference to the circumstances of their
former association would dampen Nils's weird enthusiasm. Not
really.

"Yes, I'm still there," he said. "And I've begun a collection of
rare antique instruments."

Nils's announcement grabbed Alex's attention. Alex was
still in the front of the store, feigning diligent dedication to his
menial task, out of a mixture of fascination and suspicion over
this curious caller. Nils's charisma and confidence attracted
Alex's interest, not unlike the way he had been drawn to James
Dickerson, although the present visitor was brash while the
antiquarian had been deferential. At the same time Alex did not
want to leave this imposing, magnetic figure alone with his
girlfriend to ply her with seductive stories of wealth and power.

"Alex has an interest in antique instruments," said Simone,
eager to have more than just the counter to keep Nils from
getting too close to her.

"Oh, really?" said Nils doubtfully, turning to re-appraise the
man behind him who seemed to be inordinately challenged by
whatever it was he was doing with those booklets.

Alex quickly placed Pachelbel's Canon in D-major back in
the rack for the third time. "Oh, I dabble in it you might say."
He was excited to have something in common with the local
celebrity. He tentatively approached the counter. "What are
you collecting?"

Nilson gave Alex a cool smile, and responded, turning
immediately back to Simone. "I have often said that real estate
is my pride and music is my passion. To feed my passion, I am
setting out to assemble a quartet of rare instruments made by
the great Italian masters. Over the past two years I have
acquired two violins and a cello. All that remains is to find the
right viola and the set will be complete. It will be called the
Nilsson Quartet."

"That's great, Nils," said Simone. Nils beamed proudly, but clearly he expected her to say more. After a moment she said, "Oh, you wanted to get some rosin."

Rosin did not seem to be what Nils had in mind, and it was Alex who stirred up a fresh gust of wind in Nils's sails. "What instruments did you acquire?" said Alex.

Nils now deigned to respond directly to Alex, at least for the first full sentence. "I set up a three million dollar trust that will own the instruments and ensure that the Nilsson Quartet can remain constituted after I am gone. So far, the trust has purchased two violins by the great Cremonese masters Antonio Stradivari and Guarneri del Gesù." Nils paused for the effect to sink into Simone. She inclined her head placidly. He might just as well have told her that he had used a ten-percent-off coupon to buy paper towels, at least that was the impression she hoped to achieve.

Mercifully, for Nils that is, Alex was visibly spellbound by the revelation. "You are kidding!" he said. "You have a Strad and a del Gesù? You have violins from the two greatest makers ever? You don't mess around, man. There went your budget right there." Alex knew that those instruments did not typically change hands for less than a million dollars. He remembered reading of a Stradivarius selling for three and a half million dollars.

Now Nils turned to face Alex directly. Clearly, Simone was not warming up to the topic. "There are a lot of variables involved, as you may know," said Nils. "I fully expect my war chest to carry me through. Even taking into account the newest acquisition, a 1693 cello by Giovanni Grancino of Milan, I should have just enough spare change for a viola." Here he reignited his grin and turned to Simone. "Alas, violas tend to be postscripts." If he was looking for validation, she gave no indication. Simone was pretending to be occupied setting the various rosin packages on the counter.

"These are our rosins," she said. "For a violin or viola, you can't go wrong with this professional grade light rosin. The light is also fine for the cello, but I recommend the dark rosin as the best thing for cello."

"I'm still strictly a violinist," Nils said modestly. "Although I will own a cello and a viola from among the world's greatest, I will defer to other musicians to make them sing."

"The light rosin it is," said Simone, beginning to replace the various alternatives back below the counter.

Nils did not acknowledge the rosin selection, preferring to continue musing about how his instruments might begin to sing. "You know, Simone, once I complete the Nilsson Quartet, I plan to celebrate with a performance," he said. "Naturally, I will play the Stradivarius. I was hoping I could count on you to play the del Gesù."

Are you kidding me? Play in another quartet with you? "Nils, that's very nice of you, but I couldn't do that" she said. "I'd be terrified to play such an instrument."

Alex could not believe his ears. "Come on, baby," he said, causing Simone to flinch in irritation at such familiarity in front of a customer. "Mr. Nilsson is offering the chance of a lifetime."

Simone forced a pinched smile. "I know, but I'm not the right person. Nils, you should bring in a top violinist to play. I can't do it." Simone moved quickly to close the subject. "Have you lined up a violist and a cellist?"

"Not yet," he said. "Well, I'm sorry I can't entice you."

Once Nils had paid for the rosin and the bells on the door jingled his departure, Simone turned to her perplexed boyfriend. "I don't want to hear it, Alex."

Two days later, a familiar customer dashed into the store from the gray Saturday morning drizzle. He wore khaki trousers and a red pullover fleece jacket that glistened about the shoulders with the droplets that beaded there. He carried a beat up old instrument case, but his most noticeable aspect was the bright red scrape on his left cheek the size of a maraschino cherry. "Well, look who the cat dragged in," said Simone cheerfully.

"I know," said Duncan. "It's been forever since I've stopped by. How have you been, Simone?"

"I've been great, staying busy. It looks like I've been doing better than you," she said, nodding quizzically at his injury.

"Oh, right," he said compressing the spot gingerly with the back of his damp right hand. "I was walking with my date last night and we tripped and fell." Simone's raised eyebrows suggested that he his explanation might be inadequate, but he sensed that the more he said the more he would confirm his image in Simone's eyes as a reprobate. "You had to be there."

"Ah," said Simone. She would not push it. "Are you still dating Wendy?"

"Wendy?"

"The last time we spoke on the phone, you were dating a woman named Wendy."

"Really?" he said, rifling through his recollections of dates, not even sure he had all the names on file. Now he had it. "Oh, yeah, yeah. We weren't really dating. I met her at one of the Rockin' By The Rapids concerts at the river. We just went out twice I think."

"So, tell me," said Simone, intrigued. "Who's the new girl?"

"Oh, her name's Steph—Stacey," he said. "I don't know that she's really *the new girl*. We've been out a few times."

The two continued to catch up, finally getting around to what had brought Duncan to the shop on that particular Saturday morning. "My old viola just doesn't sound right. I can't put my finger on it. I don't know if there's a crack somewhere or what."

Simone examined the instrument carefully. She smiled and pointed to the scar at the top of the scroll. "I see she still bears Beethoven's stamp of disapproval."

Duncan laughed. "She considers it a badge of honor to have aroused such ardor in old Ludwig."

Just then Alex came out from the workshop. "Duncan, I don't think you've met Alex before," said Simone. The two men shook hands across the counter.

At first, Alex did not make the connection. Then he crossed him arms and assumed a smug posture. "Actually, we met on the phone earlier in the year, but we only spoke briefly. You may not remember."

Simone's face flushed and she pursed her lips. She quickly interjected. "Duncan, the good news is that it looks like your viola is fine. The sound post has slipped out of place and needs repositioning. Alex will be happy to take care of that right now. It won't take five minutes." She gave Alex a quick, cold look in case he had any doubt about his happiness to take care of it right now.

"That's great news," he said. "While I've got it here, would you mind putting on a new set of strings. I don't need it today. I could pick it up on Monday. All I really do with it these days is give a few lessons after school, but I haven't had it restrung since...I don't know when." Duncan trailed off, realizing that he last had it restrung before the Euterpe Quartet performance.

"Simone, did you tell Duncan who popped into the shop out of the blue day before yesterday?" Alex said.

The flush returned to Simone's cheeks. "No, Duncan's not interested in every customer who wanders into our shop."

Duncan doubted that Simone's gloating boyfriend was just being sociable. "Who came in?"

"Nils Nilsson," said Simone factually.

"Which Nils Nilsson was that? I know two Nils Nilssons," Duncan said, grinning. "Was it Maestro Nils or Magnate Nils?"

"Funnily, they both walked in at the same time," said Simone falling in step with Duncan's playful allusion. Alex looked crestfallen.

"What a fabulous coincidence," said Duncan. "And what are they up to?"

"They have teamed-up to buy rare musical instruments at a cost of *millions* and *millions*."

CHAPTER SEVEN ───────────────────────────────

It was the springtime of 1931 when Nathanial Granby reappeared in Philadelphia. Few expected to see him again. He was among those who had speculated and prospered spectacularly, and whose wealth had vaporized almost instantaneously two years before. Mostly he was remembered as a gambler who diversified from playing cards to playing stocks when he realized that the latter required fewer skills, paid more and involved a lower risk of violence.

The wisp of a man who hopped expertly off the flatcar a half mile outside the freight yard at Port Richmond bore little resemblance to the "Natty" Nat Granby who moved assertively beneath his cocked Panama hat from horse track to speakeasy to country club. "Natty" Nat had a pencil-thin mustache superscripting a knowing grin perpetually impaled with a gold-inlaid Bakelite cigarette holder that secreted an endlessly twisting ribbon of pale blue smoke. Devoid of his costume, the man now landing catlike on the siding was interchangeable with the hundreds of other hobos who used this soft, high spot of turf as a transfer point. Gone were the Panama hat, the bespoke tailoring and the smoldering cigarette holder. Gone also was the mustache, replaced by the ragged stubble that ranged unchecked on his raw, lined face.

One thing was not changed. Nat still had a spring in his step. Though his torn denim trousers and shapeless, battered work boots might have suggested a different deportment, he still walked with a sort of saunter. It was with this confident stride that he reached Long's Boarding House, the first that came in his way, and knocked.   The graying, aproned woman who answered the door holding a wet mop doubted the bedraggled man's ability to afford a room until he produced four silver dollars and presented them for one week's rent in advance.

Before the week was out, Nat had bought a new suit and shoes from a department store. He was cleaned up now, though most from his former days would not have recognized this man, wearing modest, off-the-rack duds as Nat Granby. Without the Panama, the mustache and the brashly clinched cigarette holder, this man might have been any clerk in an office. He never discussed what he did to earn money, although he departed after breakfast each morning and returned only just in time for supper. When any of the other men who boarded with Mrs. Long would steer the mealtime conversation around to what Nat did for a living, he would say vaguely that he worked for the railroad. Occasionally, a new boarder would fail to detect Nat's aversion to the topic and pursue the questioning further, curious about exactly what was Nat Granby's occupation. Nat might say, "Let's not talk of work, Robert (or Sam or whatever). I get my fill of that on the job." Then he would enter into one of the anecdotes from his bottomless repertoire. "Robert, have you ever been to Florida? Well, it's an amazing place. Sometime back I was fly fishing with a colleague on the banks of the Lake Okeechobee. We were not ten feet apart. The next thing I knew an alligator as long as a Packard shot up out of the depths and dragged him under. The whole thing was over in three seconds."

Helping Mrs. Long to run the boarding house was her daughter, Gladys who at twenty-nine years old had all but resigned herself to spinsterhood. She had been engaged a few years before to a man who was killed when his car slid off of an icy road and into the Delaware River. Since the depression hit, she had worked tirelessly with her mother to run the boarding house. With nothing but toilsome labor to look forward to each day, she had not attended to her pleasant but otherwise plain appearance. Her unwashed, golden-brown hair that had been her most alluring feature was now a dry thicket. When she did take a moment to consider her appearance and her prospects, she despaired. Most often she would think of such things as she was preparing for bed at the end of her sixteen-hour day. She might notice her thick, swollen feet and ankles. Her big feet had always embarrassed her, but the endless hours without sitting had bloated them out of all proportion.

It was therefore an unimagined surprise when, two months after arriving at Long's Boarding House, Nat Granby asked Gladys Long to marry him. Granby was the last man from whom she would have expected such a thing. It was not uncommon for a boarder to flirt with Gladys or even to make more substantive advances in hopes that the rent might afford benefits beyond room and board. Granby was not such a boarder. He had a busy, sophisticated air. He was not likely to even notice someone like Gladys, let alone take an interest in her.

Gladys hardly knew how to respond to the proposal. It made no sense. Nat insisted that he had been drawn to Gladys from the start, but he had not known how to make his feelings known without seeming boorish. He wanted nothing more than to make a life and a family with Gladys. It would take him a short while to get his business affairs on the proper footing to allow him to buy her the home that she deserved. This home would also be able accommodate Mrs. Long if she chose to retire. He suggested they could marry and live together in the boarding house temporarily while he arranged his finances.

It was Mrs. Long who gave Gladys the maternal shove she needed to accept the proposal. As far as Mrs. Long was concerned Nat was the ticket out for both of them. And so, with little fanfare and less of a honeymoon, Nat and Gladys took up residence in the attic of the boarding house, freeing up Nat's room for a new boarder and, vitally for Nat, relieving him of the necessity of scrounging up four bucks a week for rent.

Ten months later, Gladys gave birth to Doris Granby, the future mother of Duncan Flowers, but for the moment just another depression-era baby living in a grubby attic. Nat had insisted all along that his affairs were coming together, although he declined to offer details and was prone to rage if the subject were not dropped. Poor Gladys had continued working throughout the pregnancy. Mrs. Long began to complain to her daughter. "Your Nat is more parasite than provider," she would say. "And before long, we'll have another mouth to feed because of him."

Mrs. Long did not have to feed Nat for much longer because before Doris was two months old he disappeared, taking with him his few accumulated belongings packed in Gladys's one suitcase, a wedding present from her mother. In his brief note he regretted that his affairs were not, after all, maturing as expected and that he would be forced to spend time on the road. He made a tentative commitment to write.

One could hardly blame ten-year-old Duncan for being confused when, on the day after Halloween, the elderly man standing on the doorstep claimed to be his grandfather, his "Pappy Nat." The man might have been playing a practical joke, pretending to be Rip Van Winkle and trick-or-treating a day late. His oversized, red polyester leisure suit looked more like a costume than the attire of a grandpa, and he was carrying something like a violin case that could easily have served as a quirky receptacle for Halloween candies.

"You're not my grandfather," the little boy said. "My PeePaw lives in Florida. My other grandpa died."

Duncan summoned his mother, who stood frozen in the doorway facing the visitor with her hands over her gaping mouth in an expression of suffocation. When her lungs began to work again, she immediately sent Duncan to his room. From behind his door he heard only his mother's voice, a mixture of anger and despair. She came up a short time later and escorted him to the front door, telling him to run over to his friend Eddie's to play for the afternoon. As his mother shuffled him through the foyer, Duncan caught a glimpse of the old man sitting on the couch in the living room. He would always remember the old man's placid, cheerful expression in contrast with the anguish on the face of his mother.

Eddie's mom sent Duncan home for dinner several hours later, having received the all-clear. By then, Duncan's father, a dermatologist, had gotten home from his clinic. The table had an additional place setting and there sat the old man. As Duncan took his usual seat, the only sound in the room was his mother stirring the iced tea pitcher. Presently, she brought the pitcher out to the table and took her place with the three others waiting there silently. Duncan's father was by turns realigning his placemat on the table and adjusting the position of the plate and silverware lying on top. The old man simply smiled, tilting his face toward the light above the table as if he were on a warm rock soaking in the down-pouring rays on the first sunny day of the year.

"Shall we say grace?" said Duncan's mother across the table to her husband, who by apparent coincidence had just completed to his satisfaction the arrangement of his tableware.

"Great God, Thou Giver of all good, accept our praise and bless our food. Grace, health, and strength to us afford, through Jesus Christ, our blessed Lord." Duncan's father paused. Duncan glanced up furtively from his lap to see his father's eyes squinting in concentration and his lips working to form some forthcoming phrase. In re-bowing his head, Duncan looked quickly at the old man who continued to bask in the incandescent light above the table. "And Great God, let us give thanks for reuniting Nathanial with his daughter, Doris and grandson, Duncan. And we are so pleased to welcome him into our home who was lost but is now found. Amen."

Over meatloaf and mashed potatoes, Duncan learned that the strange man at the table was indeed his grandfather. His mother had apparently misspoken in previously telling Duncan that her father was dead. Very much alive, the old man had helped himself to a second serving before his grandson had finished smearing his own unenticing mashed potatoes into a thin glazing over the surface of the plate.

His appetite sated and smacking his lips with some gusto, Nat described to the family his recent foray into acting. He had worked in the mountains of North Carolina at a theme park, playing the sheriff of the small frontier town recreated there. Five times a day, including Sundays, Bad Bart would attempt to rob the tourist patrons at the rustic, cafeteria-style saloon.

Each time, Nat would burst in before Bart could lay his hands on any of the diners' wallets or handbags. Nat would always try to talk Bart into giving himself up, but the incorrigible outlaw would go for his gun, forcing Nat to shoot him dead. Alas, now the season was over and there were no more tourists for Bart to assault and no more need for Nat to intervene. Thus, now was the perfect time to visit his family in Richmond.

"I've been everywhere in this great land, and I've seen everything a man can see," said Nat to Duncan. "But there was always one thing missing. Do you know what that was, young man?"

"No, sir."

"Call me Pappy, sonny. I called my grandfather Pappy and I'd be honored if you would do the same for me."

"Yes, sir, Pappy."

"Family!" said Nat plunking his right fist onto the table, fork pointed aloft. "No matter how far you travel, you must never forget your family."

This last statement seemed to spur Doris out of her silence. Duncan thought it odd that she had said nothing during the meal and that she seemed entirely preoccupied with cutting her meatloaf into minute slivers which she would then chew relentlessly. "Look at the time!" said Doris. "We've gotten so carried away with our stories that it is getting late. Duncan, you need to get up to your room. You can read your Great Brain book."

For several nights, Nat slept on the pullout bed in the family room. Duncan never saw any luggage other than the violin case. He did notice that on the third day, his Pappy had changed from the leisure suit into a pair of his dad's corduroys and a sweatshirt bearing the initials of the Virginia Military Institute, where his dad had gone to college. The home had three bedrooms: the master bedroom, Duncan's bedroom and a third that Duncan's mom used as her painting studio. Doris made portraits of children and pets. Having gained a reputation among her friends at the Junior League, she had a steady flow of commissions. With the bedrooms thus assigned, when the Flowers household entertained the rare overnight visitor, the family room served as the guest room.

Clearly, Pappy was to be more than a transitory visitor, because when Duncan returned from school on the fourth day, his grandfather had been installed in the attic. It was a walk-up attic that the previous owner had insulated with the intention of making a finished room, but never competed the job. The shuffling and thumping overhead alerted Duncan to the new arrangement. When he emerged into the dusty space at the top of the stairs he saw his mother busily sweeping while his father struggled to fit an air conditioner into one of the small windows that peeped out at each end of the attic. Pappy reclined in the white beanbag chair that had briefly resided in the family room before Duncan's mom declared it a waste of money. The old man relaxed with his hands behind his head and his feet extended before him, crossed at the ankles.

"David, you don't know how this brings back memories," said Nat. "Your grandma Gladys and I lived in an attic when we were married. We didn't have much, but we had each other. And before too long, we had your mom."

Duncan's mom suddenly stopped sweeping tossed the broom unceremoniously to lean against a nearby wardrobe. It glanced off and fell to the floor with a smack. "His name is Duncan, not David," she said, leaning over Nat with her hands on her hips.

"Did I say David?" said Nat with a quizzical smile. "More and more I just seem to forget things.

"I'll say you forget things," she said. "You remember living with mom and me in an attic. Do you remember what happened next? All I have to go by are postcards and the occasional birthday card. How's your memory about that part?"

Here, Duncan's father intervened and suggested that they leave Nat to get settled in. This was a somewhat curious proposition since Nat had no belongings other than the instrument case and as for himself, he could not have settled any farther into the beanbag. Duncan stayed behind as his parents disappeared down the narrow stairway. He rarely came up to the attic, mostly because he found it spooky, but it also had a certain mystical appeal. On the rare occasions he did come up it was with one of his parents on a mission to deposit or retrieve some relic and then beat a swift retreat. Now he would be able to explore the space with his grandfather nearby to ward off any goblins that might inhabit its dark corners.

Among the boxes of holiday decorations, the disused housewares and the cardboard wardrobes smelling of mothballs, Nat would have a cozy nook. Duncan's mom had made up a folding cot, and there was a wide selection of items that Nat could make use of as desired. So far, he had favored the beanbag, but he would later set up a bridge table and a couple of the accompanying folding chairs.

"What do you think of your Pappy's penthouse?" said Nat. "Do you like it?"

"Yes, sir."

"Please. You don't have to call me sir," said Nat. "This isn't the military is it?"

"My dad wants me to say ma'am and sir."

"Hmm," said Nat. "Well, suit yourself, but as far as I'm concerned you can just call me Pappy. You know, I used to call my grandfather Pappy, and I would be honored if you would call me Pappy too." Nat began to sit up, reaching forward as if for some unseen purchase. He got his torso about halfway raised but was unable to overcome his inertia. He collapsed back into the vinyl-encased mass below him. He looked like a great mosquito whose wings had become stuck in a globule of melted marshmallow. "This damn thing is diabolical," he said as he rolled off sideways onto all fours and raised his rusty frame to its full height, or nearly full height because he had to tilt his head to keep it out of the wooly pink insulation between the rafters. Full headroom was only available under the peak of the roof.

Nat shuffled over to the cot and sat down. "Come over here, David. I want to show you something." Nat reached under the cot and extracted the case that he had brought with him. As Duncan sheepishly took his place next to Nat, the old man arranged the case on his lap and opened it, revealing a golden-red instrument cradled in a bed of faded green velvet. "Do you know what that is, son?"

"Yes, sir. It's a violin," said Duncan quietly, still regarding the contents of the case.

"You know, I thought it was a violin when I first saw it back in nineteen and thirty-nine," said Nat. "But you know what? It's called a viola."

"What's a viola?"

"This is a viola!" said Nat, raising his voice in a flash of irritation as if such a question had no meaning. Then he came back to himself and chuckled. "A viola is just like a violin, only a little bigger. That's exactly what the man I got it from told me."

"Can you play a song on it?" said Duncan.

"No, no," said Nat. "I never had time to learn to play on it, but it's the one thing I've kept with me all throughout the years."

"Why?"

"Because the man who gave it to me told me that he wanted me to keep it as a sacred trust."

"Why did he give it to you?"

"He gave it to me because I was the closest thing he had to family. He was an old man, an old Jew. He lived in a big old house. This was in Newark, New Jersey. He had been in the jewelry business and had done very well in his day, but when I met him, he was retired and living alone. People said he had a lot of money, but besides his house and belongings, I never saw him spend any money that wasn't for necessities. Anyway, he hired me to be a sort of helper. I was his driver, his handyman. I ran his errands, bought his groceries- he ate like a bird. He let me live over his garage for no rent and still paid me fifteen dollars a week. That may not sound like a lot, but it sure beat the alternatives."

"I get three dollars a week," said Duncan cheerfully.

"Well, we might have to put in for a raise then," said Nat. "So, I worked two years for Mr. Gutmann, from the end of 1936 to early 1939. He was pretty frail when I started working for him, and after a while he needed me to help him get up and down the stairs, and during the last year he almost never went outside. One day he asked me to open up the library. It was a big room, twice the size of your living room, filled with books on every wall. I had never been inside because it was always closed to save on heat. On one of the few shelves not filled with books lay this case. He asked me to pull it down and open it up, and he showed it to me just like I'm showing it to you. He said that he had collected many instruments over the years, but this one was his pride. While all the others were stored away in New York, he could not bear to be separated from this viola."

Nat went on to tell Duncan something of where the viola came from, but the details would escape him. What remained with him was that this was a viola crafted long ago by an Italian master. "On that day, Mr. Gutmann told me that he wanted me to have this viola and to keep it as a sacred trust. He had no family. He had instructed his lawyers what to do with all of his other instruments if anything happened to him, but he wanted the viola to go with me because he said I was like a son to him."

"What happened to Mr. Gutmann?"

"You know, he died a few days later," said Nat. "So, I carried with me his sacred trust. I also got his Cadillac Sixty-Special." Nat's eyes gleamed at the reminiscence. "Now that was a car. You were really somebody when you rode in a Sixty-Special." After a moment, he seemed to find his place again. "But I didn't have the car for very long. It wasn't part of the sacred trust so I liquidated it."

Duncan's eyes bulged at the thought of a liquidated car. It sounded like something that a Batman villain would resort to, rendering his target a gurgling puddle of slime. What a strange thing to do to a car.

"I've guarded this sacred trust for more than thirty years," said Nat. "Now, David, I'm passing the trust to you. Can I count on you?" Nat slid the case from his lap onto Duncan's knees. Duncan nodded and held his breath.

CHAPTER EIGHT ————————————————————————

Alex Alvarez stood before the workbench in the back of Duval Violins. Before him lay the viola that Duncan Flowers dropped off the day before for a soundpost adjustment and a new set of strings. Nearby, Alex had been perusing several of the reference books that he acquired during his abortive foray into the world of rare musical relics. It was Sunday now and Alex had come back to the workshop, telling Simone that he wanted to do some tidying up to make the most of the wet weather. The rain had been coming down since before Duncan left the viola and now, with a stiff autumn wind from the North, the fat drops smacked the glass panes in the door at the back of the workshop.

Alex did the requested work on the viola the day before, shortly after Duncan departed. A professional luthier could have restrung the instrument and reset the soundpost in a matter of minutes, but the job had taken Alex over half an hour. Only recently had Simone trusted him with setting soundposts without her direct supervision. Even after many months of practice with this task he still struggled. To orient the tiny dowel perfectly vertically inside the body of the instrument was challenge enough, but then it had to be positioned precisely below the treble foot of the bridge and just a few millimeters toward the tail of the instrument. To accomplish the adjustment, he maneuvered a thinly curved metal probe through the f-shaped hole on the treble side of the viola. The tool had a sharp tip designed to stab into the wooden dowel and to be wiggled out once the dowel was in place. The process was not unlike building a ship in a bottle. Wrong placement would at best detract from the sound quality and at worst damage the body of the instrument. He had fumbled the dowel inside the body six or seven times. Each time he had to turn the viola face down until the tiny wooden cylinder came tumbling out of the f-hole so he could skewer it once again on the probe and start over.

It was fiddling with the soundpost on the previous afternoon that first aroused Alex's curiosity about Duncan's viola. Alex had by now worked with many violas and it struck him how this soundpost was discernibly longer than any that he had seen before. He had previously remarked that the front and back of the viola seemed more arched than normal. Duncan's viola gave the impression of a normal viola that had been overinflated. It was only upon examining the soundpost that Alex got a tangible sense of how much deeper this viola was than the ones that came regularly into the shop.

Now Alex was returning to the workshop to examine this strange viola more closely. He wanted to see what his books had to say about its features. He soon discovered that the puffed out body style had been typical of baroque instruments and was well suited to the intimate settings in which they played. The voluminous sound boxes created a rich, warm sound. This style had been supplanted by the flatter profile, pioneered by Antonio Stradivari, which had the ability to project powerfully into the concert hall settings that came to the forefront beginning around the turn of the eighteenth century.

Upon reading these commentaries, Alex's pulse quickened. He had not forgotten his misguided excitement about the Landolfi cello, but this was different. This was an instrument owned by an unsophisticated school teacher. In retrospect, the dealer on eBay was obviously knowledgeable. Other than the body style, Alex could find no other features that the books could help him with. The instrument was apparently quite old, or at least well used. The golden-red varnish was scratched and worn, and the scroll had a pretty good ding on the top. He had hoped to find a label, but there was none. Normally, labels reside directly below the bass-side soundhole. In this case, there was only a faintly discolored rectangle where a label had once been glued.

He decided to have a peek inside using an inspection mirror and a tiny flexible light. Here he found a couple of patches, but nothing remarkable. Then he caught the reflection of something interesting. It was a label. This one was affixed, nailed, to the block at the top of the viola, where the neck attaches to the body. By looking through a soundhole at a shallow angle, he could just make it out: *Nicolaus Amatus Cremonae Hieronymus et Antonius Nepos fecit anno 166_*. The nail on the right side of the label obscured the last digit of the year. It might have been a one, or maybe a four or a seven. The entire label was pre-printed, though primitively, except for the last two digits of the year, which were handwritten. When Alex consulted his Encyclopedia of Violinmakers, he found a photograph depicting a nearly identical label. The book attributed the label to Nicolò Amati, the "preeminent craftsman of the Amati dynasty and likely teacher of Antonio Stradivari."

"I tell you, little lady," Alex murmured to the viola laid before him. "I don't know if you are the real deal or what, but I see no reason for you to waste your time with that jackass Duncan. I think you and I make a much better couple."

That evening, as he and Simone shared tacos for dinner in their kitchen, Alex had a suggestion. "I think you were right when you said I should start small and work my way up in the antique trade."

"Right," said Simone after a moment. She had assumed that Alex had dropped his preoccupation with antiques. Other than his little exchange with Nils the week before, Simone had observed no further interest on the part of Alex. In fact, she was beginning to wonder exactly what his career plans were since becoming a luthier was also off the table.

"I think your friend Duncan has a nice little viola," said Alex. "I think it probably has some moderate antique value, not a lot, but some. He has not taken very good care of it. It could be refurbished and it would probably be a decent collectible."

"Okay," said Simone. "So, you want to refurbish Duncan's viola for him?"

"Sort of. Clearly, this guy Duncan is not a collector. He just wants an instrument to play around with and..."

"Excuse me," interrupted Simone. "*This guy* is a friend of mine and he also happens to be an excellent violist. I don't really care for the way you talk about him."

"No, no, baby. Don't get upset. I just meant that he is not a collector," said Alex. Then he winked at her coyly. "And can I help it if I get a little jealous of your old boyfriends?"

"He's not an old boyfriend. I've told you that ten times," she said. "So what is it you want to do with his viola?"

"You said you thought I should start small if I want to get experience with antiques," he said. "I just thought we could offer Duncan a trade-in for a new instrument, or one of the lease instruments that we take back. If we swapped him for one of the models in the thousand dollar range, I know I could make a nice profit for us after cleaning it up."

"Alex," said Simone with a tone of pleading. "Again you want me to be the one making the investment. I've said you can use the shop, but this is supposed to be your project, not mine."

"I know, baby. You are right. That is my plan. It is just that a thousand dollar instrument costs the shop less than that," he said. "I thought we could swap him an instrument and I could pay the shop the wholesale price."

Simone stared at him for a moment. It was not that selling him an instrument at wholesale was a problem. She just felt Alex's whole adventure into antiques was a waste of time. He took the same cavalier approach to it as he had done to everything else since moving in with her. Why would this scheme be any different? "Fine," she said. "If you want to offer Duncan a trade, I will sell you the instrument at cost."

"Oh, baby that is wonderful," said Alex squeezing Simone's forearm affectionately, shaking most of her taco's toppings out onto her plate. "Ooh, sorry about that. But there is just one thing," he said. "I was hoping you could be the one to ask him."

The next afternoon, Duncan bounced into the shop through the door with the jingling bells and a recently added poster for the Twelfth Annual Apple Festival. The sun had reasserted domain over the town, bathing the emerging harvest colors in encouragement. Simone was in the showroom flitting a feather duster about the tops of the cellos. She wore a snug pair of jeans with a delicate pink knit top. Duncan noticed that she was wearing her hair back. "Great day," he said. "I couldn't wait for classes to let out so I could get outside."

"Don't rub it in," said Simone, stashing the duster behind the counter.

"I know, sorry. If it will make you feel any better, I'll be laboring away after school for the rest of the week giving viola lessons," he said.

"Really? That's great. I didn't know you were so busy with music."

"Hey, a few extra bucks in the wallet never hurts," he said. "So, has Alex finished up with my viola?"

"He's out, but yes, it's all ready," she said, retrieving the case from just inside the workshop. She placed the case on the counter and opened it. "A new set of strings and a re-positioned sound post. Good as new."

"Great. How much do I owe you?"

"Well, I had something I wanted to ask you." Simone explained Alex's proposal to Duncan and offered him a trade. "I'm not knowledgeable about antique instruments, but I can say that our new ones are excellent quality. If making a swap appeals to you, I can promise you would be getting a fine instrument."

Duncan thought for a moment. "I can't do that. My grandfather gave it to me. For all I know he got it out of a gumball machine, but it was his gift to me," he said. "And anyway, I don't perform. I give lessons to teenagers who have developed a spontaneous passion for music to fulfill their after-school activity requirement. Taking lessons from me gets them out of running cross country or playing soccer or some other activity involving grunting and communal showering."

"I understand," said Simone, releasing a conclusive breath. The more she had thought about Alex's proposal, the less she had liked it. Now the whole idea was moot. She had not realized how uncomfortable it made her until now, because she felt relieved of a burden. She gazed cheerfully at Duncan, snapping the case closed and sliding it across to him, but leaving her hands lightly on top. "You've got something special here. You should hang on to it."

When Alex returned to the shop, he could not conceal his frustration at Simone's failure to close a deal. "Did you offer him a new viola, a good one, not one of the student models?"

"Alex, I made the proposal exactly as we discussed. He just wasn't interested."

"How could he not be interested? He has an old piece of junk and we are offering him a brand new instrument."

"It was a gift from his grandfather," she said. "And if he has such a piece of junk, why do you want it anyway?"

"I am just trying to get started in the antique trade— starting small like *you* wanted me to— and you don't seem to want me to succeed."

"What are you talking about? I made the offer. I can't make him take it. You should have handled it yourself."

"You could not have really tried. I think you still have a thing for that doofus and the two of you just don't want me to get ahead."

It took a pleading apology and a bouquet of assorted flowers from the grocery store before Alex could entice Simone to speak to him that evening. He had just been overexcited. He also assured her that he would no longer get her tangled in any antique dealing schemes. After a couple of weeks of reasonably good behavior on Alex's part, the two settled back into a relatively comfortable routine. The Apple Festival served as a small spark to their relationship. Alex took care of all the setting up and taking down of the booth and the two even stole a couple of hours wandering around the apple-themed festivities. He bought a pair of dried apples carved into the shapes of a wizened crone and an old geezer. He joked that they represented the two of them when they reach their golden years. Simone thought they looked more like the work of

Amazonian headhunters, but by now she had become accustomed to Alex's primitive sense of romance.

Duncan had no occasion to return to the shop over the succeeding months, which eliminated one potential source of disharmony. Still, beneath the veneer of contentment, Alex could not lose his preoccupation with Duncan and his viola. It is unlikely that he himself knew which of the two held the greatest sway over him. Had he been someone who reflected on such things, he might have concluded that his desire for the viola perfectly matched his desire to abuse Duncan. Therefore, he would have concluded that his plan to steal Duncan's viola was the ideal confluence of his two desires.

Alex decided to steal the viola very shortly after Simone's failure to make the swap for it. In fact, he probably decided unconsciously that he would get the viola by hook or by crook the moment he read the label inside. Still, he took his time. He did not want Duncan's viola to go missing too soon after he had thrown a tantrum for not getting it. It also took some time to figure out how he would carry off the theft without getting caught.

Shortly after the new year, Alex began to follow Duncan's movements. This was tricky due to his living and working arrangements. In early January, he declared to Simone that he had made a resolution to get back into shape and so he was starting a trial gym membership. Each morning he would dutifully leave the apartment at a little after seven, carrying his blue nylon duffle bag. By around nine he returned with damp hair and expressions of vitality. During the intervening two hours, he would drive his Ford Ranger pick-up over to Duncan's street and shadow his mark over the commute to River Road Academy. A pit stop in the restroom at Hank's Gas 'n' Go on the way home provided him with a few splashes to simulate the showered look.

In late January, Alex declared to Simone that the gym lifestyle did not suit him. He would not be extending beyond the free trial. He had by now learned Duncan's morning travel routine. Unfailingly, Duncan left his house each morning around seven-thirty and drove the ten minutes to school, where he parked in the same spot in the faculty lot. The dumbass was nothing if not consistent. Alex did learn two interesting things. Duncan carried his viola to school on Tuesdays and Thursdays, and he always put his keys over the visor of his piece-of-shit Honda. While this was interesting information, it did not provide Alex with a clear idea of how he could steal the viola and avoid detection. He had tried the front and back doors of Duncan's house one morning after Duncan was gone. They were naturally locked. In any case, Alex felt extremely uneasy lurking about where any neighbor could see him. He had to believe that there would be some simpler way of getting at the viola. Swiping it from the classroom was unthinkable, but perhaps something in Duncan's evening routine would yield an opening.

Now Alex needed a pretext to slip out of the shop in the late afternoons. In mid-February, he hit upon an excuse that relied upon the indulgence of his friend KG. Alex had two friends, Dwayne and KG, with whom he primarily socialized, that is to say drank beer and, depending on the season, either tossed horseshoes or shot pool. KG Benner called himself an arborist, apparently unconcerned that normally such things require certifications. He adopted this designation two years before when he began working as a groundman for Green Tree Specialists. Gordon Green owned and operated the outfit and had received his degree in forestry from Duke University. Green took tree work very seriously. That is why after two years, KG was still only allowed to feed branches into the chipper and saw up fallen debris. He also maintained the chainsaws and other equipment for the real arborists who scaled the boughs in climbing gear and performed aerobatic tree surgery.

With KG's agreement to vouch for Alex in the unlikely event that Simone should become curious, Alex told Simone that he needed to help out KG in the afternoons for a week or so. KG, the story went, needed a hand cutting up a mountain of wood that he had gotten from his tree work. Actually, this was not entirely untrue. In the tree business, a lot of wood ends up in the landfill. If a worker wants to have some dropped at his house instead, that means lower landfill fees for the business and free firewood for the worker. Because of this, KG had a healthy firewood business going on the side and he always had a mountain of wood behind his trailer.

Of course, the fiction was that Alex would be helping KG, although KG did demand one afternoon's assistance in exchange for the weeklong alibi. All Alex told KG was that he was sick of being on such a short leash all the time and he needed some space. In practice, he left the shop each day after three o'clock and headed to River Road Academy to pick up on Duncan's movements. Here again, Alex observed a reliable consistency. From his Ranger, parked in eyeshot of the faculty lot, Alex observed that each day shortly before five, Duncan would come out to his car and place his briefcase and, on Tuesday and Thursday, his viola, in the backseat before heading into a squat, modernistic building at the edge of the parking lot. In the 1960's, building such a structure probably seemed like an interesting complement to the predominately colonial architecture of the campus, but now it just looked like a drab, geometric oddity fallen from space.

At the school's main entrance stood a color-coded, carved wooden map of the campus. Alex determined that Duncan was entering building number nine, it was easy to find because it was the only building with a footprint resembling that of a space ship. Number nine was the dining hall. So the schmuck ate his supper at school every day. How pathetic. And by quarter to six he was in his crap heap Honda and on his way home.

After a week of watching Duncan's routine, Alex drummed the steering wheel of his ranger and declared, "Dude, you're not going to know what hit you." A month later, on April Fool's Day, Alex bagged his quarry.

Shortly after seven in the evening on April 1, a couple of hours after Duncan's Honda sped illicitly out of the faculty lot at River Road Academy, the phone rang at Allegro Antiquities of Boston.   James   Dickerson   was   reading   over   the dendrochronology report on a Renaissance lute that a client wished to bid on at Sotheby's.   Among the various age-verification tests available, James was partial to the technique of comparing wood grain patterns in a musical instrument to the patterns in wood samples of confirmed age from the same region. All trees in a region during a given period of time experience the same predominating weather conditions, and the ring patterns unfailingly reflect these conditions. On more than a few occasions, James had steered away from instruments whose wood was apparently derived from trees that lived after the putative maker died. At first James did not recollect the identity of the person on the phone. It had been over eight months since his unmemorable meeting with this man who apparently wandered at random into James's booth at an antique show.   But James prided himself on having a photographic memory, which served him well in a business where a flawless mental archive was one's greatest asset.

"Yes, of course," said James.   "Didn't you contact me afterward about a cello, a Landolfi I believe? How did that work out for you?"

"I decided not to pull the trigger on that one," said Alex. "I am actually calling about another instrument. I have come into possession of an extraordinary antique viola, one which I believe may have come from one of the great workshops of Cremona."

James glanced at his watch and cast his eyes heavenward in supplication. "I see," said James, offering no further encouragement. He allowed Alex to carry on with his story, which conspicuously lacked in specifics about the provenance of the instrument. Finally, as a matter of course, he suggested that Alex send him a set of high-resolution photos. These, he informed Alex, would do nothing to authenticate the instrument, but might allow James to shed some light on its nature. "The only way to authenticate an instrument is through direct examination, but I may be able to save you a lot of legwork with a quick glance at what you send me."

James placed the cordless phone back in its cradle and turned back to the lab report. Across the floor, Larry Giles was just switching off the work lights in the luthier's studio that made up fully half of the open layout of Allegro Antiquities. Larry was the other half of the business. James brought the encyclopedic expertise for identifying and appraising rare pieces and Larry had the skills of a master craftsman. Allegro could provide one-stop service for appraisals, repairs and brokerage of fine antique instruments. The shop also offered the added service of creating valuable replica pieces. Supply and demand in the limited pool of historical treasures meant that not all collectors could own an original. Allegro possessed the skills and knowledge to provide historically accurate pieces to dabblers and dilettantes as well as serious musicians and educators.

As one of the rare black men in an overwhelmingly white field, Larry Giles had received an enormous amount of advice to pursue some other line of work. The wiry, independent product of Boston's toughest neighborhoods was unfailingly polite in receiving these unsolicited tips. He continued to receive them up until he demonstrated that he had in his hands the artistry that most craftsmen can only dream of. His talent won him a coveted spot at the Civica Scuola di Liuteria in Milan. Upon returning to the States, he could have his pick of instrument makers, but he wanted to be independent. It was

James Dickerson who proposed that the two of them create the Allegro partnership where Larry could make his own instruments and have the opportunity to work with rare treasures. Larry would do all of the repair work and fabrication for Allegro Antiquities and he would create originals under his own banner of Atelier Giles. The name gave his more effete clientele the satisfaction of a label with European cachet. They pronounced his name unfailingly as *Jeel*. "Another sighting on the Stradivarius hotline?" said Larry.

"Indeed," said James, already engrossed again in the dendrochronology analysis.

"Well, I'm out of here," said Larry, smoothing down the well-manicured patch of beard in the middle of his chin. "We're jamming at Cleo's tonight. You should swing by." Larry's hobby was his trio, Pangeastica, an underground favorite in Boston. They played in a willfully bewildering style that fused any and every musical form Larry could cram into their repertoire. Backed by a keyboard and drums, Larry laid down vocals and alternated between bass and six-string guitar. He and his band mates also had the facility to pick up the banjo, the accordion, the flugelhorn and the bagpipes, among a variety of other noisemakers that served to titillate their nouveau-beatnik cabal.

It was the next day before James opened the email from Alex. To his surprise, the photo attachments did convincingly depict the characteristics of an instrument made in the style of Nicolò Amati. That the text of the label supported this impression added little since labels were notoriously unreliable, almost to the point of being irrelevant. In nearly all cases, James could disqualify, or at least discount, an undocumented inquiry based on photographic evidence alone, but this one had all the hallmarks of an Amati. The scrollwork was particularly exact. Amati typically made his scrolls more compactly than did his contemporaries. Amati imitators tended to miss this trait, focusing more on the body styling and varnishing. Still doubtful that the instrument would ultimately pass muster, James phoned Alex to suggest that they meet in Washington that Saturday afternoon. James would be attending a conference in the morning at the Smithsonian and perhaps Alex could drive up with the viola.

Four days after swiping the viola, Alex traveled to the meeting at James's hotel room, a five-minute walk from the Washington Mall. To keep his lies to Simone simple, he told her that he was going to Washington. He said he had learned about an important conference on appraising musical instruments at the Smithsonian. All true. He said he would be remiss to pass up the chance to learn from the many experts who would be convening in one place.

In the hotel room, James examined the viola carefully for several minutes, including making some ad hoc measurements with a caliper he had brought. To his surprise he still found himself unable to disqualify the viola. "This is certainly an interesting find," said James. "Now, tell me again how you came into possession of it."

"I am not at liberty to disclose the name of the owner," said Alex. He had already practiced his reply to the inevitable question. "He needs to remain anonymous."

"I see," said James.

"Yeah," said Alex. He quickly redirected the conversation. "I thought you might be able help me in two ways— for a fee of course."

"Of course."

"Yeah," Alex continued. "You see, not only do I have a seller, but I know a potential buyer. Assuming the viola is real, I was also wondering if you could be the go-between to make the sale."

"I don't understand, Mr. Alvarez," said James. "Assuming you have a reliable authentication, why wouldn't you make the sale if you already have the buyer lined up?"

"The buyer is not exactly lined up," said Alex. "I just know that he is in the market for a rare masterpiece viola. If I approach him to make the sale, that could compromise the identity of the current owner and that would spoil everything. Also, if for some reason the buyer that I have in mind does not go for this viola, you could probably find another buyer, right?"

"I see," said James.

"I figure if this viola is real, like the owner thinks it is, it could be worth twenty grand, maybe thirty. You never know."

"You never know."

Alex described Nils Nilsson's project to assemble a string quartet of rare instruments. He knew that Nils had violins by Stradivari and del Gesù. He could not recall the maker of the cello. "I think it was something like Gambino," he said, to an indulging, thoughtful nod from James. "Anyway, Nilsson has spent some big bucks on the three instruments so far and I am sure he will want a decent viola to round out the lot, don't you think? Like I said, I cannot go and ask him about this one because he would figure out who the owner is. The owner really needs to stay anonymous."

"You've made that very clear indeed, Mr. Alvarez," said James. "You have quite an interesting story here, and I must say, a very interesting instrument. I'm still not in a position to reach any conclusions. If you will allow me to take it back to Boston where I have access to the necessary resources, I can make an assessment. My fee for authenticating an instrument like this is normally..." he considered for a moment, seeing Alex's eyes begin to bulge anxiously. No need to complicate matters at this stage. "Actually, there are some preliminary evaluations I can do at no charge. We can reconnect when those are complete. Assuming the instrument does prove out, and I represent you and your client, we can always deduct my fees on the back end."

Alex thought for a moment. Somehow he had overlooked the possibility that James might want to take the viola with him to Boston. Sooner of later Simone would notice the missing case he had borrowed for this trip. She would not miss the junky old student viola that he had placed in Duncan's car to serve as a realistic dummy in case there would be a surviving fragment or two among the ashes. Removing its label, he had used the old, damaged instrument that Simone let him have the previous year to take apart and to practice basic repairs. If she ever asked about that, he could credibly say that it had served its purpose and gone in the trash. But having a serviceable case disappear, even this cheap one, might raise questions from

Simone. "I thought you would be able to look at it here and tell me if it was real, like you did with that violin you bought at the antique show last summer," he said finally.

"You are referring to the Dollenz I presume," said James.

"Yeah, I think so," said Alex. He had no idea.

"That, Mr. Alvarez, was a nineteenth century instrument of a provenance that has few, if any, counterfeits to compromise its prohibitively modest value. In any event, the seven hundred dollars I got it for was a steal based on sound quality alone, irrespective of the instrument's authenticity. What you have brought me, on the other hand, purports to be a seventeenth century creation from the house of Amati. You cannot expect me to stake my reputation on a casual perusal in a hotel room. If your client desires to make a serious sale through a serious dealer, he or she will not find a credible expert who does not require a complete qualitative and quantitative analysis under controlled conditions. Are you and your client serious, or are you wasting my time?"

The day after the theft of Duncan's car, Wednesday, the campus buzzed with the news. The event took on such significance that the headmaster, Dr. Bryson, saw fit to draft a memo to be carried home by each student describing the facts of the incident and reassuring parents that safety and security at the school remained a top priority. Mostly, the memo was to short-circuit the whirling rumor mill that by mid-day was describing crack-addled junkies carjacking Mr. Flowers at knifepoint and dumping him, naked and molested in front of the Ornery Pig Barbecue on route six.

By Thursday afternoon, the thrill had fizzled, especially since Dr. Bryson's memo had drained out all of the intrigue. At quarter to five, Duncan was in one of the small, sound-insulated rehearsal rooms finishing up his weekly lesson with Eric Fleenor. River Road Academy had a policy that required students to participate in after-school athletics. After complaints from parents of students disinclined to physical exertion, the school had broadened the policy to allow for music lessons as an alternative to athletics. This loophole created a minor musical renaissance within the student body. Although few of the sport-dodgers knew what a viola was, let alone had any interest in playing one, Duncan landed four students. These had been slow out of the blocks to sign up for the available options. Most enlisted in guitar lessons with Kurt Kleinbach, the woodworking teacher who had been strumming Bob Dylan songs since his college days in late 1960's Berkeley, California. Kurt was also Duncan's occasional supplier of fodder for the *Puffmeister*. The guitar lesson calendar filled quickly. The next desirable option was to take piano lessons from Erma Tomkins. Once her docket was full, the choice for the remaining students was to take viola from Mr. Flowers or be damned to odiferous locker rooms and calisthenics on wet sod.

The lessons with Eric Fleenor were the most challenging for Duncan. Eric had zero aptitude for the viola. To a great degree, this was a function of his pudgy little hands, dimpled at the knuckles. His sausage-like fingers fumbled on the fingerboard like elephant legs on a tightrope. Duncan was beginning to despair of Eric's ability to master the most basic techniques that he would need to play in the end-of-term recital required of all those in the after school music track. If he failed to make progress, next fall Eric's expansive rump would be squeezed back into a pair of River Road Ravens gym shorts to galumph around the intramural field with the rest of the PE herd.

"Eric, I think that's all for today," said Duncan. "I really need you to make the most of your practice time each day. Are you getting in the half hour that we've agreed to?"

"Yeah, I guess," said Eric. He already had his instrument in its case.

"Well, don't guess," said Duncan. "Make sure. You've got to master two octaves of the scales we've been working on. The only way to get it is to put in the time."

"Yeah, I know," said Eric.

"We meet four more times before the recital. Are you still planning to play Witches Dance?"

"Yeah."

"Alright," said Duncan, patting Eric on his pillowy shoulders. "Let's work on that too. We want to really nail it for Ms. Tomkins and the music committee."

"Yeah, okay," said Eric, padding out of the room and banging his instrument case on the doorframe.

Duncan wondered whether Simone had any idea of the abuse that the Duval rental instruments suffered at the hands of these thoughtless kids. He was putting away his own Duval loaner that he had picked up from Simone at lunchtime. It occurred to him that he was in no position to judge the thoughtlessness of his students. It was he who left his car perpetually unlocked and who treated his grandfather's viola with no more care than one would give an old umbrella.

"Hi, Duncan." Sarah Bugbee had opened the door and was poking her head in with her always-optimistic smile, and, it seemed to Duncan, was blushing slightly. "Are you finished for the day?"

"Hi, Sarah," said Duncan. "Yeah, all finished. Come on in."

"I didn't want to bother you," she said. "I just thought I would see how you were doing. I just feel terrible about what happened."

"Oh, I'm okay," he said.

"I heard they found your car," she said brightening again.

"Yes, they did," he said. "But, I'm afraid it was totaled. Whoever did it left it behind The Furniture Bonanza that went out of business last summer. They parked it next to a dumpster and set it on fire."

Sarah's eyes widened in amazement and she grasped Duncan's wrist. "No, they didn't!" she said.

"Yeah, can you believe it?" he said. "It mostly just toasted the interior. I'm surprised there wasn't a big explosion or something."

"Do they know who did it?" said Sarah with a look of distress as if the culprit might be lurking nearby.

"It was probably some kids. Probably not River Road kids— more likely just some hoodlums," he said. "The police told me they found a bunch of empty malt liquor cans and the car was covered with graffiti. Kurt Kleinbach gave me a lift down to the police lot today to see if there was anything I could salvage. There was nothing worth saving. I did grab my viola case out of the back. It was cooked, but I couldn't just leave it to be junked with the car. You know, Sarah, I got that viola from my grandfather when I was eight years old. That was the one thing he left me." The image of his old companion scorched on the floorboards came back to him along with self-recrimination for his negligence.

"Oh, you poor thing," said Sarah. She looked like she was going to cry. "I wish there was something I could do."

The intimacy of the rehearsal room and young Sarah Bugbee's gentle empathy aroused a swell of gratitude in Duncan. "I just really appreciate you looking in. You're such a good person." He reached out and touched her shoulder. Then he stroked her hair, brushing his fingertips lightly around her ear lobe. Sarah closed her eyes, her head listing slightly into his caresses. Not wanting to favor one ear over its counterpart, his other hand joined in the attentions. By the time Erma Tomkins strode into the rehearsal room, Sarah had clambered up onto Duncan and was wrapped around him like a three-toed sloth clinging to a tree trunk. Duncan staggered slightly to maintain balance with his newly acquired passenger, whose tongue was exploring his palate with the aid of a relentless suction.

"Excuse me!" said Erma. "What do you two think you are doing?"

Sarah released the vacuum on Duncan's mouth. Duncan's already somewhat bewildered expression translated into one of terror. "Oh, my God," he said, panting with the renewed free-flow of air to his lungs.

"Have you lost your minds?" said Erma with her hands on her hips, glowering at the enwrapped pair. Duncan still swayed under his burden. If anything, Sarah was squeezing him tighter. "Sarah, honey, can you please get down."

"Okay," said Sarah, sliding back to the floor. "I'm so sorry. It's all my fault."

"Sarah, you just need to go on home," said Erma. "I'm going to have a little talk with Mr. Flowers."

"Go ahead, Sarah," said Duncan. "It's okay."

After Sarah had unhooked her hair from behind her ears and disappeared behind the soundproof door, Erma turned to Duncan, two red, plastic orbs quivering indignantly below her own earlobes. "Have you gone completely crazy?" she said.

"I don't know what happened," he said. "We were just talking, and then... I don't know what happened."

"Well, I know what happened, Duncan," she said. "You have no self-control and, frankly, no self-respect."

"Hey, now. Come on, Erma," he said. "Okay, I made a mistake. We got a little carried away. We should've taken it off campus. But give me a break. We were—thought we were—in private, after hours. And we're both consenting adults."

"Then why don't you act like one?" she said. "For the past several years I've watched you behave more like a teenager than a grown-up. I know about your gallivanting social life and I see you rolling in here bleary-eyed and bed-headed every Friday and Monday morning. I don't believe for one second that you are any more interested in Sarah than you are in any of the other women you hook up with. She's barely half your age for heaven's sake."

"Is that what this is about?" he said. "Is this about you being jealous? You weren't so pious when it was you and me in the wrestling room after chaperoning the homecoming dance."

"Duncan, listen to me," she said. Her voice was now quiet and deliberate. She was not going to let this encounter devolve into a silly argument. "I frankly don't care what two adults do together in private. What I care about is when a friend of mine willfully harms himself. You're a good guy, Duncan. I can't just watch you flounder like this."

"Harm myself?" Duncan said. His tone still had an edge of defensiveness, but Erma had gotten his attention. "You're not making any sense."

"I know you were hurt by the divorce," she said. "But at some point, you have to pull yourself back together. Nobody else is going to do it for you."

"What are you talking about?" he said. "I'm together. It's not like I'm pining away in some garret."

Erma sat on the stool in front of the upright piano. She motioned for Duncan to take the folding chair that was the only other furnishing in the small, white room. "Would you say you are happy?"

"Oh, please," he said impatiently. "Yes."

"Is there anything you would change about your life if you had the chance?"

"No," he said, but then added, "I'd like to have my old viola back."

"Your viola?" she said. "That's the one thing you would change? Why is that?"

"I had a responsibility to keep it safe, and I didn't do it. I guess I didn't take it seriously," he said, his voice trailing off.

"Hmm." Erma shook her head in disappointment. "Well, it's late. Can I give you a ride home?"

After Erma dropped him off, Duncan once again recognized the familiar sounds of his neighbor Willie working in the garage next door. "*Mister* Flowers," said Willie in his eternally benevolent way when he saw his neighbor standing in the garage's side entrance. "Come on in my friend."

"Hey, Willie," said Duncan. "How's it coming with the Ranchero? Did you find the short?"

"Yeah," said Willie. "It took me half the night last night. I can tell you that Mrs. Hamilton was not happy. She doesn't like being up in the bed while I'm piddling around down here. She's worried I might fall out. She's always worrying me about my blood pressure"

"Well, it's good that she's looking out for you," said Duncan.

Willie laughed. "You ain't lying," he said. "Say, any news about your car?"

"Yeah," said Duncan. "The cop that wrote up the report phoned me yesterday. Whoever stole it just abandoned it and set fire to the interior. It's a total loss."

"I guess you'll have a little insurance coming?"

"Yeah, I haven't followed up on that, but whatever it is it won't be much."

"The good news is now you won't have to replace the head gasket," said Willie. "You just let me know when you're ready to look for your next car. I'll help you out." He pulled two beers out of the old GE and handed one to Duncan. He slid the two aluminum folding chairs out from the wall. Their hollow tubing grated thinly on the concrete. "I'm knocking off early. I can't have Mrs. Hamilton worrying." He lowered his bulk into the rickety frame, which gave a few squeaks but otherwise fulfilled its duty without complaint. He took a healthy slurp from his beer. The can looked miniature in his massive grasp. "They burned up the interior. Damn, that must have been a sight."

"That wasn't the biggest sight," said Duncan. "They spray painted penises all over the exterior. The cop said it had to be some juvenile delinquents out for a joy ride."

"Penises?"

"Yeah, big, fat penises. On the hood, the doors, the roof, everywhere."

"Good God," said Willie. "What about your viola?"

"It was still in the back seat, but it was cooked. I dropped it by my house earlier today. The case is a charcoal mess. I only glimpsed inside at the viola. The strings all popped and the whole thing is a sort of burnt caramel color with spidery cracks running everywhere. I just shut it back up and left it on my kitchen table."

"What a shame," said Willie.

"Yeah," said Duncan, staring at the pull-tab on the top of his still-full beer can. "I really screwed up. I was never careful with that viola, at least not since I was a kid. Unless it was hot outside, I would just toss it in the backseat of my unlocked car with the keys dangling over the visor. This was just bound to happen. I'm such an idiot."

"No need to go beating yourself up," said Willie. "That don't do any good."

"Well, I need to turn over a new leaf," said Duncan. "I won't even tell you about the stupid shit I did at school today. I've got to start taking things more seriously."

"Can I get you another one?" said Willie, pressing himself up from his chair. It twisted plaintively out of shape, but managed to recover in anticipation of Willie's return. Duncan shook his head to decline the offer. "Well, I'm still a little parched. I better have one more."

"Willie, you talk to a lot of people. You must have some advice for me."

"I can give you advice on cars," Willie said. "I can give you advice on hair cutting. Otherwise, I'm mostly in the listening business."

"Come on Willie," said Duncan. "I've blabbed away to you enough over the years. You must have some advice for me."

"What did you mean when you said you have to take things more seriously?"

"I just meant that I've got to start being more responsible, doing things like locking up my viola, or getting a new gasket for my car when the oil is leaking," said Duncan.

"Well," said Willie, tilting back his thick head and pausing to pour a stream of beer into his mouth. "It sounds like you have it all figured out already. Better overall care and maintenance. Right?"

CHAPTER ELEVEN ———————————————————

Duncan ran into the kitchen hugging his prize. His mother was chopping vegetables on the cutting board. She called over her shoulder for the excited eight-year-old to slow down. His father was leaning back against the counter nearby, drinking his ritualistic evening scotch on the rocks. "Look what Pappy gave me."

Duncan's mother did not acknowledge the boy's announcement, but his father set his drink aside and squatted down to examine the acquisition. "What have you got there, sport?"

"It's a viola," said Duncan. "It looks just like a violin, but it's not a violin. It's bigger. It's called a viola."

His mom's chopping was becoming more determined. His father said, "Well, that's a mighty fine gift from your Pappy. Did you say thank you?"

"Yes, sir."

"Good boy. Let's have a look." Together they laid out the case on the floor and examined the viola inside. Duncan's father lifted out the instrument and held it like a ukulele, strumming the untaut strings tunelessly and singing with a falsetto warble, "tip-toe through the tulips with me-eee."

"Ed!" said Duncan's mom over her shoulder. "You all shouldn't play with that thing in the kitchen."

"Okay, son," said Duncan's father. "Let's put it away. You need to take good care of this. Musical instruments aren't toys. You know that, right?"

"Yes, sir," said Duncan. "Pappy told me that I have to always take care of it. He told me all about it. It's very old and could be in a museum. It came from Italy. He was given it by a rich man who wanted Pappy to have it instead of sending it to a museum."

Duncan's father glanced quickly in the direction of his wife who was now tossing salad in a large bowl, jabbing two wooden implements erratically into its leafy depths. Shreds of lettuce and other vegetable fragments were flying onto the counter. Dr. Flowers smiled at his son. "That's quite a story Duncan. What a special gift. Now take it on up to your room and wash up for dinner."

Before long, Duncan wanted to learn to play his new instrument. Just taking it out from under the bed to admire it lost its appeal within a week. He asked his mom if he could take lessons. She advised him to take it up with his father. His father thought learning an instrument was a tremendous idea, and why not the viola? "Now, son, I'm happy to pay for you to have viola lessons, but studying music is serious business," his father said. "You have to take it seriously. Do you understand?"

"Yes, sir."

Duncan did take it seriously. He took his lessons once per week from Mr. Poojari, a prim and precise little man from Bangalore, India. At first they lasted half an hour, but Duncan was so diligent about practicing between lessons that within several months, Mr. Poojari suggested that Duncan was ready for a full hour. It was a proud afternoon for Duncan when he excitedly gathered his parents and Pappy in the living room and played a rendition of "If I Were a Rich Man" from the popular Broadway play, Fiddler on the Roof. The play had been made into a movie that came on TV a few months before. Duncan's mom declared at the time that Fiddler on the Roof was her favorite musical ever, and she adored Tevye's rendition of "If I Were a Rich Man." Duncan wanted to surprise her and worked on the piece for weeks with the help of Mr. Poojari. His mom proclaimed with glassy eyes that Duncan was her perfect little fiddler. The sound of that melody from his fiddle and the stirring effect it had on his mom would always be with him.

When he began at Grove Avenue Middle School two years later, the music teacher, Mrs. Boykin, was so impressed that she made him first chair in the string band, even though she normally just seated students alphabetically. When he reached eighth grade, she selected Duncan to play a solo recital at the fall assembly, another exceptional distinction.

Duncan would always remember his parents and his Pappy sitting in the front row of the auditorium. By then, Pappy had slipped into a mercifully blissful senility. His grinning face wagged like a tick-tocking metronome as Duncan played the second movement to Telemann's viola concerto in G-major beside Mrs. Boykin's bouncy accompaniment. Pappy had turned to Duncan's mom during the raining applause. "That boy playing the violin looks just like David!" he said. She only smiled and patted him on the hand, having long since become reconciled to her father's presence in the family's home and his advancing dementia.

It wasn't until after Pappy died, when Duncan was in ninth grade, that his mother took him aside and shared some of her childhood experiences. Duncan had had a friend over from school and she overheard Duncan telling the story of the viola, how it was a rare Italian masterpiece that belonged in a museum but that his grandfather had passed down to him instead. After the friend went home, she sat Duncan down in the living room. "Duncan, you know we all loved Pappy very much and he gave you a very special gift," she said. "And Pappy was full of stories. They were great stories, but you have to realize that they were only great stories." She went on to tell Duncan about her difficult childhood in her father's absence and of his incurable propensity to weave tales that allowed him to avoid facing life. "In a lot of ways, he never grew up to learn that sometimes you have to do things that are serious and aren't any fun."

Duncan's face reddened. He didn't know if he were angry or sad. "You shouldn't say such mean things about Pappy."

"I'm not trying to be mean. I want you to have fond memories of him. I just didn't want you to mistake his stories for reality. You should cherish the story about your viola like you would cherish a favorite bedtime story, but at the same time you need to know that the story isn't true."

Duncan did not want to believe what his mother told him, yet he suspected as much, at least subconsciously, all along. Pappy's stories were always so far fetched, but Duncan adored them and the storyteller. Pappy was a chauffeur, a cowboy, a circus entertainer, a balloon pilot, a train engineer, a sheriff— once for real and once as an actor—and even a Hollywood movie producer. Duncan had to admit that these tales were implausible, except that when Pappy told them, he made them real. He became the man he described. It took some time, but finally Duncan had to admit to himself that his mother was right. Pappy probably picked up that junky, bloated viola in some trade, probably on his way into town from that theme park in North Carolina, or wherever he was really coming from. Both Mr. Poojari and Mrs. Boykin had remarked on his viola's oddly arched belly. They agreed that it had a good sound— rich, though not strong. Now he realized that it likely had an odd shape and underpowered sound because it was just a cheap, amateur job, but it was Pappy's gift to him and he cherished it.

High school marked a new phase for Duncan. Music became less of a priority, in part because of the demystified status of his instrument and in part because he had become more interested in his social standing, especially with respect to his female counterparts. He played in the school orchestra, but he avoided taking it as seriously as he once had. He even toyed with pursuing a degree in music in college, but this was more out of a lack of better ideas than a true passion. By then he was well established on the path of least resistance and he ultimately found that math was the perfect major for him since he was naturally good at it and since it never required any term paper writing.

"David," his Pappy was fond of saying before he slipped out of coherence. "Life is too short to spend it playing other people's games by other people's rules. You just play your own game and you'll have a lot more fun."

When Duncan got home from drinking his half beer at Willie's, he stood in the kitchen staring at the charred viola case that he recovered from the police lot earlier in the day. It lay inert in the middle of the kitchen table. A dusting of ashy flecks had accumulated on the table around the perimeter of the case. He pried up the latches and peeked inside. He plucked out a small, clear plastic bag containing something like shredded tobacco or Italian spices. It was the bag of pot that he had bought from Kurt Kleinbach while Kurt chauffeured Duncan on the midday run to the police lot and to Duval Violins to pick up a loaner viola. "Dude, you've got to be way bummed about losing all your shit," Kurt had said before suggesting that a little weed could go a long way to easing a troubled soul. Duncan had fed the last of his stash to the Puffmeister two nights before and so he figured it would be prudent to re-stock.

Duncan stared for a moment into the sealed clump of marijuana resting in his hand. He glanced from his palm to the scorched sarcophagus lying on the table before him. After a moment, he turned and walked to the bathroom where he inverted the bag over the toilet and tossed the emptied plastic pouch into the wastebasket. Leaning forward to flush, he paused, stood back up, unzipped his pants and relieved himself on the discarded contraband that peppered the inside of the bowl. Then he flushed.

Back in the kitchen, Duncan fumbled around in the drawer below the telephone. He pulled out a wad of expired coupon fliers and a bare roll of aluminum foil before finding the River

Road Ravens student and faculty directory. He phoned Sarah and apologized for letting himself get carried away. He had expected her to be distraught; he certainly was. Curiously, she seemed to be her typical ebullient self. He could have been just as easily apologizing for bumping into her tray in the cafeteria line. At school the next day, when he passed her in front of Dr. Bryson's office, she flashed him an undiminished, flirtatious smile. Duncan only managed to nod awkwardly and continue briskly down the hallway.

On Saturday, he was up well before his customary mid-morning revival hour. Whether spring was making a particularly brilliant debut or whether his mood made him more attuned, he had to pause on his crumbling walkway and draw in a balmy breath of blossoming morning air. It certainly helped that for the first time in recent memory he was up and about in the world before noon on a weekend without his brainpan throbbing and his mouth tasting like a fermented bar rag.

"What a great day!" he said to Simone before the tiny bells on the shop door had finished their welcoming jingle at Duval Violins. She smiled at him from her stool behind the counter.

"Hey there," she said. "What are you up to?"

"Not much. I'm really just stopping in to say *hi*."

"Isn't that nice," she said. "It's been pretty quiet here. I'm just minding the store and catching up on important reading." She held up the cover of the magazine that had been laid out in front of her. It showed a famous Hollywood couple walking down a matrimonial aisle. Between their radiant faces on the cover floated a pink cartoon heart rent in half. The headline read *Divine Duo Divorce During Honeymoon*. There was a smaller headline announcing *The Amazing Pickle Diet*. "So, how is the loaner working out?"

"Oh, just fine. Thanks for helping me out until I get a new one," he said. "Listen, I actually wanted to come by to apologize to you."

"Apologize? What for?" she said.

"Well, for all those times I phoned you in the middle of the night to hit on you, and all the way back to that night in your apartment after the quartet. You are a good friend and I've acted like a dolt."

Simone gave him a quizzical but sympathetic smile. "Duncan, that's all part of your charm. You don't have anything to apologize for. Anyway, I can't remember the last time you phoned me in the middle of the night." Now she laughed. "I was beginning to think you didn't like me anymore."

"Are you kidding?" he said. "It's just that I finally got the picture that you had a boyfriend. Admittedly, I was slow on the uptake, but I eventually got it."

"Yes, well..." Simone started a small flurry of activity tidying up the counter, putting away the magazine, re-aligning the stapler beside the cash register and straightening the ink pens in the can that looked like a miniature bass drum. "Anyway, you mentioned yesterday that you got your viola back. Do you think it could be repaired?"

"I think that would be like trying to uncook a slice of crispy burnt bacon," he said. "But you know, maybe I could have it cleaned up somehow for display. It may not have been worth much, but it was pretty special to me."

"I know," she said. "You told me about getting it from your grandfather. He sounded like quite a character. We'd be happy to take a look at it if you want."

The shop door jingled. Alex leaned his head partially in. "Okay, I'm on my way to the Smithsonian thing in DC. I'll see you this evening," he said. Now he saw that Duncan was there talking to Simone. He seemed perturbed and mildly confused. "Oh, hey," was all he said, still remaining outside and peering in.

"Alex, come in for a second," said Simone. "There's something we want to ask you about real quick."

Alex hesitated. "Uh, can it wait? I should get on the road. The thing starts at two."

Simone crossed her eyes in mock vexation. "Just come in for one second, Mr. Busyguy."

Alex's head dropped in resignation. He came in. He was carrying a viola case. "I just don't want to be late to the conference. It only lasts three hours and I'm already pushing it."

"What's in the case?" said Simone.

"It's... for the conference," said Alex. He stared down uncertainly at the case hanging by his side. "It's just one of our student violas. They suggested that we bring an instrument so we can have a... hands-on reference during one of the lectures."

Simone's brow knitted slightly and her head tilted. Then she shrugged her shoulders and said, "You know about Duncan's viola, right?"

"Oh, yeah," said Alex, turning to Duncan in faux earnest. "That was a terrible thing. I heard your car and viola were burned to a crisp."

"Well, almost," said Duncan. "The fire kind of fizzled. The cop said whoever did it probably threw some gasoline or lighter fluid inside, but once that was burned up, everything just sort of smoldered. Of course, the car is a total loss. What a mess."

"Oh," said Alex. "And the viola. I suppose there was very little left of that."

"Actually, it survived, sort of," said Duncan. "Maybe because it was down on the floor. It's pretty cooked, but it's in one piece. I haven't even taken it out of the case. I was thinking I might get it cleaned up, stabilized, whatever, so I could display it."

"So, I suggested to Duncan that he bring the viola to the shop so you and I could take a look at it," said Simone. "That's all I wanted to ask you about. Don't you think we could have a go at refurbishing it to a presentable state?"

Alex's mouth had dropped open in dismay. "Uh, I don't know. I'm guessing it's too brittle. It would probably fall to pieces if you even mess with it," he said. "I mean I just don't know what to tell you."

"Well," said Duncan. "I haven't decided what I want to do. It's just a thought."

"Listen, I better run," said Alex distractedly. He glanced at Simone as he headed to the door, case in hand. "See you tonight, baby."

"Okay," she said pantomiming a look of bewilderment to Duncan. "Have fun."

CHAPTER THIRTEEN ─────────────────────────────

Boston was not leaving winter behind without a fight. James Dickerson dodged out of the bone-chilling April gusts and into Allegro Antiquities. Larry was already busy in his workshop, clamping a set of C-bouts into a violin mold for one of his Atelier Giles originals. He looked up as James bustled through the door. "Hey, what's up? How was DC?" said Larry.

"A lot warmer than Boston," said James.

"What's in the case?" said Larry. "I knew you couldn't come home empty-handed."

"I never do; do I?" said James. "This, my friend, is a most interesting item. Why don't you have a look and tell me what you think?" James placed the inexpensive, canvas-covered case on the workbench. Larry looked at James for some indication of what to expect, but got none.

"Okay, I'll play," said Larry. He popped open the case and opened it. "Hmm. What have we here? High arch. Nice color. May I?"

"By all means," said James, giving a fluid wave to indicate that Larry had full license to examine.

Larry lifted out the viola carefully, but with the deft precision of someone accustomed to handling delicate artifacts. He explored the surfaces with his hands and his gaze. From above the workbench he pulled down a magnifying glass affixed to an extendable arm and equipped with a fluorescent light. Larry continued the scrutiny for about half a minute. "Very, very interesting," he said finally. "Graceful, confident f-holes. Elegant scrollwork." He frowned at the deep scratch on the top of the scroll, rubbing it empathetically with his thumb. "I love the varnish— translucent red with a golden fire beneath." Running his finger along the thin, black double-line of pear wood at the perimeter of the face, Larry nodded appreciatively. "The purfling is so fine, perfect, as close to the outer edge as only a master would dare to go."

"So, who do you think made it?" said James.

"That's your department," said Larry. "I know craftsmanship, but I can't keep up with every luthier who ever lived, like you can. I see it had a label at one time, but I guess it was removed."

"You don't want to venture a guess as to the provenance," said James.

"I'll guess Italy in the seventeenth century, or at least that's what it's supposed to look like," said Larry, slipping the instrument back into its compartment. "But judging from the cheapo case and the fairly recent scratches, I'd say you got this at a pawn shop."

"You're not far off," said James. "Actually, the man who brought it to me must think I am a pawn broker who deals in pilfered antiquities with no questions asked."

Larry laughed and clamped James on the shoulder. "I assume you didn't ask any questions."

The corners of James's mouth turned up minutely as he snapped the case shut and slid it under his arm. "I have been engaged by a client to perform an appraisal. Allegro Antiquities is nothing if not discreet."

"So who made it?" said Larry.

"I'll let you know when I figure that out."

On the following Wednesday James beckoned Larry over to his office in the rear of the shop. They could leave the front unattended because it was always locked. They received clients by appointment only. To enter Allegro Antiquities, discretely located in a classic Georgian row house in Beacon Hill, was to enter a sphere of grace and culture. The clientele paid as much for the exclusive image as for the tangible artifacts they purchased, and for most the image was the greater attraction.

The antiquities side featured several ornate oriental rugs, substantial carved wood moldings, a sprinkling of eighteenth and nineteenth century oil paintings, and museum-quality displays of numerous rare instruments, some behind glass, others standing or hung in the open. The workshop side conveyed no less an image of classic sophistication. Larry had taken great pains to create a display as much as a practical work space. The cabinetry and bench surfaces alone were works of woodworking artistry. A variety of wooden moulds and instruments in various phases of repair or construction dangled from above. On the wall hung Larry's array of luthier's tools, many of which he had acquired while in Italy. There were files, gouges, saws, knives, planes, clamps, and a collection of neatly organized bottles, canisters and sachets containing glues, varnishes, oils, powders and color extracts. For the most part, he preferred to use the same tools and techniques that his predecessors had used for hundreds of years.

It was in the back of the shop, behind the front façade, where the wheels of the operation turned. It was to this crowded wheelhouse that James had now invited Larry. Here was the cluttered repository of James's collected books and files from thirty years in the business. Many of his reference materials, meticulously jumbled on shelves and in teetering stacks, were themselves historical rarities.

"What's up," said Larry. He was wearing a well-used, moss-green apron and wiping his hands with a rag.

"You remember my little acquisition from my DC trip?" said James. "Well, the evidence is in and it is intriguing."

"Oh, really?" said Larry, dropping into the nineteenth century, Shaker chair that stood across the desk from where James sat looking at his flat screen computer monitor. The monitor stood incongruously as being among the few items in the room that could not have been made before the industrial revolution. Not only was it decidedly modern, it was decidedly cutting edge modern. James may have been a man drawn to antiquity, but he was no Luddite. In fact, he embraced the forefront of whatever modern technologies might enhance his access to the past. He also took pride in his ability to evolve with the modern marketplace. He personally developed and maintained the company's website and published a monthly e-newsletter to help grow and maintain a burgeoning mailing list of well-heeled potential customers.

"I called in a favor and had Chuck expedite the lab work for me," said James. "I ordered two reports. First, here's the x-ray fluorescence analysis." James clicked his mouse twice and rotated the high-definition, large screen monitor so Larry could see. "Here, I'm looking at the chemical composition of the varnish. I want to see if this is something that perhaps a Cremonese master would have used or is it something more modern. You can take one look at the instrument and tell it has an old-style oil varnish and not a spirit varnish, but here's what the analysis shows."

Larry squinted at the tables of values and the accompanying line chart that looked like the readout of a heart monitor on a patient having an infarction. "Am I supposed to get something from all this?" he asked.

"Do you see the spikes here and... here?" said James. "Those are the levels of iron and arsenic, both highly typical of the varnishes used in the days of Stradivarius. If this were a later varnish, I would expect to see spikes for manganese, cobalt, maybe copper, zinc."

"Come on, James," said Larry. "Even I can tell this definitely ain't no Strad."

"I didn't say it was," said James. "Now let's look at the dendrochronology." James made a few more clicks with his mouse, pulling up a new image on the screen, what appeared to be the cover sheet of a report. James scrolled down through several pages of dense text to a graph with three lines zigging and zagging in nearly identical paths across the chart. "This chart considers wood samples and tracks the spacing between growth rings from year to year. Obviously, higher growth years are higher on the chart and the reverse for lower growth. The blue line represents the grain of the spruce from the viola's belly. The red line is the maple from the back. The black line is our reference baseline."

"What did you use as a reference?" said Larry.

"Ah, yes," said James. "I had a feeling about our specimen and so I asked Chuck to use data we have from a 1666 Italian violin that I brokered through Tarisio three years ago. As you can see, the growth rings from our specimen align almost exactly with those of the reference sample. So, it is highly likely that the wood used in our specimen and in the reference sample came from trees that grew in the same region during the same time frame."

"Okay, you've got a region and a timeframe, but do you have a maker?" said Larry. "Who made the 1666 violin that you used as a specimen?"

"That instrument was made by Nicolò Amati," said James. Larry looked incredulous, but James continued. "The Cremona masters took great care in selecting their woods, which could come from hundreds of kilometers away, having been floated down the Po. It is rather interesting that the wood in our specimen should be so closely identified with the wood that we know Nicolò Amati selected for one of his masterworks."

"Interesting, but are you suggesting that your client's viola is actually by Amati?"

"Let me show you a couple of other things," said James. A few clicks later, a photograph appeared on the screen. "What do you see?"

"Okay, it's a label," said Larry. He read the faded text. "Nicolaus Amatus Cremonae Hieronymus et Antonius Nepos fecit anno...." Larry squinted at the image. "The date is sixteen sixty-something. I guess somebody put a tack through the last digit. It looks like the label's tacked on the block. This is the label from the 1666 violin that Tarisio sold?"

"No," said James placidly. "It is a photograph that I had Chuck take of the interior of our mysterious viola. Of course, what's in a label? But I want to show you something else." A few more clicks. He pulled up a black and white image of a viola, viewed straight on. "This is an authenticated viola by Nicolò Amati that is at the Henry Ford Museum. Now we'll trace the shape of the instrument." A thin red line spontaneously coursed its way around the viola's edges and f-holes. Then with a click the viola disappeared leaving just the hollow red outline on an otherwise blank screen. "Okay, we both know that once a master created a successful mould for a given type of instrument, it became a trademark template. Let's see how our mysterious viola stacks up with the Amati trademark." With a final click, the image of their specimen instrument appeared. The red outline matched every contour precisely.

"Not bad," said Larry, nodding his head in appreciation of the evidence laid out by his partner. "So, what's your final assessment?"

"Well, the odds of an authentic Nicolò Amati viola appearing out of nowhere nearly three and a half centuries after it was made are so slim that they are effectively zero."

"So, this is an amazing fake?" said Larry.

"All I'm saying is that, in my experience, such a thing does not appear with no historical evidence to support it," said James. "That's why I began looking for a possible thread that may link our specimen to its putative heritage." He spun his chair around and lifted a hefty tome from the credenza and transferred it to his desk with a thud. "One useful place to look is always *The Strad*. Just about any significant occurrence in the world of strings has been covered in this journal. I just so happen to have every issue since 1890. This volume contains 1940, 41 and 42. I searched my online sources and found reference to an Amati viola that disappeared in 1940 and hasn't been seen since. Allow me to read to you from the June 1940 issue of *The Strad*." He drew open the bound set to a place he had marked with a letter opener whose handle was in the shape of a treble clef sign.

NOTES and NEWS— Gutmann Collection Donated to Met— The Metropolitan Museum of Art is the beneficiary of the stringed instrument collection of Mr. Abraham Gutmann, passionate patron of music and founder of Gutmann Jewelry in Manhattan. Mr. Gutmann died last year at the age of 81. He was an avid and gracious collector, frequently lending his fine instruments to promising musicians who could not otherwise afford instruments commensurate with their superlative abilities.

In March of this year, Mr. Gutmann's executors transferred title of 22 stringed instruments to the museum, including... Let me just skip ahead to the most interesting bit. *A local dealer, Blaise Rosat, familiar with the Gutmann collection has asserted that a rare 1661 viola by Nicolò Amati should have been part of the estate. Representatives from the Wurlitzer Company, which stored the collection, provided documentation with the transfer confirming the completeness and accuracy of the pieces that they delivered to the Museum. They did, however, confirm that they represented Mr. Gutmann in the 1922 purchase of a 1661 Amati viola from a private collector in Britain, but that viola was never placed in storage with Wurlitzer. No trace has been found of the mysterious Amati viola. Police authorities are investigating a possible link between the disappearance of the Amati and that of Mr. Gutmann's automobile, which was also absent from the estate.*

James replaced the letter opener and closed the book, giving it a crisp pat that caused a small grey cloud to erupt from the dingy cover.

"Nice," said Larry.

"My friend," said James, rubbing his hands together and revealing the sly smile that he only allowed himself within the confines of the back office. "I'd say we have ourselves a live one."

CHAPTER FOURTEEN ————————————————————

At the end of April, a brief but torrid preview of summer overtook spring in central Virginia, giving occasion to several analysis articles in the local paper, including one decrying the havoc caused to the seasonal cycles by those selfish citizens who insisted on lighting their homes with incandescent bulbs. Nils Nilsson had just finished reading this particular article and was gazing pensively out the window of his office suite on the twenty-third floor of the Nilsson Center. He picked up his phone and pressed the top speed-dial key.

"Yes, Mr. Nilsson," said Norma. She had been at Nils's right hand for over ten years and was never more than one press-of-a-button away. Her short-cropped hair and unflagging precision gave her somewhat of a military air. But her value was not in her undeniable ability to follow orders. It was in her knack for anticipating her boss's needs and filling them before they arose.

"Norma, will you get me a meeting with Hans," he said. "I want him to pull together some thoughts on how we might integrate more green energy features into Nilsson Town Center. I want to make sure that my mall is attractive to everyone, including global warming kooks."

"Will do," she said. "While I've got you. I have a caller on the other line named Dale Overby. He says he deals in rare musical instruments. He's calling from Los Angeles. I was going to take a message."

"Nah, just put him through," said Nils. "If he's going to get up at six in the morning to phone from the west coast, I'll see what he has to say."

Several seconds later, the call arrived at Nils's phone. As usual, Nils staked out the dominant role. "Mr. Overby, I've got about two minutes. What's on your mind?"

An erudite, vaguely British accent came over the line. "Fair enough, I'll get right to it then Mr. Nilsson. I know you are very busy and I appreciate your consideration. I assist clients in buying and selling rare musical instruments. I don't normally initiate client contacts, but I have run across your name too many times now not to introduce myself. The world of musical antiquities is rather small and I must say that the recent acquisitions of your trust are impressive. The Nilsson Music Trust has established an enviable reputation."

If Mr. Overby was hoping to flatter Nils, he had succeeded, but Nils was not one to let that compromise his hardnosed business demeanor. "I appreciate that Mr. Overby. I've got about another minute. Make the most of it."

"Not a problem, Mr. Nilsson," said Overby, utterly unperturbed. "I simply wanted to introduce myself and to make you aware, if you are not already, that Overby International has enormous connections in the world of rare instruments. To the degree that your organization is seeking to add to its collection and may find that the public auction market is not offering a satisfactory selection, we have the ability to tap into private avenues. The big auction houses have big corporate overheads to maintain and charge correspondingly hefty fees. Many sellers, frankly, can't be bothered, and that's where Overby International comes in. We offer efficiency. With your permission, I'd like to send you some information about us. You may also be interested in our website at OverbyInternational dotcom. It provides an overview of our services and also lists several opportunities that we currently have available, including two pristine baroque viols, a Ruggieri cello and an Amati viola. You won't find any of these instruments under the hammer in New York or London."

"I appreciate the call Mr. Overby," said Nils. "Send me your information. We'll keep it on file and contact you if we need anything. How's the weather out there?"

"Eternally balmy," came Overby's undiscouraged reply.

"Wonderful. Have a nice day." After Nils ended the call with a perfunctory jab, he contemplated the bright morning skyline, uninterrupted across two entire walls of his vast corner office. He could just make out the grayish purple silhouette of the Blue Ridge Mountains to the west. He tapped the top speed-dial key. Norma picked up.

"Do me a favor," said Nils. "See what you can find out about this guy Overby who just called. You might start with his website, OverbyInternational dotcom. I'm heading over to Monument Municipal to check on progress at the golf course. I intend to remain ahead of schedule so those slugs at City Hall can see what productivity looks like. Then I'm with the lawyers. You can tell me what you find on Overby when I get back this afternoon." He tapped the key again to end the call without waiting for a response.

At a little after two that afternoon, Nils strode off the elevator and past Norma's desk. He was speaking to someone on his cell phone, but interrupted himself in midsentence to say to her, "I'm ready for you." She grabbed a manila file folder whose tab was already identified by an adhesive strip from her prolific label maker. It said simply *OVERBY INT'L*. She took her customary place across the desk from Nils, who was already oscillating impatiently in his oversized black leather rolling chair as the party on the cell phone talked. His starkly barren, clear acrylic desktop sat dramatically atop an artistically engineered frame of chromed tubular steel. He snapped the cell phone shut and dropped it into the side pocket of his charcoal gray suit jacket.

"Is Hans lined up?" he said.

"Hans is flying in on Wednesday," she said. "He says he's excited to work on more green concepts. I took the liberty of suggesting that they should be at least financially neutral."

"You're damn right," said Nils. "What else?"

"I've done preliminary research on Overby International."

"Alright. Let's hear it."

"Well, they have a very elegant website describing them as brokers of high-value antique instruments, based in Los Angeles. There's a bio of Overby there. It says he is British and worked for a dealer in London called Digby & Sons Limited until coming to the states in 1989 to start his own firm. The sight lists a number of trades that they have brokered. Other than their own website, there's nothing I could find online about them."

"That's all you've got?" said Nils, raising his eyebrows and leaning forward.

Norma responded to Nils's impatient question by simply turning to the next sheet in her file. "I looked into the transactions that they claim to have brokered and I did indeed find references to the sales on various trade sights, but they don't say who the brokers were."

"What else?"

"I phoned the auction house in New York where you purchased the instruments in the Nilsson Quartet and asked about Overby. I spoke to Franz. He said he did not know Overby, but he found him listed in the dealer database, registered with the same contact information as appears on the website you gave me."

"So that's it?" said Nils. "Nobody knows this guy?"

Norma turned over the last sheet in her file. "I found a web page for Digby & Sons Limited. It wasn't much more than the company name, address and a blurb about them. I phoned and spoke to a man named Derek Wingfield-Digby."

Nils smirked. "Now there's a name with character. That beats 'Øystein' hands down. What was he like?"

Norma paused and glanced upward. "He was a bit... stodgy," she said. "His photo appears on the web page. He looks like Sherlock Holmes's Dr. Watson. Apparently, he is the current owner of the firm. He confirmed that Overby had been one of their representatives. He told me that he took a 'dim view' of people like Overby."

"Now we're getting somewhere," said Nils. "What's his beef with Overby."

"He claims that Digby & Sons provided Overby with the best training in the business, making him into a leading expert. He says Overby repaid their investment in him by going off on his own and becoming a competitor."

"Hmm. Interesting," said Nils.

"Wingfield-Digby said that Overby was more interested in profits than tradition. He suggested that he was probably more at home with us Yanks." Norma closed the manila folder on her lap. "That's all I have."

"Excellent," said Nils. "I consider that a glowing endorsement. I'm liking this Overby more and more."

Norma departed and Nils spun around to the minimalist computer monitor and wireless keyboard on the acrylic and steel table behind his desk. Nils hated to have cables cluttering his office. As with his telephone, Nils had insisted that what few cables could not be eliminated should be run invisibly through the tubular supports of the furniture. He pulled up Overby's website and made his way to the section called *New Opportunities*. He found the viola that Overby had referenced. There was a front-view photo with the caption *Viola by Nicolò Amati, 1664*.

Nils twirled back to his desk and picked up the phone. Looking back to his monitor to confirm the numbers at the bottom of the screen he punched in the desired digits. After a moment a man's voice issued a greeting. "Overby International, may I help you?"

"Nils Nilsson for Dale Overby."

"Yes, of course. One moment please."

Half a minute later, Overby's voice came on. "Mr. Nilsson, what a pleasant surprise," said Overby. "What can I do for you?"

"I'm interested in your Amati viola."

CHAPTER FIFTEEN ─────────────────

James Dickerson tilted his head heavenward as he crossed the granite plaza toward the office building that was his destination. He paused momentarily to bask in the beneficence of the noonday sun. James was always a fastidious dresser, but today a bowler hat topped off the look of his double-breasted, powder-grey pinstripe suit, precisely knotted silk tie and laboriously polished black wingtips. He carried at his side an oblong aluminum case.

As he exited the elevator on his destination floor, a middle-aged, efficient looking woman greeted him and offered to take his hat. "Did you have a nice flight, Mr. Overby?"

"It was lovely," replied James's alter ego, his accent now modulated several degrees east of his normally intercontinental timbre.

"Mr. Nilsson is ready for you. It's right this way," she said. "May I bring you a coffee? Mineral water?" Overby smiled appreciatively, waving his hand to decline the offer. She directed him through the open office doorway that seemed to extend upward to twice his height.

"Mr. Overby!" called out Nils, circumnavigating his iceberg of a desk with his hand already extended in greeting. "What good fortune that you could make it out here so quickly."

"I am always on the move," said Overby. "I'm engaged for several east coast meetings over the next several days and then I'm over to Italy and on from there to Tokyo. But I'm always reachable through my office and always working to serve my clients."

"Let's see what you have brought," said Nils.

"May I?" said Overby nodding toward the immense desktop.

"Of course," said Nils.

Overby laid the aluminum case carefully on the transparent surface. From his jacket pocket he retrieved a key and unlocked the case's two security latches. He popped them open along with the two additional latches. "This case is hermetically sealed and humidity controlled. It can sustain a fall of three meters onto concrete with no damage to the contents." Now he lifted open the case, revealing its precious cargo. "This, Mr. Nilsson is a rare masterpiece. It is an authentic viola made by one of the greatest luthiers in history. Nicolò Amati not only produced great instruments such as the one before you, but he is responsible for passing the art down to other great masters. I know you have an appreciation for Amati's artistic descendents, among whom are counted some makers already dear to you, such as Grancino, Guarneri del Gesù and Stradivari. Should you decide to purchase this instrument, it would be a crowning element for your collection."

"Who is the owner?" said Nils.

"The owner is a member of the Saudi royal family," said Overby. "My client is in the process of divesting himself of selected assets to raise cash. He is not using the public auction markets because he would prefer not to draw attention to his financial... affairs."

"How much is your client asking?" said Nils.

"The asking price is one hundred twenty thousand dollars." Said Overby. "I have had this commission for about ten days and there are several clients showing an interest. I fully expect to get the full price, probably during my east coast swing."

"I'd like to examine it," said Nils.

"Of course," said Overby. "By all means. The instrument is in playing condition and has a smooth, full sound. The only requirement is that we wear gloves when handling the instrument, at the request of my client." Overby retrieved a pair of white cotton gloves from a compartment inside the case and handed them to Nils. He also produced a pair of his own from his jacket pocket, and both men donned their protective layers.

Nils held the viola up to the light, eyeing it inexpertly from various angles. He squinted over the left sound hole. "What the hell? Why is there no label?" said Nils.

"That is one of the fascinating and unique features of this viola," said Overby. "In fact, there is a label." He assisted Nils in catching a glimpse of the label tacked to the interior block at the base of the neck. "It was likely moved during the eighteenth century when it would have been taken apart and modified, as virtually all baroque instruments were, to meet classical playing demands."

"Wait a second," said Nils. "You're telling me that this instrument has been through some chop shop?"

"Hardly, Mr. Nilsson," said Overby. "I am referencing the types of modifications that, I assure you, also would have been carried out on your other masterpieces. Instruments that were built to play Bach were not particularly suited to play Beethoven. To evolve with the demands, strings needed to be tighter, soundposts and base bars had to be strengthened. The necks got a little longer to maintain the tonal properties. They tilted backward. These inevitable adjustments meant disassembling and reassembling the instruments, but the most important element was always unchanged: the soundbox. The body of the instrument, the shape, the placement of the f-holes, even the varnish— there is where the magic resides."

"Why have I never heard of this before?" said Nils.

Because you have more money than sense, thought Overby. "I'm sure I don't know, but I anticipate you will do your due diligence. I have brought with me the paperwork that we discussed." Overby extracted a large envelope from the compartment in the top of the case. He removed some papers and laid them out on the acrylic surface. The first was a yellowed, official looking document in a plastic sleeve. "Here is the certificate of authenticity, by Digby & Sons Limited, dated 1906."

"You worked there didn't you?" said Nils.

"I did, many years ago," said Overby, adding with a dry chuckle, "Of course, this precedes my tenure there by a few years. The house has been in the business since the 1820's. They've become somewhat of an obscurity, but they are still at it. I run across old Derek Wingfield-Digby in London, now and again." Overby turned back to the documents before them. "Next, we have a photograph of the label that is affixed to the block."

"I can't read the full date," said Nils. "What's that spot?"

"Whoever relocated the label tacked it to the block rather than gluing it," said Overby. "The spot you see on each end is a brass tack. The one on the right obscures the last digit of the year. You can just see the downstroke of the four, making the date 1664. Your certificate of authenticity bears out the correct year, which Digby & Sons would have corroborated through various historical resources."

"Uh huh."

"Personally, I think the affair of the label lends this specimen an added cachet," said Overby. "Finally, here is our standard consignment agreement, the same one I emailed you a few days ago."

"Yes, I've read it," said Nils. "It's fine."

"With your signature, Mr. Nilsson, you will have the instrument at your disposal for twenty-four hours in order to undertake professional evaluations as provided in the agreement," said Overby. "I know that is a very short window, but I'm afraid it is all that we have available at this time."

"Don't worry," said Nils. "I'll make the most of it."

"With your permission, and as a small consolation, I'd like to come back at the end of the day tomorrow, around five. I'll be in a teleconference until then. That will give you a few extra hours on top of the agreement."

"Fine," said Nils. "Come back at five. I will have the viola ready for you."

An hour after Dale Overby departed the Nilsson Center, Nils bounced through the jingling door at Duval Violins. It was over half a year since his last visit, where he announced his project to assemble a quartet, and now his look of perpetual confidence had a triumphant edge. To his annoyance, Simone was helping a woman and her elementary-school-aged daughter. Simone stood behind the counter holding a student violin. The woman seemed distraught, while the daughter was content to stare at her mother's leg while tugging downward on the hem of her own pink t-shirt, causing the neck opening to distort and stretch toward her navel.

"We've checked it out," said Simone reassuringly. "Everything is fine. We've reset the bridge. They can get knocked over. It's not a big deal. The key is to keep the instrument in its case whenever its not being played." The woman expressed her gratitude to Simone and then began scolding her daughter for stretching the t-shirt, which was just the sort of thoughtless behavior that had knocked over the bridge on the violin. The woman became startled when she realized a tall, distinguished man with an important looking case was standing behind her, and she made a flustered exit, tugging her still-expressionless child by the wrist.

"So, how is my beautiful friend Simone?" said Nils as the bells signaled the all-clear.

"Hi, Nils," said Simone. "We haven't seen you for a while."

He lowered his voice confidentially. "I came by because I have something I want to show you." Nils lifted up the aluminum case and patted it with his free hand.

"What have you got there?"

"I am about to make an important acquisition and I wanted to get your professional opinion." Simone noticed that his tone sounded more amorous than professional. "It's the viola that will complete the Nilsson Quartet Collection."

"Congratulations."

"I thought you might take a look and let me know what you think," said Nils. "I wanted to give you first look at a 1664 masterpiece by Nicolò Amati." He slid the case onto the counter.

"I should get Alex to come out and take a look," she said. The less alone time with Nils, the better. "He's the real specialist when it comes to antiques." Before Nils could respond, she had poked her head through the door behind the counter and invited Alex to come have a look.

Alex appeared. When he perceived that Nils was at the counter, his expression became guarded. "Hello, Mr. Nilsson."

"Hello," said Nils, his enthusiasm on the wane. "I have come into possession of a viola by Nicolò Amati. I thought you might be interested in having a look."

Alex laughed nervously. James had called days ago to say that he was initiating discussions with Nils, but Alex had not expected things to move so quickly. He certainly didn't expect Nils to show up in the shop with the instrument. "Sure, sure. We would love to have a look." He glanced quickly at Simone who was watching him. "What a surprise."

Nils popped open the latches and revealed the instrument inside. A bit of zeal returned to his expression as he assumed the demeanor of a proud father gazing upon his first born. "There she is, a real masterpiece." Nils said. He turned to Simone and gestured toward the case. "Please, feel free. You just have to wear these gloves." Nils lifted the lid to the little compartment where the gloves resided.

Simone demurred and invited Alex to do the honors. He awkwardly pulled on the gloves and lifted out of its repose the viola that he had only recently stolen from Duncan Flowers. A knot had formed behind his sternum and dampness was spreading across his scalp. Nils had assumed a commanding posture, with arms crossed, to observe his prize being taken through its paces. Alex looked sheepishly upon the object in his hands. "Well... uh, let's see what we have... very, very nice." Nils inhaled deeply, his nostrils flaring approvingly at this meaningless assertion.

Alex began to relax. Maybe this could be fun. "Oh, yes!" said Alex. "Wonderful color. Such craftsmanship." He squinted into the soundholes and looked up toward the neck. The light was bad, but he glimpsed the corner of the label, which he already knew was there. "And there is the trademark Amati label. Interesting. Stuck to the block. I have never seen that before.

That is something special." Nils nodded with increasing appreciation for Alex's apparent insightfulness.

Simone stared at Alex in amazement. Had she misjudged his commitment to becoming a serious antiques specialist? As Alex continued his inspection with a running commentary of banalities, a blemish at the top of the scroll caught Simone's eye. "That's funny," she said. "Let me take a look at that."

Simone's request reminded Alex that he was in fact in a dangerous situation. "You said you did not want to examine it," said Alex, turning slightly away from her under the pretense of locating the most favorable lighting.

"Well, I changed my mind."

Alex forced a chuckle. "Too late! You missed your chance. Anyway, you are not wearing gloves." After another minute of feigned assessment, Alex placed the viola back in its case and returned the gloves to their compartment. "Mr. Nilsson, this is an amazing acquisition. You should be very proud."

"I must say, I'm quite satisfied," said Nils. He looked over at Simone. "Please, have a look if you'd like." He raised the lid to the compartment holding the gloves.

Simone had lost interest. The blemish on the scroll reminded her of the one on Duncan's viola, but this was not his viola. She had no desire to get into a tug-of-war with Alex just because he thought he was an expert and she was not. "It's a nice looking viola," she said. "I don't need to pull it back out." She changed the subject. "When did you buy it?"

"Technically, I haven't bought it yet," said Nils. "I have it on twenty-four hour consignment during which I have the option of obtaining expert analysis."

Simone laughed, genuinely amused. "I hope we're not your experts!"

Nils formed a magnanimous grin. "Simone, I consider you to be among my most relied-upon advisors." Alex assumed that Nils meant *you* as in *the two of you*. Simone knew that he did not. Simone was Nils's idea of a potential lay. "In fact," Nils continued, "I already have all of the validation I require. One of my talents, enabling me to succeed time and again with multi-million dollar projects, is knowing when I need more information and knowing when it's time to strike. When I see what I want, I go for it."

"Well, you are making a great move in going for this Amati," said Alex.

"That brings me to the second reason for my visit," said Nils, intensifying his gaze upon Simone and deciding to pretend that Alex was not there. The man's presence was an inconvenience. He was not certain of the extent of the relationship between Simone and this guy Alex, but a little competition never discouraged Nils. "Now that the Nilsson Quartet Collection is complete, I will be putting on a reception to introduce it to the world. I will of course need three musicians to join me. I will play the Stradivarius, and Simone, I would still like for you to play the Guarneri del Gesù violin."

Although Nils had floated this idea before, Simone was momentarily speechless. Alex held his breath. When Nils had made the invitation several months before, the thought of being in the inner circle of such important treasures beguiled Alex. That was before he had engineered the sale of Duncan Flowers's stolen viola to Nils. Now Alex feared the potential for Simone to somehow make the connection. It had not occurred to him that Nils's interest in Simone was far more carnal than musical.

"Thanks, Nils," Simone said finally. "I can't do it. I just wouldn't be comfortable playing such a treasure."

Nils tried to no avail to convince Simone to play at the reception. Finally, he snapped shut the aluminum case and departed. He had not lost any of the confident self-satisfaction that he arrived with. Nils had not closed the deal he had in mind, but there were always more deals.

CHAPTER SIXTEEN ─────────────────────

At half past ten the next morning, the cell phone lying on the passenger seat of Larry Giles's rented Chevy Malibu warbled the opening frenetic piano riff from Blue Rondo A La Turk. He verified the incoming number on the phone's tiny screen, flipped it open and held it to his ear. "Yo."

"Where are you now?" came James Dickerson's voice over the line.

"I'm sitting outside of an enormous construction site for a shopping mall," said Larry. "He's been here since eight. I'm looking at his Mercedes parked outside the construction trailer right now. What about the package?"

"The package hasn't left his office downtown since he brought it back there yesterday," said Dickerson. "I'm observing its position right now." James had placed in the viola case a GPS transponder, the type designed for owners to track down lost pets by consulting mapping information on the Internet.

"So he only took it to the one place?" said Larry.

"That's right, Duval Violins" said James. "I just drove by there to get a closer look at whom he might have been talking to. They opened at ten. A woman opened the shop. I didn't get a look at her, but she was accompanied by the same fellow who brought us the package."

"What!" said Larry. "You gotta be kidding me."

"Relax," said James. "We've got no worries."

"Are you serious?" said Larry. "The buyer probably told them about the whole..." They had agreed not to use any names on the phone. "The whole LA broker scene and he probably also told them the price."

"Allow me to remind you that those possibilities are not insurmountable for us," said James. "If the seller learns of the little broker charade, what's he going to do? I assure you, it's nothing we couldn't rationalize to him. Meanwhile, if he finds out about the price, he will be thrilled. We would have plenty of leverage to negotiate a fair split, perhaps not as generous as we had hoped, but that was always an inherent risk."

"I just don't like the way all these people seem to be so chummy," said Larry. "I don't like not knowing what all the relationships are."

"We know enough," said James. "The buyer has proven to be every bit the arrogant egomaniac that we suspected. He hasn't even obtained an expert opinion on the package. As I expected, this is a hobby for him. I'm sure he's a wizard at building malls and skyscrapers, but he's a fool when it comes to what we're dealing with here."

"Why is he visiting the seller?" said Larry. "It doesn't make any sense. You said the seller didn't want the buyer to know who he was."

"That's right," said James. "We don't know how the seller got this package in the first place, but we can be damned sure that it wasn't, shall we say, *proper*. We've known all along that the seller and the buyer have some sort of relationship; after all it was the seller who told me about the buyer's interest. So yesterday's little visit shouldn't be shocking."

"I still don't like it, man," said Larry.

"I admit, I wasn't delighted by that little visit yesterday," said James. "But we're still in an excellent position. After the shop opened this morning and I saw that our seller was one of the principals, I phoned him. I told him I was checking in and wanted to let him know that I was in town and in discussions with the buyer. He told me, exactly as we knew, that the buyer dropped in yesterday causing him an embarrassing surprise. He scolded me for not informing him that I was already in town. Naturally, I apologized profusely—short notice, things moving quickly, that sort of thing."

"He's got to be wondering what's going on."

"Just listen," said James. "His only complaint was about the surprise. Otherwise, he made no mention of the LA dealer and as far as the price, he was anxious to know whether I thought I could negotiate in the range that he had originally suggested, which is a tiny fraction of what we're dealing with."

"He's probably just playing with you, trying to catch you in a lie"

"You don't know this bloke," said James. "He's a bit of a dunce. Honestly, this deal is no stickier than any we've done before. I say we proceed according to plan and we will get the maximum pay-off. If the buyer decides he's not interested, we can find another outlet. If he buys and later decides to get curious about the viola's provenance, he won't get much help from our LA colleague or his frumpy former employer in London. They will be together on permanent sabbatical."

"Alright. Fine," said Larry. "So, you're ready for the next move."

"Precisely. I'm going to ring Nilsson and shake things up a bit."

Inside the construction trailer of Crane & Jensen, Nils and two other men stood before the long conference table where the project manager held his daily meetings before sunrise with the representatives from the major contractors on the site. The Nilsson Town Square project was just in its early stages of moving earth and installing underground utilities. For now, morning meetings involved only a handful of people, who arrived and left in barely enough time to drink a Styrofoam cup's worth of burnt coffee. Within two months, the sessions would involve a raft of representatives and last up to two hours as the Crane & Jensen project manager would have to through a myriad of competing priorities and last-minute adjustments to the schedule.

The three men were examining a set of drawings and schematics that covered the length of the sixteen-foot conference table. One of the men was Hans Schweitzer, the architect of the Nilsson Center and now of Nilsson Town Square. A top priority for Nils was always visual impact. He unfailingly put his name on the projects that he built and he insisted that the projects make a visual statement. "Anybody can put up buildings. I create landmarks." With the Nilsson Center, Hans created and delivered a striking aesthetic crescendo in the midst of the city's relatively bland downtown business district. The brash, silver-blue tower gave the impression of an inverted chrome and glass icicle. Naturally, there were vocal detractors who claimed the structure was an architectural atrocity that vandalized the town's traditional themes. But within a few years, most had to admit that the feature brought a welcomed spice and distinctiveness to the skyline.

The third man at the table was Clement Brown, a twenty-two year veteran project manager for Crane & Jensen. He had built factories, skyscrapers, theme parks and military complexes on three continents. He got this assignment because he was the best when it came to delivering big projects on time. C&J won the bid based on a fixed price with significant rewards for coming in early, and significant penalties for coming in late.

"The next item is the roof structure," said Hans. For two hours, the three had been discussing Hans's proposals for making the buildings more environmentally friendly, or at least more *environmentalist* friendly. "While keeping the same basic look, I am recommending what we call a 'green roof.' It will in fact be planted with indigenous grass or ground cover—I haven't yet determined the variety—in order to achieve two things..."

"Hold up, fellows," said Clement. "These changes are starting to mount up big time. I'm all for green buildings. My last two projects were LEED certified, but you're starting to talk about significant modifications to the plan. This is going to mean a major review of cost and scheduling."

Nils smiled gamely and clapped the project manager on the shoulder. "Clement, I *want* you to review the program. I fully expect that now you'll be able to bring it in sooner and at a lower cost." Nils's phone began chirping inside his jacket pocket. He recognized the Los Angeles area code and surmised it must be Overby. Indeed it was Overby, calling on the pre-paid cell phone he had picked up at a convenience store and set up with an appropriately misleading number.

"Mr. Nilson, I'm terribly sorry to disturb you," said Overby. "I trust your expert assessments of the Amati are proving satisfactory."

"I don't know yet," said Nils. "I'll let you know at five."

"I'm actually phoning about the pick-up time," said Overby. "There's been a development that will require that I collect the viola by two o'clock, strictly according to the consignment agreement. One of the other clients with whom I am scheduled to meet this week is leaving the country, returning unexpectedly to Madrid. I will need to pick up the viola and take it out to the airport. He is flying in expressly to see the Amati."

"Just what the hell is this, Overby!" said Nils, stepping out of the trailer and into the wasteland of red clay that would be more conducive to shouting. "We discussed five o'clock and now you're trying to hotbox me? I don't appreciate being jerked around. What kind of bush-leaguer do you think I am?"

"I understand completely your frustration," said Overby. "I assure you that this development is as much a surprise to me as it is to you. At the same time, I am obligated to ensure that my client's instrument receives optimum exposure to prospective buyers. I hope you can understand the position I am in, and I must make arrangements with you to collect the Amati by two o'clock."

"Based on the way you do business, you can pick it up right now for all I care," said Nils. "See Norma; she'll hand it over."

"Thank you, Mr. Nilsson," said Overby. "Again, I'm terribly sorry about this unforeseen circumstance and that we won't have had time to discuss your impressions of the Amati when I pick it up. With your permission, I will be pleased to come to your office at five o'clock as we had previously arranged and discuss your interests."

"You better hope the other buyer comes through, because I seriously doubt I'll be interested," said Nils, crisply clapping his cell phone shut before Overby could respond.

From the parking lot of Swifty's Speed Stop, across the four-lane turnpike from the mall construction site, Larry Giles observed as Nils Nilsson made another short call. Where the previous conversation resembled an irate baseball manager cursing an invisible umpire over a called strike three, this one was as relaxed as it was brief, and Nils turned blithely back into the trailer. When Blue Rondo A La Turk kicked in a moment later, Larry picked up his phone and related to James what he had observed.

"I'd say things are right on track," said James.

"I hope you know what you are doing," said Larry. "The guy looked pissed-off to me."

"I doubt he's annoyed," said Larry. "He's an actor, a showboat. You said he looked calm when he made the next call. No doubt he was letting his assistant know that I will be dropping by. We're fine. I'm going to his office to pick up the viola. I'll meet you back at the hotel."

At precisely five o'clock, reciprocal to his visit earlier in the day, a perfectly pressed Dale Overby stepped off the elevator on the twenty-third floor of the Nilsson Center, bowler in one hand, brushed aluminum case in the other. Norma was there to greet him and she escorted him to the plush seating area outside of Nils's office. Her instructions were to make Overby wait for twenty minutes before showing him in. The visitor suffered this sanction with equanimity and with the consolation of imported mineral water and the latest editions of The Financial Times, The Wall Street Journal and several major business magazines. These were complemented by a conspicuously placed stack of Enterprising Virginia magazines from six months before, featuring *Nils Nilsson, Real Estate Visionary*. The cover photo presented a headshot of Nils scowling shrewdly with one eyebrow raised and his chin resting contemplatively on his fist. The viewer could just glimpse Nilsson's Patek Philippe watch with matching platinum cuff links. A small sticker at the top of each copy invited visitors to *Please take one, compliments of The Nilsson Group.*

"Overby, I'm not interested in playing games," said Nils, coming around his desk to confront the visitor whom Norma had just shown in. "That's not how I operate."

"Of course not, Mr. Nilsson," said Overby. "I have the deepest respect for your reputation. I hope you will respect my commitment to delivering expert, personalized service to my clientele. I don't want to waste your time. I have returned to discuss your interests in the Amati. As a result of my consultation at the airport, I have received a final-offer bid for the Amati in the amount of $160,000. I have until seven o'clock—about an hour and a half from now—to deliver the Amati back to the airport or to obtain a higher bid."

"You must be joking!" said Nils. "You think you can just swish in here and jack up the price by a third?"

"It is not uncommon when dealing with particularly desirable instruments that a competitive bidding situation arises, even when the piece is not being sold in the auction market," said Overby. "I would add that at auction you typically would not have had a twenty-four hour loan of the piece and you would have only seconds to decide whether you want to top a competitor's bid."

Nils glared at Overby for several long seconds, assuming the scowl that the agent had seen on the cover of Enterprising Virginia. Overby endured the look placidly, with the demeanor of a man awaiting a bus. "I want to have another look at it," said Nils finally.

"By all means," said Overby. He moved forward toward the desk. Nils remained implanted in position, causing Overby to detour around him. The agent placed the case gently on the acrylic surface, retrieved his white gloves from his jacket and put them on. Once he had opened the case, he plucked the other set of gloves from their recess and presented them to Nils, who snatched them and impatiently yanked them on. Overby observed as Nils examined the instrument, in much the same way that Alex had done, without any obvious notion of what he was looking for.

"I really don't have time to screw around with this piddly deal," said Nils finally. He continued to eye the viola, turning it over, rotating it, hefting it. Overby stood by impassively. "I'll give you your one-sixty plus a thousand."

"That's excellent, Mr. Nilsson," said Overby.

"My accountant for the Nilsson Trust will have gone for the day. I can get you the check tomorrow."

"Not a problem," said Overby. "Actually, I will furnish you with the SWIFT code for the client's account at UBS, Zürich. I have with me a purchase agreement already signed by my client. I am authorized to execute it with a buyer for any amount that exceeds the client's reserve price." Overby reached nimbly into his breast pocket and removed an envelope from which he slid two copies of an agreement signed by His Highness Khalid bin Nayyan. He placed them side-by-side on the desk. "With your signature here and... here, you will take over the honor of owning an historic masterpiece of baroque violin making. You can see the relevant bank transfer information in section twelve, labeled *payment*."

Nils read over the agreement quickly, apparently finding no cause for concern because he snatched from Overby's fingers the Mont Blanc fountain pen that the agent had deftly produced with a flourish. A moment later, Nils and Overby had signed as buyer and witness respectively.

"Mr. Nilsson, it has been my pleasure to meet you and to do business," said Overby. "I hope you will think of Overby International in the future when you find yourself in the market."

Only now did Nils allow a gleaming smile to break over his expression. The game was over. He had what he wanted all along. He did not begrudge the increased price he had to pay in the end. He would have paid more if it were necessary. Now his quartet of Italian masterworks was complete. "Thank you, Mr. Overby," said Nils. "I appreciate you bringing this viola to my attention. I'll place the order for the wire tomorrow. When do I get possession?"

"You have possession," said Overby. "I have one copy of the agreement. You have the other along with the case, the certificate of authenticity, the photograph of the label, and of course the Amati itself."

The Admiral Suites Hotel was directly in the approach path to runway one-six of the regional airport. The night-blue sky had almost entirely extinguished the faint pink glow at the western horizon line and would certainly complete the job within minutes. Alex Alvarez alighted from his Ranger pick-up. The truck's rusty springs acknowledged his departure, and the door let out a metallic yelp as it slammed shut. He entered the hotel, by-passed the reception desk and went directly into the Admiral's Quarters. This was the name of the hotel's dimly lit, nautical-themed bar that might have just as appropriately been named the Admiral's Mausoleum.

The evening's sparse selection of patrons was a mélange of regulars and budget-stricken business travelers, mostly drinking alone. It took a moment for Alex's eyes to adjust to the shipwreck murk, but soon he spied the face of James Dickerson, the one person in the bar who had looked up when he entered.

"Good evening, Mr. Alvarez," said James. "I'm so glad you could join me. I'm catching a late flight back to Boston and I wanted to brief you personally before I leave." James motioned for Alex to take the seat opposite him in the booth.

"Yeah, I was wondering how the deal was going," said Alex. "And I wasn't sure when you would get around to telling me about it since you already forgot to mention that you were in town."

"I hope you can forgive me for that gross error," said James. "I got the call from Nilsson. He had a spur-of-the-moment opening to see me. I jumped on the next flight and saw him straight away. That's no excuse, I know, but I hope you will appreciate that my intentions were focused on getting the deal done."

Before Alex could reply, a waiter appeared at the table. He wore a white, waist-length cruise ship jacket with gold fringe epaulets and big brass buttons. His expression said, "If you can refrain from commenting on my silly costume, I can refrain from polluting your drinks."

"What will you have?" said James. "I'm already one gin and tonic ahead of you." Alex ordered a draft beer and James pointed at his glass of melting ice to signal a repeat for himself.

"Now that's taken care of," James continued, "let's get down to business. I have wonderful news. When you first showed me the Amati, you had already estimated a price range. I must admit that I had to withhold judgment because there are so many factors involved, but in the end, I concluded that your range was quite realistic. Well done. And once I cleaned the instrument to enhance its presentation, I tended to suspect that we were looking at the top end of your range."

"So what did you get?" said Alex impatiently.

"I'm pleased to tell you that we got your best case scenario price." James paused to lean his head over the middle of the table, lowering his voice to a satisfied, confidential whisper. "Thirty thousand."

"Yes!" said Alex, attempting to whisper but nonetheless drawing head turns from several of the bored patrons. Just then the waiter returned and deposited their drinks.

"I would say that we have something to drink to, wouldn't you?" said James, raising his fresh drink.

"You are damn straight," said Alex, meeting his companion's glass half way. He immediately gulped down nearly half of his beer. This action left his upper lip drenched and dappled with foam. If the Admiral's Quarters served non-stale beer, Alex would have acquired a full moustache. In one motion, he wiped his mouth with the sleeve of his beer-drinking arm and plunked the glass back on the table. "So when do I get my money?"

James smiled and nodded earnestly, like a doctor preparing to explain to an anxious patient that although the surgery was a complete success, it may take a little while before the patient can expect to jog on his new prosthetic knee. "It shouldn't take much time at all," said James. "We closed the deal a couple of hours ago. Nilsson will transfer the funds tomorrow, that's Thursday, and…"

"Wait a second," interrupted Alex. "You mean to tell me that he has not paid you? He has the viola and you have like an IOU? What the hell?"

There was a momentary tiger flash below the surface of the antique dealer's decorous eyes, although Alex failed to perceive it. "I completely understand your concern," said James. "I have a fully executed purchase agreement obligating Mr. Nilsson to effect full payment within twenty-four hours. This is a standard arrangement. It is not uncommon for a transaction to take several days to settle. In the meantime, it is preferable for the buyer to take possession, *and liability*. Having closed the deal, the last thing we want is to be babysitting the instrument and it gets damaged or stolen."

"Fine," said Alex, glowering at his half-empty beer glass. "When do I get my money?"

"As I was saying, Nilsson will wire the funds tomorrow. It can take a couple of days for the transfer to complete. I expect to be able to get you a payment by next Wednesday, a week from today."

"I was hoping we could do this deal in cash or a check made out to cash," said Alex tentatively, continuing to address the beverage in front of him.

Believe me, I was planning on paying you in cash. "That would be rather irregular." James lifted his eyebrows in an approximation of dismay. "I'm not accustomed to executing large transactions in cash."

"Yeah, well, that is how I need to do it. I have my own client and he insists on cash."

"I see," said James. "Well, I'll be in Boston. You certainly don't want me mailing you a stack of bills. I can either wire the funds for you to pick up at a check-cashing bureau or I can send you a cashier's check made out to cash. The former is the more anonymous, but involves fees. In the case of the latter, a bank may require you to deposit the check, which may or may not meet your client's needs."

"How much would it cost to wire the funds—the anonymous way?"

"Of course, that is a function of the amount," said James. "The gross is thirty, less my commission of fifteen percent, that makes twenty-five five. I have expenses of roughly fifteen hundred, for cleaning, documentation, travel and for the protective carrying case..."

"Holy shit," hissed Alex, leaning onto the table, causing it to slant toward him . "You never said anything about all these costs. You are trying to ream me big time."

"Sorry?" said James. He was enjoying this little teaching moment. "Exactly what are you referring to?"

"I am referring to six thousand in charges for carrying out a sale where I already identified the buyer," said Alex through clenched teeth. "Maybe you had to fly down here. Fine. Maybe you put in some time. Fine. But not to the tune of fifteen percent. I sure as hell did not ask for that secret agent metal case that I saw Nilsson carrying."

James reached into his jacket pocket and pulled out his cell phone and began to punch keys with his thumb. "Mr. Alvarez, I do not care for your tone," said James. "Nor do I care to do business with people who misrepresent who they are. You led me to believe that you were an instrument dealer who needed assistance on a sale, but obviously you know nothing of this business. As a professional courtesy, I performed extensive analysis on your instrument to authenticate its origins. Normally, I charge thousands for this analysis alone, and yet I have foregone those fees. I am charging you only the standard representation fee plus out-of-pocket expenses. It is becoming clear to me that I should not be a representative on this transaction at all." James pressed the send key on his phone and placed it to his ear.

"Who the hell are you calling?"

"I'm ringing Nils Nilsson," said James. "I will advise him that he should contact you directly to make payment arrangements. You can pay me my expenses and I will return to dealing with people who have a modicum of respect for the legitimate marketplace."

"Hey, hey now! Hang that up. We can work this out. I was just trying to understand the costs. I never said I was not going to pay. Hang it up. Come on."

James lowered the phone and put it away. "Do you now have an understanding of the costs?"

"Yes, I got it now," said Alex. "You don't need to be so touchy. So, that leaves me with a net of twenty-four."

"That leaves you with a net of twenty-four *minus* any wire fees," said James. "You should understand that wire fees for transferring that amount from point to point anonymously would be about a thousand dollars, but that's your call. Otherwise, I can overnight you a check."

"Son of a bitch," said Alex. He directed this epithet toward the acoustical tiles above. The seafaring theme had apparently not extended all the way to the ceiling. He drained the remaining half of his beer and swabbed his face, this time to include his neck since some of the gush had dribbled down his chin. "Fine. Do the wire so I can pick it up in cash. By the time this is done, there won't be anything left."

James chuckled magnanimously. "Mr. Alvarez, I would suggest that your client has done quite well for himself. At the end of the day, he will *net* around twenty-three thousand on a transaction that could easily have *grossed* less than that. In my book, that's a big win. Your client should be very pleased with your performance."

As the afternoon sun of early May cast long shadows across the showroom at Duval Violins, Duncan and Simone stood facing the wall that featured the current selection of violas. Duncan had tried them all and was still uncertain about the sound he wanted to get from his new instrument. He was used to the warm, mellow tone that his old viola produced, but he enjoyed experimenting with the power and projection he could get out of the ones on display.

"I can see you're not bowled over by anything so far," said Simone.

"I don't know. I think I'll just keep test-driving until one grabs me. I guess they don't make them like my old one anymore."

"You never know," she said. "You'll find the one that's right—or it will find you."

"No doubt. Meanwhile, I've got my loaner to tide me over. I'm in good shape," he said. The two walked back toward the front of the shop and Duncan continued, "You'll never guess what I got in the mail today."

"What?"

"I got an invitation to the *world premiere* of the Nilsson Quartet Collection," he said. "Is he for real? What the hell is he up to?"

"God he doesn't waste anytime," said Simone, as much to herself as to Duncan.

"So you know about this?"

"I suppose I do," said Simone. "Do you remember last fall I mentioned to you that Nils had dropped by bragging about buying antique instruments? Apparently, he set up some kind of trust to create a quartet of Italian rarities. He had already made a start, including purchasing a Stradivarius violin. He was going to spend *millions*." For the last word, Simone effected her best Nilssonian hauteur.

"And now he's throwing a reception to show off his collection?"

"Exactly," said Simone. "Only his collection wasn't complete until last week. He bought a rare Italian viola by Nicolò Amati. I know because he brought it in here to show off. And now he already has invitations out for a reception. Of course, he was already talking about a reception last fall. He no doubt had all the plans in place."

"Wait a minute. Nils brought his new acquisition in here?" Duncan grinned and gave Simone a teasing poke in the arm, while tiny pangs of jealousy began to burst in his belly. "I had no idea you were so tight with Nils."

Simone's cheeks flushed. "I am *not* tight with Nils Nilsson," she said, realizing that her hands were inadvertently flailing in support of her denial. She stifled them by crossing her arms securely. "Actually, Nils was showing the viola to Alex because he knew Alex was interested in antique instruments."

"And did you get to see this rare Italian viola?"

"Barely. Alex pretty much monopolized it," she said. "To tell you the truth, from what little I did see, it reminded me a lot of yours. It had similar reddish coloring and a high arching top, like yours did."

"That's me: old school," said Duncan. "The next time you get in some priceless antique violas, let me know. I may be interested."

Simone laughed. "That's good to know. I should be getting in a truckload next week. Anyway, now you know what you've been invited to."

"Is it just me or does this guy have some nerve inviting me to his quartet party after what he did at the last quartet party? I'm completely mystified. Did he invite you?"

"I haven't gotten an invitation, unless it came in today's mail." She walked behind the counter and picked up a small stack of mail out of a basket on the shelf behind the counter. She quickly located the heavy gauge, glossy burgundy envelope with silver lettering.

"That's it," said Duncan. "Open it up. You'll get a kick out of it."

Simone did so and slid out the matching card. She read the contents aloud.

Mr. Nils Nilsson cordially invites you and your guest to experience the world premiere showing and performance of the Nilsson Quartet Collection© of Italian Masterpieces. The Nilsson Music Trust has located four of the world's finest treasures of musical craftsmanship and united them into a quartet of incomparable, harmonious beauty.

Antonio Stradivari, violin, 1678
Guarneri del Gesù, violin, 1719

Giovanni Grancino, cello, 1693
Nicolò Amati, viola, 1664

The Nilsson Center Plaza
Saturday, June 14
Seven O'clock
R.S.V.P.

"Damn. Wouldn't you know it? The fourteenth I'm supposed to be washing my hair," said Simone, tossing the invitation back into the mail basket. "I imagine your schedule prevents you from attending as well."

Duncan was fidgeting with one of the pens from the miniature bass drum next to the register. "Well, actually... I'm planning to go." Seeing Simone's mouth drop open, he hurried to explain. "Ever since my viola was stolen, I've been giving a lot of thought to how I've been living my life over the past several years. It didn't take much to realize that I've been living like an overgrown sophomore. It took a little more to figure out why that might be. I think at least some of it has to do with losing Claudia, and rather than pulling myself together like an adult, I decided to pretend that I don't need anybody anyway and I'm just going to make life a big party. It's time that I started the pulling together I should have done long ago."

"It sounds like you've done a lot of soul searching. Good for you," said Simone, with a steady, encouraging gaze. "But how does attending Nils's ego-fest help you? Personally, I do my best to ignore him."

"That's just it. I want to ignore him, but the more I pretend that I don't give a crap, the more miserable I am. I want him to be the silly curiosity that I know he is, but it still eats me up that Claudia was attracted to that guy over me. I'm galled that he would invite me to his garish self-tribute. And that's why I've decided to go. I want to inoculate myself against these stupid memories that I have blown out of all proportion and allowed to dominate my life. It's time to *get over it.*"

Simone nodded thoughtfully. "I guess that makes a lot of sense."

"In fact, I came by today mostly because I wanted to see if you would go with me to the reception." Again Duncan found himself hastening to explain himself given Simone's increasing look of dismay. "Please don't take it the wrong way. I'm not trying to hit on you or ask you on a date. I'm just asking for your support. I can't face this thing alone. Besides, you've got your own invitation. You could think of it as carpooling."

"Oh, well then," Simone said with a laugh. "That changes everything. I can't think of anything I would like to do less on that evening, but if carpooling is involved, count me in."

"Really? So you'll go with me?"

"Sure. I'll go," she said. "I'd go with you anyway, but what you said makes sense. I think in my own way I hide behind my work and the shop as an excuse to avoid getting involved in the flow of things just because I might have to deal the odd annoyance, like a Nils Nilsson. You're the one who got me out of my little shell once before and I really appreciated it. I had fun playing in the quartet even though it didn't pan out."

"Great. Now I'm pulling you right back into the same scene," said Duncan smacking his forehead theatrically.

"But that's just it. Like you said. Maybe we both need to get our feet wet again and learn that the water's just fine. So what if we got a little up our nose before?"

"Or filled up a lung or two."

The front door swung inward with a jingle and in sauntered Alex. He had just collected a little over twenty-three thousand dollars from the check-cashing agency. The last several days had given him time to appreciate the perspective that James had given him. Twenty-three grand was not a sum to sneeze at for the equivalent of a few days work. And there was the bonus of getting to stick it to that jackass Duncan Flowers.

"Hey, Alex, long time no see," said Duncan.

Alex stopped dead, speechless. He instinctively patted the front of his denim jacket, the inside pocket of which held most of his plunder. He had put a thousand into his checking account, but decided against putting more in for fear of drawing attention. He would visit various branches over a couple of weeks until it was all in. That meant he still had a bundle thicker than a pack of cigarettes riding on his person, which was only supposed to be the case until he could get it hidden in the workshop. He would take care of this chore straight away if it were not for the unwelcomed visitor.

"Duncan Flowers. It has been a while," said Alex, somewhat regaining his composure, determined to relish the encounter. "What brings you here this afternoon?"

"I'm still in the market for a new viola. Simone was showing me a couple of models that the shop just got in."

"So have you picked one?"

"Not yet, but I'm not in a rush. The loaner's got me covered for now," said Duncan. He turned back to Simone behind the counter. "Well, I'd better get on the road. Thanks for your help, Simone. I'll stay in touch and we can figure out later about carpooling to the thing in June."

After Duncan had departed, Alex watched the door jingle to a close and then turned back to Simone with an expression like he had just taken a swig of sour buttermilk. "Why is it that your old boyfriend always comes sniffing around here when I'm out?"

"Most things happen around here while you're out because you're usually out," she said evenly. "For example, you left here an hour and a half ago and I had no idea where you were."

"I told you I was running to the bank. I ran a couple of other errands. What is the big deal? I am on top of my work."

"I don't appreciate you always making snide comments about Duncan. He's a friend of mine. He was never my boyfriend. And he comes in here because he's a musician and we're a music shop. He may potentially be spending a few thousand dollars on a new viola."

Alex made a sigh and smiled. "Let's not argue. I'm sorry," he said, beginning to move around the counter to the workshop door. "So, what are you carpooling to?"

"Now that Nils bought that viola, he's going ahead with his reception to show off his quartet. Duncan and I each got an invitation and we thought we would ride together. You're welcome to come too if you want. I can bring a guest."

"Duncan can't go to that reception," Alex blurted reflexively. "That's ridiculous." He stood motionless and looked at Simone, eyes unblinking.

"What are you talking about? We're both going."

"Well, you need to tell him not to go." Alex stammered as he imagined the disaster of Duncan discovering his old viola at Nilsson's reception. "Uh... he's got no business hanging around Nils Nilsson. Why would he want to do that... after the thing with Duncan's wife?"

"I'm sure Duncan would appreciate your concern, but I think he can decide for himself," she said. "And at this point, we're both planning to go. Would you like to join us?"

"No!"

"Suit yourself. I would think a collection of antique stringed instruments would be right up your alley."

Alex sensed that he needed to settle down and think. Simone was bound to wonder about his strong reaction to this reception. He made an effort to chuckle and wag his head sagely. "I guess I was just surprised about Duncan attending the reception. I might attend with you. It might be pretty cool to see the whole collection."

"Whatever. Here's the invitation if you want to see it." Simone reached behind her and plucked the burgundy envelope from the basket.

"That reminds me," said Alex in an approximation of nonchalance. "I have been thinking about Duncan's old viola. It is such a shame what happened. And I feel bad that I have not always been very welcoming to him. He is your friend and that means I consider him my friend. I would like to do something for him. I would like to refurbish his viola, like he mentioned before—free of charge, on my own time."

Simone tilted her head in puzzlement. "You want to do this for your *friend* Duncan?"

"I know. You think it is strange that I would offer this. I just want to show you—and Duncan—that I want to be part of the friendship. Please, will you extend the offer to him? If it comes from you, he will know it is sincere."

CHAPTER EIGHTEEN ─────────────────────────────

As far as Duncan was concerned, few sensations could match the pleasure of strolling across the campus of River Road Academy on a ripe, balmy Friday afternoon in May. This represented the apex of possibility. The weekend lay ahead and shortly behind that, summer break. This time around included new possibilities as well. He was working on the new Duncan, the mature Duncan. Where at first he had feared what dreary existence his metamorphosed self might lead, now he had come to embrace the transition. His end-of-week promenade took him along a dappled path above which towered sturdy pines. Over the past week, the azaleas, nestled in flossy beds of pine straw, had exploded into impressionistic splashes of pink and white. Ancient dogwoods sprouted youthful foliage, dropping the occasional downy flower to spiral onto new-cut turf.

He meandered from Harrison Hall and past the old chapel that had once been the entire school when it was Mrs. Harrison's School for Boys. He would have gone to the cafeteria for a quick and cheap dinner, but it had stopped serving evening meals now that sports and other after-school activities had ended for the year. Exams were in full swing and in one week, commencement would release the students into three months of sultry southern summer. He reached the faculty parking lot beyond the cafeteria and was headed across to River Road to catch the bus. He would deal with getting a new car over the summer. In fact, he had come to appreciate being car-less. Miraculously, life was not only feasible, but also pleasant without an automobile.

He had for some time noticed that no other staff member used his old parking spot. The spaces were not assigned. He wondered whether avoidance of his spot was in deference to him or because his use of it had caused it to look like a treacherous tar pit. Still considering the parking preferences of his colleagues, Duncan became aware that a car had pulled up beside him. It was a gray sedan and the passenger side window lowered as it came to a stop at his side.

"Need a ride, stranger?" said a woman's voice from within.

Duncan leaned over to see Simone behind the wheel. "Hey! What a surprise," said Duncan. "When my normal chauffeur went on vacation, I had no idea the agency would send you as a substitute. I prefer you to Jeeves, but my Bentley has a hot tub and a wet bar."

"You'll have to settle for a Taurus," she said. "It has partial air-conditioning and AM-FM radio."

"I had no idea. I'll take it. Plus, I've always secretly wanted to know what it was like to ride in the front." He jumped in and Simone drove on.

"Seriously, what brings you out to this neck of the woods?" Duncan said. Another thought immediately occurred to him and he made a gasp of mock horror. "Are you playing hooky? How did you get out of the shop during working hours."

Simon laughed. "Alex is minding the store. We close in less than an hour. I'm pretty sure he won't get into trouble. It was such a great day that I decided to get out for a drive. I had something I wanted to chat with you about and I took a chance on catching you on your way to or from the dining hall that I know you adore."

"What can I say, I'm helpless in the kitchen," he said. "Having the dining hall is like living at home with mom except at the end you put all the dishes on a magical conveyor belt."

As Simone drove and watched the road, Duncan could look at her without worrying that he was making her uncomfortable. He appreciated that today she had her hair pulled back again, unveiling her fine Mediterranean features, her soft bronze skin and the gentle curve of her neck. She wore a cotton tank top, and he could follow the curve as it continued along the peek of her shoulder, down her bare, taut arm and all the way to her delicate violinist fingers gently grasping the steering wheel.

Duncan became aware that this was about the time when his old self would actuate some sort of crude overture. He considered with some satisfaction that he was not his old self and sat back simply to enjoy the unexpected ride with a friend on a glorious spring afternoon. "So, what did you want to talk to me about?" Duncan said.

"It has to do with Alex and it may have something to do with your old viola," she said. Now she was staring intently at the road ahead. Her voice quavered slightly. "You're the only person I have to talk to."

Duncan suppressed the reflex to blurt out something like "what the hell would Alex have to do with my viola?" Instead he went with "You can talk to me anytime. Tell me what's up."

"Well, things haven't been going so well between Alex and me. We sort of dove headlong into living and working together. It feels like we skipped right over getting to know each other and marriage and honeymoon and jumped right into being a mired old couple that barely tolerates each other." Simone turned away and looked out the window beside her. She re-focused on the road and resumed. "The reason I'm telling you this is just that I've come to realize I don't understand Alex. He behaves so strangely sometimes."

"Like how?"

"He acts strangely about you."

"About me? What about me?"

Simone explained the various incidents she could remember. There was Alex's odd insistence about making a swap for Duncan's viola. There was his befuddlement at learning that the burned viola might be salvageable. There was his agitation when Nils came by with the Amati viola, and Alex's apparent determination that Simone should not get a close look at it. She related that on this last occasion she had noticed a similarity to Duncan's viola, including a deep scratch on the top of the scroll. The crowning incidents were Alex's dismay about Duncan attending the reception and Alex's newfound passion for refurbishing Duncan's charred viola.

"I can only make sense of these events in one way, and you're going to think that I'm crazy," she said. "I think Alex is somehow involved in stealing your viola and selling it to Nils. I think Nils now has your viola. I think the one that you have at home must be a substitute."

By the time Simone completed her account, they had been parked in front of Duncan's house for several minutes. Simone remained with both hands on the wheel peering straight ahead.

Duncan had just taken the story in and still did not seem ready to formulate a comment. After a moment, he said, "Simone, I see how Alex has acted a bit strange, but it doesn't mean he stole my viola. Don't forget, it also involved stealing my car and burning it and painting penises all over it."

This detail broke Simone's hypnotic state. "Painting what?"

"Didn't I tell you about the penises?"

"No. I think I would remember that."

"Well, there were penises painted all over the car," he said. "In any case, it's a pretty big stretch to imagine Alex going to all that bizarre effort over my viola."

"Maybe so," said Simone. "But I find it hard to imagine any other way to make his weird behavior add up. You told me your grandfather gave you the viola. Do you know anything about its history?"

"No. I know what he told me, but if you knew my senile, raconteur grandfather you wouldn't put any stock in that."

"What did he tell you about it?"

Duncan hesitated. He knew the truth would provide Simone with misleading encouragement. "He told me it was very old and came from Italy. He said it could be on display in a museum."

On cue, Simone turned fully in her seat to face him, breathing in with an open-mouthed gasp. "Exactly! Somehow Alex knew that and he stole it and—I don't know how—sold it to Nils."

Duncan could only smile and look down at his knees. He thought for a moment, wanting to find a tactful way to get Simone to drop her wild theory, even if it did reflect poorly on Alex, who was a jerk and not good enough for her. "Actually, there's a simple way to test your idea. We can go inside and take a look at the viola in my case. We may be able to put this to bed right now."

Simone brightened at this suggestion. She had completely overlooked the usefulness of this key piece of evidence. Together they went up the crumbling sidewalk and into Duncan's house. As he unlocked the door the realization struck him that Simone had never been inside his house, and his Spartan, neo-dorm room décor would probably solidify his standing in her eyes as a pitiful man-child. At least he had recently begun to apply himself to keeping the place clean. During the preceding couple of weeks, he had reacquainted himself with the vacuum cleaner, the mop and the toilet scrubber. He even bought a spray can of stuff for dusting and before he knew it, he had wiped down nearly every surface within reach. The place still had a faint synthetic lemon scent. He could console himself that Simone would not experience the grubbiness that characterized his home during the past few years, during which his housekeeping was limited to the sporadic use of a broom and dustpan.

He invited Simone to have a seat on the futon sofa, inwardly cringing that he still had that old futon sofa. "Can I offer you something to drink? Beer? Soda? I don't have any chilled wine, but I've got a bottle of Merlot."

"I'll have whatever you're having."

"Dos cervesas coming up." Duncan returned a moment later with two sweaty green bottles and placed them on the recently cleared coffee table. It occurred to him that coasters might be appropriate, but he had none. Coasters had been superfluous when every table was already covered with newspapers, magazines and the odd moldering t-shirt. "There we are. I'll go grab the viola."

Duncan disappeared into the hallway where Simone could here him rummaging in a closet. He came back with the case. It was wrapped inside of a black garbage bag. He eased the case out of the bag and placed it on the coffee table, tossing the bag under the table. "It's such a charred mess that I had to put it in something," Duncan said. He carefully pried up the latches and gently lifted the lid."

The two looked silently at the cooked contents with a mixture of fascination and revulsion. "Do you think we could take it out?" Simone said finally.

"We can try," he said. "So far, I haven't even touched it. Here, I'll do it in case it falls apart. That way I'll be the one responsible for trashing it."

"Maybe you shouldn't," she said. "It's not right for you to have to do this just to satisfy my neurotic theory."

"Are you kidding? I'm dying to find out. Really. I'm not worried about damaging it any more. I'm starting to feel silly for holding on to the thing at all." He rubbed his hands together and leaned over the case. He turned to Simone and assumed the comically intense look of an action movie character about to diffuse a time bomb. His fingers gently grasped the neck while those of the other hand slid carefully beside the body so he could raise the instrument without undue pressure on any one section. No sooner had he begun to lift that the whole front of the viola separated from the body and the neck began to cantilever, entirely severed from its base.

"Oops." said Duncan. "I guess that didn't work out too well."

"Actually, I should have expected that, and it's not such a terrible thing," Simone said. "These instruments are held together by glue, and the heat would have broken down the bonds. Re-gluing won't be a big deal as long as the parts are more or less intact." Now that the viola had disintegrated into its various components, Simone felt less anxious. "Let's have a look at some of the pieces. We know that your viola had a pronounced arch on the belly." She lifted off the badly scorched front of the viola and examined it.

"What do you see?" said Duncan.

"I don't know. It's so warped. I can't tell the natural contour. What do you think?" She handed the piece gingerly to Duncan.

"I might as well be looking at a slice of burnt toast. I don't know."

Simone glanced at the scorched interior. "Well, it has no label. There would at least be some charred residue if there had been one."

"My viola didn't have a label either."

"Yeah, I remember," she said dejectedly. "But the real telltale sign is on the scroll, the *mark of Ludwig*!" She lifted the neck out carefully. The loose ends of the popped strings quivered about like the still-animate antennae of a squashed bug. She turned the scroll so they could both examine it. The head of the case, and therefore the corresponding part of the instrument inside, had received the most intense heat. Where the outer covering on the lower part of the case was simply charred into an ashy crust, the top third of the case was left with fully exposed wood, burned nearly through. As a result, the upper neck, peg box and scroll of the viola were charbroiled into a blackened, crackly remnant.

"It looks like even Ludwig's mark can't survive the fires of Hades," Duncan said finally. "I can barely make out the natural ridges of the scroll. There's no way that scratch would be visible. I know it's not what you were looking for, but I think the easiest explanation is that this is my viola. It got burned up because like an idiot I left it in my unlocked Honda that some kids decided to use as a disposable party parade float."

"We still don't know for sure," said Simone, trying to convince herself as much as Duncan.

"Well, we can't always know everything."

"Maybe, but we can still check out Nils's viola," she said, pleased to realize that there was still an open avenue.

"You're not going to let this go?"

"Nope. And you and I will have the perfect opportunity to check out his viola when we go to the reception."

"Great," said Duncan, shaking his head in good-natured resignation. "Well, now that we have demolished this thing do you want to take it to Alex for my free refurbishment?"

CHAPTER NINETEEN

Although the calendar indicated spring would not end for another week, that did not prevent a sweltering stickiness from engulfing the town. Walking out of an air-conditioned building meant ambush by a smothering, hug of mugginess. The reverse transition brought the equally disquieting sensation of being summarily freeze-dried. Even at half past six in the evening, the thermometer hovered at ninety-degrees, which was only half the story given the day's steaminess.

With the shop closing early on Saturdays, Simone had done some shopping but had used much of the afternoon to sunbathe on the small, private terrace that was enclosed behind the shop. Creating this miniature recreation area was one of the few enhancements she had made to the property since her father left the shop to her. Simone always adored sunshine and this was her way to escape into the sun. Living in the apartment above the shop placed certain limitations on privacy. Before enclosing the back garden, she felt uncomfortable relaxing outside and either abstained or felt obligated to retreat to a park. Now she could steal sunshine anytime. When she was not keeping one eye on the shop, she could read for hours in her Adirondack chair on the mossy stones and lose herself in the lazy burbling of the little fountain and the warm rays that glided down through the swaying branches of the old Poplar tree.

With plenty of time before her evening's engagement, she had gone up to the apartment to shower and don a cream-colored, sleeveless dress that ran faithfully over the contours of her petite figure and ended above tanned calves. A matching satin ribbon held her dark hair back. The wooden stairs descending from the apartment resounded as Simone hurried down in high heels, purchased that very afternoon at Saxon Shoes. She popped into the shop and back to the workshop where Alex was busily working on completing the refurbishment of the charred viola entrusted to him by Duncan. When she entered, she found Alex about to apply a coat of lacquer to the reassembled viola. It was no longer black. All of the charred areas and most of the original stain were rubbed away. The instrument looked like a once elegant sand sculpture after sitting out in the rain. The headstock had been the most damaged in the fire, and now the scroll was reduced to a raw, withered fist. The f-holes, once gracefully fine and curving, were now yawning caricatures of their former beauty. At this stage, there were no strings or bridge or a tailpiece for anchoring the strings to the bottom of the instrument. Alex had removed the endpin and inserted a foot long wooden dowel into the hole. This temporary "tail spike" made the viola look like a miniature cello. By holding the instrument by the neck, he could gently rotate it on the dowel and have a stable arrangement for applying lacquer with the brush in his other hand.

"So, what do you think?" he said. "It took hours to sand off all the charred wood, but it is back together and I am just going to put on a couple of layers of polyurethane to so it will be sealed and protected for display. I think it is going to look like a kind of funky work of art." He looked up from his work to focus on Simone, who was now beside him. "Damn! Look at you. Why don't you ever get dolled up like that for me?"

"I'm just dressed for the occasion," she said. "I invited you to come, but you said you weren't interested."

"I would be like a fish out of water in that swanky scene," he said. "I do want to see the instruments, but I know they will be on display in the Nilsson Center for a while. I will swing down there next week maybe."

"I would have thought swanky would be exactly your scene now that you're tooling around in that new Lexus." Simone was still annoyed that Alex showed up at home two evenings before driving a newly purchased black IS sedan. That event had been the catalyst for an argument where Simone questioned how Alex could make such a major purchase out of the blue without so much as a word to her, and where Alex complained that he should be able to make personal financial decisions without checking first with his "boss." The confrontation ended in a standoff, which meant Alex assumed the subject was closed and Simone added it to her growing list of reasons to draw up Alex's walking papers.

Simone realized that by mentioning the car she was liable to slip into another confrontation about this sore point so she redirected the exchange by nodding toward the subject of Alex's labors. "When will it be ready?" she said.

"It will dry overnight and I will string it up tomorrow. You can tell Duncan that his heirloom will be ready for pick-up on Monday morning."

"Great. He'll be pleased. I know he appreciates you doing this for him."

"Not a problem. Glad to do it."

"I'm off then," she said. "I can't imagine staying long. I'm sure I'll be home by nine or ten."

"Take your time. I am leaving in a few minutes to meet Dwayne and KG at The Cavern to shoot some pool. They also want to take a spin in the Lexus. They are so jealous."

Duncan and Simone exited the elevator from the underground parking deck and entered the vast lobby of the Nilsson Center. Hans Schweitzer had designed the lobby to be an extension of the granite plaza that spread abundantly outside his signature structure and surrounded a massive granite and white marble fountain. The lobby ceiling, painted ice blue, arched some five stories above. A highly choreographed system of lights and projections created the impression of a dynamic sky above. It shifted through the moods of rosy dawn, brilliant afternoon, contemplative twilight and starry night.

As with the building itself, Nils wanted this event to make a splash. The three hundred guests would enjoy the best in music, refreshment and comfort. Because his concept called for completely opening the lobby to the plaza, now cordoned off by velvet ropes, Nils's organizers had imported an armada of portable industrial air conditioners as well as a set of fans positioned on the street side of the fountain to take of advantage of its evaporative potential. At least for a few hours, a small plot of the downtown district would, with a herculean effort, defy the heat that radiated relentlessly everywhere else.

The string quartet performance would take place inside the lobby, where a stage was constructed in front of the Central Virginia Bank branch. CVB was a major creditor of the Nilsson Center and just about every other project that Nils undertook. Girardi's, another stalwart of the Nilsson Center's plaza-level establishments, was providing most of the food and refreshments, including a table serving Italian ice cream. The gelati stand was a hit from the start.

Guests were still arriving, mostly from the Hollywood-style, red carpet valet parking arrangement on the Main Street side of the plaza. More than twenty college kids, uniformed in black pants and gold waistcoats, whisked the vacated cars into the bowels of the parking garage and made the sweaty slog topside for the next run. Simone and Duncan had skipped past the block-long line of gleaming luxury cars and dipped directly into the deck, agreeing that self-parking would be much simpler. Duncan had observed the queue as they approached and said, "Oh, my God. Keep going. I can't take the paparazzi. Those vultures are waiting everywhere I go."

"Fine, Duncan," Simone had said. "But don't you think your life would be more enjoyable if you would embrace your celebrity instead of trying to run from it?"

The two strolled across the lobby, taking in the atmosphere, including a piped-in melody of baroque recorder music. Presumably, the organizers did not want the background music to be a direct competitor of the evening's main attraction. Simone pulled Duncan to the centerpiece of the lobby, acting as a counterbalance to the grand fountain out on the plaza. An ice sculpture as high as two men formed a replica of the thirty-story Nilsson Center. Given the skyscraper's existing likeness to an icicle, the frozen sculpture was a virtual duplicate in miniature. At its base, against each of the sides, leaned chiseled stringed instruments, representing the four instruments in the Nilsson Quartet Collection. The cello towered up to the twentieth floor while the violins and the viola reached the tenth and eleventh floors respectively. Spreading out from the street-level of the icy skyscraper was a panoply of culinary creations. Duncan eyed a platter of complicated salmon and crab canapés, each topped with an olive slice and a precise dollop of some coral-colored cream. Simone tapped him gently on the forearm.

"You might be interested to know that Claudia just arrived," she said, peering out toward the effervescent scene emanating from the red carpet on the plaza.

Duncan appeared uninterested, shifting his glance over to a meticulously stacked and aligned arrangement of asparagus spears. The card before them declared in a flourish of calligraphy that they were sautéed in butter and garlic. A small parenthetical below this statement clarified helpfully that they were *nut free*. Duncan was doing his best to appear preoccupied even though he had the sudden sensation of impending diarrhea. Having allowed for a sufficient demonstration of indifference and having gauged that he could manage preventing his bowels from exploding, he followed Simone's line of sight out to the plaza. Indeed there was Claudia, swathed in a sheer, emerald green dress that draped elegantly down to her ankles. Her shoulders were bare and about her neck hung a considerable string of pearls.

Since their split, Duncan had not seen Claudia to speak of. They moved in entirely different social circles and neither had attempted to maintain contact. And yet after all of this time and cutting through the space of the buzzing reception he sensed that her sharp, gray-eyed gaze was as acute and arresting as it had been on their first date at the Café Provençale. She did not see Duncan and Simone, for the moment beyond her immediate scope of observation, but clearly Claudia was not dazed and doe-eyed in the midst of the sparkle and pageantry. Duncan had no doubt that she was already taking an inventory of who was present, what they did and what would be their assigned priority during her evening's networking.

Only now did Duncan realize that Claudia was not alone, but at the side of a tall man, clearly in his middle years, who wore his thick brown hair boyishly long and waggishly disarrayed. His attire was relatively daring in comparison to his conservatively clad peers. Rather than the basic black tuxedo, Claudia's escort wore a deep blue velvet smoking jacket. His open collared silk shirt emanated a faint lilac sheen.

Duncan only allowed himself a couple of blinks in Claudia's direction before redirecting his attentions to the cornucopia at the base of the frozen skyscraper. He did not perceive the instant during which Claudia's roving surveillance of the crowd registered him and Simone and assigned them a priority for her rounds. This was a high priority indeed because Duncan and Simone had only just finished populating their tiny porcelain plates with savory hors d'oeuvres when Claudia glided up between them from behind.

"I thought I saw the two of you back here," she said, placing a light hand on their respective shoulders.

Simone was the first to respond. Claudia's sudden appearance not only took Duncan by surprise, but it had caused him to cram the entire canapé he was sampling unceremoniously into his mouth. For the moment, he could only smile dumbly and brush toast crumbs from his chin. "Hi, Claudia," said Simone. "You look stunning. I love that dress."

The two women exchanged enthusiastic compliments about their respective wardrobes, hairstyles and girlish figures while Duncan contributed supportive, fascinated nods and struggled to reduce the glutinous mass in his mouth into a state that might slide safely past his windpipe. Finally, Duncan threw caution to the wind and swallowed so that he could speak. Other than the sensation of having a boiled egg nestled behind his sternum, he felt fine. "We just need Nils and we'll have our old quartet back together," he said. "Not that I'm suggesting we should literally get back together. It would just be funny." *I'm such an idiot.*

"You know what? I see someone I need to say 'hi' to," said Simone. "I'll catch back up with you in a few minutes." She turned and in a moment the now-swarming lobby crowd had engulfed her and her bobbing white hair ribbon.

"So, Duncan, how are you?" said Claudia, choosing not to consider the merits of Duncan's suggestion for a funny reunion. "I can't believe it's been, what, five years."

"Yeah, I know," he said. "I'm doing great. Still teaching. Staying busy. How about you?"

"I can't complain." Claudia seemed to be resisting a smile. "I made partner at Brice, McMillan and Schober back in March."

"Hey, congratulations. I didn't know they had three names on the firm. Is that new?"

"Oh, the third name is for Brent Schober. They made that change two years ago, figuring that since he was single-handedly responsible for landing accounts worth almost half of the firm's turnover, it might be politic to put his name on the door. Actually, he and I came together tonight."

"Ahh, well you *have* been doing well for yourself. Are you two serious?"

Duncan thought he might have glimpsed an uncharacteristic shade of insecurity cross Claudia's face. Or it might have been the play of one of the projectors that was sending wispy, gray-orange clouds across the simulated sunset sky above. "Oh, who knows," she said. "We both work so much that there's hardly any time for much else. But things are good. So. You and Simone. I guess you two kept things going. That's great."

"What? Oh, no. We just rode together. I'm not really seeing anybody right now. That is, tonight I'm not seeing anybody. Otherwise, I'm seeing a lot of people. But not Simone." He noticed that Claudia was just watching him, observing him as he blathered on. "Do I sound like an idiot? Because if I do, you should know that I realize I sound like an idiot. Some people sound like idiots and have no clue. Me, I'm very aware of it."

Claudia smiled warmly. "You don't sound like an idiot. You do seem a bit, I don't know, anxious maybe."

"Yeah. I didn't really eat anything today. I think I'm just feeling a little giddy," he said. "So, who will be playing in the quartet tonight?"

"I have no idea. You can bet Nils will be playing, but I haven't spoken to the man in four years. You wouldn't believe what a shallow prick he is." She noticed the uptick in Duncan's eyebrows and laughed. "Or maybe you would. Anyway, he's so far in the rearview mirror that he doesn't seem real."

"I guess I'm that much farther in the rearview mirror," said Duncan.

Claudia scanned Duncan's face for a thoughtful moment. "Duncan, there's no comparison. You and I had something very special. You have such charming humor and wit. It turned out that we were out of synch, but I'll never stop appreciating what we had. You taught me a lot."

"I taught you?"

"Yes you did. You taught me that career and achievement aren't everything. You might not believe me to look at my crazy work schedule and making partner and all that, but at least now I'm better at putting those things in perspective." Claudia shrugged. "I'm still a work in progress I guess. It's taking me longer than you to find that peaceful equilibrium."

Something over Duncan's shoulder caught Claudia's attention and her eyes darted over and quickly back, "Well, I've got to scoot," she said. "Brent is determined to introduce me to the president of CVB. He wants us to play golf with him and his wife. Can you believe it? I've become a golfer." By now she was waving back to Duncan as she receded into the swirl of guests.

The soft recorder music, now barely discernable beneath the din, ceased, supplanted by a pervading baritone voice that one might hear on the radio or announcing prizes on a game show. "Ladies and gentlemen, may I have your attention please. The evening's entertainment—the world premier performance of the Nilsson Quartet—is about to begin. Kindly make your way to the lobby stage area and take your seats." A few guests began to peel off and file into the rows of folding chairs with burgundy slipcovers set up before the stage. Of the rest, about half continued their conversations while the others headed for the bars or the restrooms or both.

Duncan decided that a beer was in order and entered the scrum of mostly men at the nearest beverage table. "Can you get me a glass of Chardonnay?" Simone had appeared at his sided. "I'll get us a seat and a couple of programs. Look for me on the left side toward the front. I want us to have a good view."

The announcer's voice prodded the crowd once more, and Duncan made his way forward, drinks in hand, to where Simone was sitting. He asked her if she recognized the voice, but she said it was not familiar. Within a few minutes the assemblage was deemed reasonably complete and a little round man wearing a black tailcoat took the stage, bathed in a blue spotlight, and trotted on dainty feet to the microphone. Duncan turned to Simone excitedly. "I knew it. That's the guy who does the Chevy ads."

"What?" said Simone, puzzled. "I don't watch television."

"You don't know him? He used to be Skipper the Clown on channel six when I was a kid. You can't tell me..."

"Shush." Simone gave Duncan's knee a benign smack. "I need you to pay attention."

"Ladies and gentlemen," said the round man. "I'm Skip Melvin, and on behalf of the Nilsson Music Trust I'd like to welcome you to this premier of one of the finest quartet collections the world has ever seen. This evening will afford you the opportunity to hear them play, and after the performance to view them here on stage where they will be on display. And without further adieu, let's bring out the man, the visionary, who made this collection possible. He's a man who needs no introduction, Mr. Nils Nilsson." Skip Melvin graveled up his honey-smooth voice and gestured to stage right, releasing the blue spotlight to pan in welcome of the evening's self-appointed hero. Melvin's expertly crafted crescendo triggered a tumult of applause and even a few inspired, or perhaps hired, cheers.

Nils took the stage, followed by his three fellow musicians. Nils was empty handed, but the others were equipped with their instruments. While the three took their places standing beside the chairs already positioned for the performance, Nils and the blue spotlight moved to the microphone at the front of the stage.

"Thank you, Skip, and thanks to all of you who have come this evening to celebrate this fine collection of Italian masterpiece instruments. Tonight you will hear them played humbly by me and my colleagues, to whom I will introduce you in a moment. This evening is intended to mark the formation of the collection, but it is the intention of the Nilsson Music Trust to hold auditions to form a world class, virtuoso quartet that will tour and bring the joy of these masterworks to audiences far and wide. The charter of the Nilsson Music Trust—a non-profit charitable trust— is the preservation of important musical instruments for the purpose enhancing the public's understanding and appreciation of our musical heritage, especially through live performance. Tonight I hope to whet your appetite because there is a lot more to come from the Nilsson Music Trust. I look forward to supporting its work, and I hope you will too."

"Of course, the main attraction tonight is the instruments themselves," Nils continued. "So allow me to share a little background with you. Our first instrument—the oldest— is a viola crafted in Cremona by Nicolò Amati in 1664." As Nils made this brief introduction, the violist stepped forward to join Nils at the front of the stage. "This evening, Dr. Theo van Winkle, music director of our own Church Hill Philharmonic has agreed to sit in on viola." Next to Nils, Theo gave the impression of a mischievous old elf.

Simone turned to Duncan and whispered, "Check out Theo. Doesn't he look great? He hasn't aged a day."

"Yep, and he still doesn't own a comb."

Now, with Theo at his side, Nils gave an abbreviated discourse on seventeenth century Italian violin making in general and the Amati dynasty in particular, starting with Andrea Amati, the patriarch and proceeding to Nicolò, the grand master. "I'm taking a little more time with this instrument because its creator was the direct or indirect teacher of those who created the other instruments on this stage. Grancino's father was an apprentice, Guarneri del Gesù's grandfather was an apprentice and there is strong evidence that Antonio Stradivari developed his craft in Amati's workshops, though it is unclear whether he was a formal apprentice."

"Does the viola look familiar?" Simone whispered to Duncan. "What do you think?"

"I can't really tell from here," said Duncan. "The color is certainly similar. I don't know."

Nils finished with the viola and moved on to the 1693 Grancino cello. The musician was Martin Tubbs who had played with the Philharmonic but was now with the Tidewater Symphony. Next came the 1719 del Gesù violin, likely the most expensive acquisition, but for once Nils abstained from punctuating his speech with dollar signs. The svelte, young Japanese violinist named Kiku Yoshida stepped forward. She cast a blushing glance at Nils as she presented him with the violin for his commentary. Both Duncan and Simone simultaneously flipped in their programs to her short biography. She was a graduate student at Westham University, studying early music.

Duncan leaned over to Simone. "I hear there's going to be an intimate party on Nils's sofa after the show."

"Shush!"

"And now our fourth and final instrument," Nils continued. "Completing the Nilsson Quartet Collection is a 1678 violin by Antonio Stradivari." Here an attendant mounted the stage and delivered the masterpiece to Nils. As with the others, he gave a short history of the instrument and its famous maker. In all, he spent half an hour declaiming on the collection. He then announced that he and his colleagues would play an excerpt from Beethoven's string quartet number sixteen.

Simone nudged Duncan with her elbow. "Now we can hear what that viola sounds like."

The quartet played only the first two movements. The musicians demonstrated technical precision. Either by design, out of trepidation or simply due to limitations of skill, the four did not explore the dynamic opportunities offered by their precious instruments. At least that is how Martha Clayhill, cultural reviewer for the local paper, would describe the performance. Her overall assessment of the collection and the mission of the Nilsson Music Trust would nevertheless be enthusiastically favorable, delivering Nilsson with the positive PR spin he was always looking for.

When the performance was concluded and the audience had expended a healthy, wine-enhanced shower of applause, Nils announced that the instruments would be arranged on stage for viewing. He invited the guests to continue to enjoy the food and refreshments and to visit the display on stage at their leisure.

Now that the drone of surrounding conversations had settled onto the revived backdrop of tootling renaissance recorders, Simone quizzed Duncan impatiently. "Well, what about the viola? Didn't you think it sounded just like yours? It sounded to me just like in our old quartet. We worked on the exact same piece."

"I don't know what to say. I just can't tell. For one thing, I never really heard anyone else play my viola. I always heard it playing right under my chin." He saw the exasperation building in her expression. "Look, Simone, I'm not trying to be contrary. I just honestly don't have a strong feeling one way or the other. When the crowd thins out we can walk up and take a closer look. Maybe the Maestro will have left the stage by then."

Three beers and two Chardonnays later, Simone insisted that it was time to make their move. Nils was still positioned proudly with his collection, expounding on its wonders to the now dwindling string of viewers. "If we wait much longer, they're liable to pack up the display and we'll miss our chance," she said.

"Why the hell not," he said, feeling somewhat fortified for the encounter. "I'll even lead the way."

Nils was just bidding goodnight to a clutch of observers as his former band mates approached him and the cordoned rectangle that enclosed a velvet-draped table displaying the collection. Two security guards stood discreetly at the back corners of the display. Two others took up stations at the back of the stage.

"My old friends, Simone and Duncan," said Nils with apparently genuine affection. He kissed Simone on the cheek and shook Duncan's hand vigorously. "I'm so glad you could make it."

"Congratulations on a successful launch of your collection," said Simone. Duncan could think of nothing constructive to say.

"Well, thank you," said Nils. "And remember, it's not my collection. It belongs to the trust, which has its mission that will go on after I'm no longer around. That's what makes me the proudest."

"So here they are," said Simone. Duncan was still trying to formulate something constructive to say. "All gathered in one place three hundred years after they were made and halfway around the world. The viola was your last acquisition. When you stopped by the shop, you didn't mention where you got it. Was it at an auction?"

"I bought the other three at auctions up in New York, but as I've learned, masterpiece violas are much harder to come by. I bought the Amati from a dealer out of Los Angeles called Overby International. I don't mind telling you that it cost a bit more than I had anticipated, but it was worth it."

"How much was it?" blurted Duncan. His mind had been churning so chaotically to locate some inoffensive contribution to the conversation that it had become addled.

Nils seemed pleased to address the question, as if he had just been asked the name of his tailor. "I set up the trust with three million and used most of it on the first three instruments. I had counted on landing a viola for somewhere in the hundred thousand range, but in the end I paid over one-sixty for it. Worth every penny."

"Such an amazing collection," Simone said, turning wide, awestruck eyes to Nils. The disconcerting image of Sarah Bugbee flashed in Duncan's head. "You're going to think I'm such a nuisance, but I'd really love to get a close look at the viola. I should have taken advantage when you came by, but I was just so intimidated by it. I've been kicking myself ever since."

"Don't be silly," said Nils. "For you, Simone, anything." He lifted the velvet rope from its post and motioned for them to join him inside. The sudden incursion stirred the guards from their tedium. As he re-hooked the rope, Nils smiled at them reassuringly and said, "Not to worry officers. These are authorized personnel."

Nils lifted the viola from its stand and presented it to Simone for inspection. She made a show of examining its various elements, but turned her attention quickly to the scroll. "My goodness," she said. "I see it has a few bumps and bruises. Look at that scratch on the scroll." She held the scroll up so Duncan could have a clear look. "Do you see that Duncan?"

"Yes, I see it," he said.

"This is an instrument more than three centuries old," said Nils. "Marks like that only add to the character, and certainly they have no effect on the sound quality."

"Of course not," said Simone. Nils seemed to interpret her triumphant smile as euphoria from holding his masterpiece. She returned the instrument to him. "Thank you so much, Nils. This has been a real thrill." As Nils replaced the viola in its stand, she turned her back to the table and mouthed to Duncan, "I told you!" Duncan was still trying to process what they had seen, on top of general agitation from his first encounter with Nils since the Euterpe Quartet's fateful debut night.

"Can I play it?" said Duncan suddenly. He spoke as someone awaking from a dream uttering the words that jolted him back to consciousness.

"Excuse me?" said Nils, turning back from replacing the viola.

"Um, can I play the viola?" said Duncan. "I mean just a few notes."

Nils looked mildly annoyed. He glanced at Simone who just shrugged meekly. She already had one hand on the velvet rope preparing to exit.

"I've only ever played basic violas," Duncan continued. "And it would be such a... privilege to one time play a few notes on an authentic masterpiece."

Nils squared his stance and scrutinized Duncan with one eyebrow raised skeptically. Duncan simply awaited a response. Simone had not moved, her hand still poised on the rope.

Nils rubbed his chin. Perhaps he was wondering whether Duncan might commit some misguided act of retribution against Nils even though Nils considered himself just the innocent beneficiary of Duncan's marital negligence. Finally, he said, "Why not? These instruments are to be played and you certainly are an excellent player. Be my guest." He stepped aside and gestured for Duncan to help himself.

Duncan took up the bow that lay behind the instrument and tightened the hairs with the screw at the end. With the bow in his right hand, he took up the viola with his left and positioned it under his chin. He composed himself to play and it suddenly occurred to him that he had no idea what to play. His mind was a blank. He glanced nervously over at Nils, who stood stone faced, and Simone, who looked almost scared. "Um, I guess I should play something. Heh, heh, I must have forgotten how to play." A couple of the diehard guests, still haunting the lobby were drawn to the scene, perhaps thinking there would be an impromptu concerto. At least it would be better than watching the ice tower melt.

Duncan squinted in concentration. After a moment, his bow began to carve out a Yiddish flavored melody. In his mind, he heard Tevye the milkman singing, "If I were a rich man, Ya ha deedle deedle, bubba bubba deedle deedle dum." He opened his eyes in amazement. The piece just sort of played itself. He had not even thought of it in years. He looked around sheepishly. Nils, Simone and the few guests who had been drawn like moths to the spectacle gawked at him in disbelief.

Nils was the first to reanimate. His tone indicated that he was not amused by the use of a rare antiquity for playing novelty ditties. "That's an interesting choice of music for you to play on an Italian masterpiece. I hope you had fun." Nils held out his hands to indicate the immediate return of the viola would be appropriate.

When they were securely in the elevator on their way back to the parking deck, Simone finally burst out in perplexed amusement, "What the heck was that all about? We established that it's your viola. I may not be sure what to do next, but I never would have thought to play show tunes."

"What we do next is absolutely nothing," Duncan said calmly.

"Are you kidding? Your viola has been stolen. We know who has it, and you want to do nothing?"

The elevator opened and Duncan held the door so Simone could exit. "Simone, I hate to tell you this, but that is not my viola."

CHAPTER TWENTY

On Sunday morning after the reception, Simone emerged tousle-headed and yawning from the bedroom. She wore one of Alex's large flannel shirts and a pair of pink socks. Alex had risen only a few moments before and was pouring water into the top of the coffee maker.

"Hey, good morning," said Alex. "The coffee is coming up. I am in the mood for some scrambled eggs. Are you interested?"

"Yeah, sure. Thanks." Simone sat absently in one of the vinyl covered kitchen chairs and stared out the window.

"I hope I did not make too much noise when I came in last night. Dwayne and KG and me must have shot twenty games of pool." Alex finished breaking four eggs into a warped plastic bowl. As his hands busied themselves with beating the eggs, his eyes subtly scrutinized Simone. "So... how was the reception? Any big surprises? I mean... was it a spectacular event?"

This line of inquiry seemed to jostle Simone back to wakefulness. She looked up at Alex, who reflexively focused his full attention on the bowl of frothing yellow slime. "What? No there were no surprises. Did you think we would have a surprise?"

"Uh, no. Well, you know, given the history between Duncan and Nils, I did not know if things might get a little weird." He stopped beating and smiled. "But really, I just meant to ask whether you had fun."

"It was fine," said Simone, and she turned to look out the window again, drifting back for a moment into dream-frosted thoughts. A little thermometer clung to the outside of the pane with clear suction cups. Despite the tarnished pewter skies hanging over mid-morning, the mercury had already risen to eighty-two. "You forgot the alarm last night," she said finally.

"What?" Alex was pouring the eggs into a black iron skillet sitting on the neon-blue flame of Simone's ancient stove.

"The alarm. You went out without setting the alarm," she said. "I had to put it on when I got home. How many times have I told you about setting the alarm? Our whole livelihood is in that shop."

"Oh, my God." Alex made to slap his forehead with his non-pouring, left hand. Since he held a dripping fork in his left hand, he could only make a token tap with the back of the hand. A small eggy glob flipped into his hair without his notice. Simone said nothing about the glob, not wanting to distract attention from the issue at hand. "After you left, KG called to say they were waiting on me and I kind of rushed out. I must have been in such a hurry that I forgot to set the alarm. I am so sorry. Stupid." He gave himself another thwack, accenting his disheveled coif with another undetected spatter of goo.

Simone had to suppress amusement with the unintended consequences of Alex's self-flagellation. "Please, please. If there's one thing we can't get lax on, it's setting the alarm."

"I know. You are absolutely right. It will not happen again," said Alex. He tended the eggs for a moment, gently prodding them with a spatula. "The good news is that Duncan's viola is ready, except for putting on the strings, which I will take care of today. After we eat, would you like to come have a look?"

"Yeah, sure." Simone stared out at the dull sky. She had been certain that Nils had acquired Duncan's viola and that somehow Alex was involved. Now nothing made sense. On the drive home she had insisted that Duncan was mistaken, but he was equally insistent that while the Amati looked just like his, right down to the scratch, it was absolutely not his. He was adamant that Nils's viola failed to deliver the right sound quality for that goofy tune. She found this absurd, but she had no basis to argue against it. The only option now was to let the subject go, even though she could not bring herself to drop entirely the theory that Nils had Duncan's viola. In the end, if Duncan did not care, why should she?

After breakfast, Alex led the way down the stairs to the front door of the shop. He flashed Simone a sheepish smile and shrugged before keying in the code to disarm the alarm. Simone closed the door behind them with a jingle and they went back to the workshop door behind the counter.

"Well, at least I did remember to lock up the workshop door," he said, as if to himself, and flipped the deadbolt. He opened the door and stepped through. With Alex in front of her, Simone could not see the sight that caused Alex to cry out in dismay as soon as he was inside. "Holy shit! What the hell happened in here?"

The workshop was in a state of devastation. It looked as if the hand of a giant had picked it up like a doll's house and shaken it vigorously. The workbench was overturned. The cabinet doors all dangled open with the contents of the shelves strewn everywhere. Spray painted on the lower panel of the back door was an exclamatory "Fuck." A vaporous odor of varnish pervaded the air. Intermingled with the noxious fumes was another scent: stale beer. Among the flotsam scattered about the room were perhaps a dozen empty malt liquor cans. Alex quickly threw open the back door to allow for ventilation.

He turned back to Simone. She said nothing. She just stood in the workshop doorway with her arms crossed staring inscrutably at the wreckage. Alex hesitated, uncertain of what to do next. Finally, he said, "I'll call the police."

An hour later officer Bert Dixon arrived at the premises to conduct his interviews and determine what, if any, investigation was warranted. He would note that he spoke to Simone Duval and Alejandro Alvarez, a.k.a. Alex Alvarez, cohabitants of the apartment above the shop, which was owned by Ms. Duval. The report would reflect that Mr. Alvarez supplied the majority of the information required while Ms. Duval seemed withdrawn and dejected.

"You believe the perpetrators broke in between seven and ten yesterday evening, is that correct?" Broken glass crunched under the sole of Dixon's patent leather shoe. The officer jotted notes on a clipboard, the base of which he rested on the prodigious bulge of his belly. He pinioned his hat under one arm while fingers of sweat crept down the sides of his face from his prickly, tawny flattop.

"That's right," said Alex. "Simone and I went out for the evening just before seven. We had separate appointments. She got home a little after ten. I got home around midnight."

"How do you know this didn't happen in the middle of the night?"

Alex explained about the alarm. "They apparently got in by busting out that pane in the back door and reaching through to unlock it. Fortunately, the workshop door kept them out of the shop. I guess when they left they happened to shut the back door. If they had left it open, the alarm panel would not have let Simone activate the system when she got home." Alex noticed that officer Dixon did not seem to be listening to his explanation but was eyeing him strangely. He shifted uncomfortably under the policeman's scrutiny. "What is it? What's the matter? Doesn't that make sense?"

Dixon continued to survey Alex with a suspicious squint. "You know you have some kind of yellow gunk in your hair?"

Ten minutes later, Dixon was putting the finishing touches on his clipboard notes. The three were now in the front of the shop. Simone had been propped meditatively on her stool behind the counter virtually since Alex phoned the police. Alex and Dixon now stood in front of the counter concluding the interview.

"So the only things missing were the three tools you listed plus the violin?" said the policeman.

"Uh, it was a viola," said Alex.

"You didn't say it was a violin? Well, I'll need to fix that." He sought out the erroneous entry on the clipboard for correction. "You'd think I'd have learned the difference by now. I had a case a couple of months ago involving a stolen viola. You seem to be part of a regular viola crime spree."

Alex laughed uncomfortably. The officer did not seem to notice the malignant glare that Ms. Duval directed at Mr. Alvarez as a consequence of the officer's comment. "They would have to be some pretty stupid crooks to steal this viola. It was severely damaged, virtually worthless except for some sentimental value," Alex said. "If this were some kind of viola spree, they would have forced their way into the front of the shop don't you think?"

"You're probably right, Mr. Alvarez. No, I suspect this was just some kids up to mischief on a summertime Saturday night. Beer drinking, vandalizing, the graffiti on the doors, pretty typical."

"On the *doors*?" said Simone. The two men had almost forgotten that she was sitting there before them. "They wrote on more than one door?"

"Yes, ma'am. There was the F-word on the rear entrance door and there was the... male genitalia on the other side of that door there." Dixon pointed his ball point pen at the workshop door.

"Oh, I see," said Simone shaking her head in wry disbelief.

"I know," said Dixon. "It's disgusting. I'm sorry I had to be the one to tell you."

When the policeman had driven away in his patrol car and Alex came back into the shop, Simone remained on her stool and surveyed him coolly.

"I am so sorry, baby," said Alex. "I am such an idiot. I am going to clean everything up and put it all right. I will pay for it myself so you will not have to claim insurance."

"I see," she said evenly. "And what will you do about Duncan's viola?"

"Well, I do not know. I will find out from Duncan what he thinks is fair. I mean the thing was just a burnt up shell."

"I've actually got a much better idea."

"Okay, baby. Just name it."

"Pack up all your shit and get out."

Simone phoned Duncan as soon as Alex sped away from the shop, in the throws of a tantrum that was far more theatrical than emotional. Alex had assumed for quite some time that his cushy arrangement with Simone was approaching the end of its shelf life. In any case, his fortunes were on the upswing. The dummy viola that inconveniently survived the fire lay in fragments in a dumpster behind The Cavern bar. He now had a foot firmly in the door of the antiques trade with its lucrative market opportunities. If he had to, he could pave his way to get up and running by doing carpentry work on the side. These were the thoughts that dominated Alex's mind as the rear wheels of his Lexus screeched away from Duval Violins.

"Holy cow, what a mess," said Duncan when he arrived in response to Simone's call. "You can't really believe that Alex did this. I mean, my God."

"That's exactly what I believe, Duncan," she said. "He trashed the place to cover up his real motive, which was to eliminate the evidence. Your viola was the only thing taken other than a couple of cheap hand tools."

"Simone," Duncan implored patiently. "I thought we put to bed the theory about my viola being stolen and sold."

"You put it to bed. I wasn't so sure, but this confirms to me that something strange is going on and Alex is obviously in the middle of it."

"Isn't it possible that this is simply what it appears to be?"

"You mean that a group of kids broke into a violin shop before ten o'clock on a Saturday night to have a beer party and spray paint penises?"

"Well, yes," he said hopefully. And then, "Penises?"

They were standing in the middle of the workshop. Simone turned and swung the door to the shop closed, revealing a bulbous, cartoon cock and balls outlined in fuzzy red. "Have you ever seen something like that before?" she said.

Duncan smiled. "I'm not ashamed to admit that I have, on a few perfectly innocent occasions, seen men's genitals. What of it?"

Simone punched Duncan's arm. "You know what I mean. You told me whoever stole your car painted it up the same way."

"Mmhmm. Very interesting," said Duncan, rubbing his chin in mock contemplation. "The penis is sort of a calling card, like the mark of Zorro, and Alex must be... the evil Doctor Wang!"

"You're not funny," said Simone, annoyed at Duncan as well as at herself for laughing.

"I'm sorry," he said sympathetically. "I shouldn't kid around. I admit that it is odd that the two events have such similar hallmarks. At the same time, drinking beer and painting asinine graffiti could describe the behavior of just about any juvenile delinquent. Maybe the same hoodlums happened to commit both crimes, I don't know. It still doesn't make sense to me that Alex would do such stupid things, even if he is a colossal jerk."

"But don't you see?" she said. "Both crimes involve your viola, and we've talked about what a weird obsession Alex seems to have with your viola, up to and including his insistence to get it into the shop for him to refurbish." She gestured toward the wreckage at their feet. "And this supposedly random act occurs while he's refurbishing it."

"You're right," he said. "These are some pretty weird coincidences. Maybe Alex *was* involved. I'm not convinced of that, but even if he was, I'm over it. I got an insurance payout on the car that was more than I would have gotten on a trade-in, and it was high time for me to get a new car anyway. I've lost my grandfather's viola, which is a bummer, but somehow losing it has caused me to take stock of my life. For the first time in years, I feel like I'm really starting fresh with all sorts of possibilities ahead. Frankly, I'm happy to move on, and I'll help you get the workshop cleaned-up. It'll be good as new."

The bells on the front door jingled, as someone must have entered the shop. Simone moved quickly to the front, where she found Alex making his way in with a large cardboard box.

"Why are you here, Alex?" said Simone, her arms crossed tightly across her stomach.

"I am just getting my stuff, like you said. I feel bad about what happened and I understand why you are upset. I came in to let you know that I was going to start boxing up my stuff in the apartment."

Duncan now emerged from the workshop. "Oh, hi, Alex."

"I see it did not take you long to come to the rescue," said Alex, eyeing Duncan suspiciously, but then reminded himself that it was he, Alex, who had won the skirmish over the viola. "I am sorry that your viola got stolen again. You may have heard that I don't work at the shop anymore, but I am sure Duval Violins will compensate you fairly for your loss."

"You said you came to pack," observed Simone flatly.

"Yeah, that is right. I am heading upstairs to pack," said Alex, beginning to withdraw to the front door. "Oh, say, Duncan, what did you think of Nils's collection last night? He spent some big bucks on those instruments. I hear he paid twenty or thirty grand for that viola. How about that for a viola? Can you believe it?"

"Actually, he told us that he paid a lot more for it than that. I think he said he paid more than one-sixty for it," said Duncan.

Alex stopped cold, with one hand on the doorknob while he gripped the mouth of the box with the other. "You are full of shit. He did not pay any one-sixty for that viola."

Duncan shrugged. "I don't know what he paid, but I don't know why he would lie since all the purchases were part of a non-profit trust and will be public information. Plus, one-sixty is pocket change next to what he probably paid for the other instruments."

Alex stood paralyzed for several seconds. The only signs of animation were the pulsations of his jaw muscles. "That son-of-a-bitch," muttered Alex with no attempt to camouflage his rage. He flung open the door and stormed out. The box in his trailing hand wedged in the closing door. Duncan and Simone watched the box collapse and distort as Alex's disembodied hand yanked it viciously through the opening. Next they heard a car door slam, an engine thrum to life and rubber yelp against asphalt as roaring energy transformed violently into motion.

Duncan stood blinking for a moment in the now peaceful room and then turned to Simone, who peered smugly back at him. "Okay, I get it. Something weird's going on with Alex and the viola."

Duncan and Simone spent most of the rest of the afternoon back in the workshop restoring things to order. The overturned workbench posed the most strenuous challenge, but grunting together the two set it upright and slid it back into its place. After that, the rest was mostly a matter of putting items back on shelves, on hooks or, as needed, in the large green garbage bin that Simone had Duncan drag in from the back garden. As they bent their backs to their chore they discussed how they might decipher the strange events in which Alex seemed to be involved.

"Who do you think is the 'son-of-a-bitch' that Alex is referring to?" said Duncan, leaning momentarily on his broom. "Is he talking about Nils? Nils is after all a son-of-a-bitch?"

"That wouldn't make any sense. If Alex was involved in stealing the viola, how could he be mad at Nils for paying *too much*? The more Nils paid, the more Alex would make."

"But Nils does not have my viola. It looks like mine, but it's definitely not mine."

"Don't you think it strange that Nils's viola looks identical to yours, right down to that accidental scratch on the scroll? There's no way that's a coincidence."

"I don't know what else to tell you. It's not my viola."

"I believe you," she said. "So, if it's not yours, the choices are that it is either an identical twin that freakishly received the exact same injury on the scroll *or*..." She waited for Duncan to fill in the blank.

Duncan shook his head skeptically. "You mean to say that Alex somehow made a near perfect replica of my viola?"

"Not Alex, but someone Alex was working with, someone who sold the replica to Nils for a price far higher than Alex was aware of."

"This is all so far fetched. Granted, it might hold together in theory, but the thought of Alex engineering the theft of my old viola so some mysterious person can make a replica of it for sale to Nils Nilsson is just too wild."

"Maybe," said Simone. "But it wouldn't hurt for us to do some poking around, just for fun. There's nothing wrong with having some fun is there?"

Duncan reluctantly agreed to participate in Simone's endeavor of "fun," but insisted that he was not interested in anything that involved confrontations or tediously skulking around like a private detective. They started with an internet search for Overby International, the name Nils had mentioned at the reception. After a quarter of an hour putting in every spelling and cross-reference term they could think of, they came up empty.

Next, it occurred to Simone that Alex's phone records might provide a clue. "He and I have a shared cell phone account. Oh, God, that reminds me I'll need to deal with that," she said. "Anyway, if he was making calls to Mr. Son-of-a-Bitch on his cell phone, the number will appear on our monthly bill." She pulled open a file drawer from the cabinet behind the counter and located a file labeled *Utilities/ Phone*. She opened the manila folder and plucked out a few of the phone statements closest to the front. Spreading them out on the counter before them she began to scan the calls assigned to Alex's cell phone.

"This number appears a lot," said Duncan pointing at a string of digits that repeated sometimes two or three times on a given date. "What's that?"

"Oh, that's his friend KG," she said. "He might be able to cut you up a stack of firewood, but he's no luthier. I'm pretty sure he's not a rocket scientist either. Neither is this one." She pointed to a number that she identified as belonging to Dwayne. "And this is my cell. This is the shop. Our apartment. This is Alex's sister in North Carolina. Here are a couple of local numbers I don't recognize." She ticked the unfamiliar ones with a pencil.

"Six-one-seven. What area code is that?" said Duncan, indicating a couple of entries in early April.

Simone pulled down the phone book from the shelf and consulted the area code table in the front. "Apparently, it's for Boston."

"Who does Alex know in Boston?"

"I don't know," she said, adding two little graphite checks.

When they had gone through the three statements on the counter, they surveyed the accumulated tick marks. There were nine marks attached to an assortment of local numbers, two of them appeared twice, the rest were unique. The Boston number had a total of five hits, three in April and two in May.

"Do you remember when your viola was stolen?" asked Simone.

"How could I forget?" he said. "It was April Fool's Day. Rather poetic I have come to decide."

"Look at this, the first call is on April first at seven nineteen in the evening. That's just a couple of hours after the theft, right?" said Simone turning to Duncan excitedly. "I say we start with this one."

Duncan agreed to stand nearby with moral support while Simone dialed the number. He said that calling strangers to inquire about their involvement in crimes was not his idea of fun, and he had signed on for fun stuff only. Simone accused Duncan of being a chicken, a claim to which he enthusiastically assented, and she picked up the shop phone and dialed the Boston number.

An erudite voice came on the line. "Allegro Antiquities. This is James Dickerson."

Simone hung up the phone immediately. "That's him!"

CHAPTER TWENTY-ONE —————————————

From behind his desk in the rear of Allegro Antiquities, James heard the echoed sound of someone entering the front door and re-closing it firmly. A moment later, Larry appeared at the threshold of James's cluttered lair.

"What's got you popping in here on a Sunday?" said James peering above the half-rimmed reading glasses that aided him in perusing an original edition of Appelbaum's The History of the Lute, published in 1859, that he had recently obtained.

"I just want to get another coat of varnish on a violin I'm making for a dude in Manhattan. It's a sweet piece of work, if I do say so myself." Larry turned to head back up front.

"You'll never guess who rang a few minutes ago," said James.

"Nope. I never will," said Larry, but he lingered briefly in the hallway to hear the revelation.

"It was our friend Alex Alvarez."

This news drew Larry into the office. "Well, we knew he would probably phone sooner or later. Lord only knows what took him so long. What did he say?"

"Actually, he said nothing. He rang off without speaking, but I could see from the caller ID that it was he. It came from Duval Violins, where he works."

"I guess he called to complain and then got cold feet." Larry spun around the Shaker chair in front of the desk and sat down heavily with his arms resting on the back.

"It would appear so," said James. "He's likely ascertained by now that the sale price was slightly higher than he realized."

"You don't think he knows about the swap?"

"I really doubt it. Reproductions from Atelier Giles are the best in the world," said James with a sly nod to his colleague. "Nilsson would have to figure out about the swap and then somehow Alex would have to hear about it. First of all, Nilsson didn't even take the prudent step of having the viola evaluated during the twenty-four hours when he had the original. Clearly, authenticity was not a concern. But sooner or later some expert will get a look at the viola and raise suspicions. My guess is that Nilsson would try to avoid any publicity or scandal. He's the kind of guy who can absorb this kind of loss and would prefer to do so rather than look like a cretin."

"No. He wouldn't want that." Larry smiled. James had shown him a souvenir copy of a magazine featuring Nilsson. The guy came across as a narcissist. "And our tracks are covered?"

"We've left not so much as a fingerprint," said James, removing his eyeglasses and tossing them onto the open book before him. "Messrs. Overby and Digby have melted into the mist. The only way he could track us down is through Alex Alvarez, who may be an imbecile, but he's smart enough to quit while he's ahead."

Larry pursed his lips and gazed down at his arms, propped on the chair back. After a moment of reflection, he said, "Alright then. So what about the second half of the endeavor? Any prospects for the Amati?"

"Now, now, we mustn't be hasty," said James. "As I said from the beginning, the 'second half' as you call it may be a long time coming. Even though we have an authentic Amati, verifiable as the one lost from the Gutmann estate, a public sale would be too risky. Even a private sale can attract attention. Just this morning, I saw online a reference to Nilsson holding an event over the weekend where he debuted his new collection, including the viola. He will be getting, if he hasn't already, calls from specialists in the field wanting to get a look at his acquisition."

"So when's the right time to move the instrument?"

"Unless the perfect opportunity falls into our laps, it may be prudent to sit on it for a few years," said James. Seeing Larry straighten his back at the suggestion of such a long wait, he added, "Don't worry. We'll get it done, but we've got to do it right. I'll likely work with some contacts I have on the continent who can serve as middlemen and cover the trail to Allegro Antiquities. Even though our piece is authentic and dated three years older than Nilsson's, we don't want anyone connecting our future sale to Nilsson's fake. I certainly don't intend for Nilsson to somehow see my smiling face pop up in a trade announcement about an unearthed Amati viola."

"Not to mention the true owner of the viola seeing it," said Larry.

"Good point," said James. "It's still a complete mystery how a dolt like Alex got such a treasure. All we know is that it disappeared from Gutmann's estate under highly dubious circumstances three generations ago. I can't see any real threat coming from the 'true owner,' but it does remain an intriguing riddle."

James's cell phone emitted a muffled buzz and began to sidle across the stack of reports on the corner of the desk. He plucked it up and read the caller ID. What he saw inspired an amused grin. He looked across at Larry and waggled the phone. "It seems our friend's cold feet have warmed up." James flipped open the phone. "Hello. James Dickerson here."

"Dickerson, you sissy-ass dirt bag, did you think you could steal from me and get away with it?" said Alex through the phone.

"I'm sorry? With whom am I speaking?"

"You know goddamn well who this is. I am the guy you shafted for a hundred and thirty thousand."

"Ah, Mr. Alvarez," said James, smiling benevolently for Larry's benefit. "I'm so sorry you are upset. Ironically, I should be the one who am upset with you and yet I have let it go like water under the bridge."

"What the fuck are you talking about? How would you like to be *sleeping* in the water under the bridge?"

James sat up in his chair, his expression grey and grim. He was no longer interested in entertaining Larry. "Let me explain something to you, Alex. You are a petty thief. You stole something and you wanted to fence it. I am not a fence. I don't know anything about this money you claim you are owed. I would suggest that you consider your situation and be thankful that you aren't in jail. If you continue harassing me, that's precisely where you are likely to end up."

"You are not just going to walk away from this deal with my money."

James modulated his voice into a more avuncular tone. "Alex, for your own peace of mind, it is important that you get a grip. I don't know anything about this money you are talking about, but I do know that the last time we spoke, you were in high spirits and feeling successful. I recommend that you regain that positive outlook. Don't be the greedy monkey who loses everything because he wouldn't let go of the trifles in the jar."

"Fuck you, James Dickhead and your fucking monkey…"

James held the phone away from his ear so that Larry could clearly make out the gist of Alex's apoplectic rant. Through the phone's earpiece, the compressed warble gave the impression of a tiny man yelling up from the bottom of a drain. Although the diatribe had not abated, James spoke into the handset perfunctorily before clapping it shut. "Thank you for ringing, Mr. Alvarez. Have a nice day."

The female voice delivered its message in the rapid monotone of a cattle auctioneer, informing the passengers that the Embraer jet would touch down at Logan International Airport in approximately twenty minutes. Duncan insisted on the window seat because he said looking out the window made him less terrified. Although he skipped the complimentary dinner service, he drank a couple of beers. These were not complimentary, and together they cost as much as he would have paid for a case of beer at the Food Lion, but he rationalized the expense since he was taking them for medicinal purposes.

He enjoyed them about as much as taking medicine. He stared out his window and began to feel a little less tense. The second beer hummed warmly in his chest. For the first time, looking along the wing that extended out toward the red, western horizon, he noticed the small, skyward-pointing triangle at the end. It gave the impression that the maker had turned up the wingtip. Were these flourishes necessary or just fashionable? He was beginning to enjoy this little meditation on aircraft design when Simone, in the seat next to him, nudged his elbow.

"How are you doing over there?" she said above the squeezed whir of cabin noise. Duncan seemed disinclined to chat during the flight so she had engrossed herself in the novel that she brought along, but she could no longer focus on reading, and she was finished perusing the glossy photos of the airline magazine.

"I feel much better, but I'm looking forward to getting back on solid ground."

"I really appreciate you going along with this," she said. "I hope you can think of it as a sort of vacation. I'm looking at it that way, at least in part. I can't remember the last time I closed down the shop when it wasn't a holiday."

"It's not much of a vacation," he said. "You're just closed tomorrow and Saturday."

"For me, a three day break feels like a sabbatical," she said. "By the time we get to the hotel, it will be around eight. After we check into our rooms do you want to go out for a bite?"

"Yeah, sounds fine," he said. He glanced out the window again. The tiny roads and buildings below had grown since his last observation. "We've got to get clear on what we're doing tomorrow. I'm happy to tag along on this, but I'm really not comfortable with anything that might get sticky. I'm still not sure why we don't just call..." He realized that fellow passengers might take an inopportune interest his conversation. Given that they had been conversing as if each were hearing impaired, he leaned closer to Simone. "I don't know why we can't give the police the information we have and let them investigate."

Simone smiled and gave Duncan's forearm a pat. "Come on. This is a harmless adventure. Think of it like one of those safari vacations where you never leave the safety of the Land Rover." Duncan shook his head skeptically, and Simone continued. "Seriously, I would feel foolish going to the...you-know-who right now because what do we really have? We've just got Alex's strange behavior and a viola that looks like, but isn't, the one stolen from you. All we would succeed in doing is coming across as nutcases. I can only imagine Maestro Nils's reaction to the claim."

"Okay. That's fine," said Duncan. "We can do our little charade. It might even be fun, but I still don't know what you think you're going to find out. Even if you are right and this guy has the viola, I can't imagine he will have it in the window with a price tag on it."

Simone did not respond immediately. She seemed to be contemplating the air vent above her head. "I'm not sure what we'll find out," she said finally. "We won't know until we get there. We'll just have to visit the shop and make our inquiries as discussed."

"And what if we come up empty? I don't want things to get sticky. I'm not up for confronting the guy and accusing him of something."

Simone smiled. "If we come up empty, I will forget the whole thing. We can sight see and make the most of our mini-vacation, and I will go back home and begin enjoying my new Alex-free life."

By ten in the morning, the narrow Beacon Hill passage already felt like an oven. An American flag hung motionless above the baking cobbles on the street below. This would be a day where Larry Giles would enjoy the out of doors by observing it from his air-conditioned workshop. Larry was more of a nocturnal creature anyway. To move about the streets on a hot summer evening made his senses tingle with anticipation. The night meant live music—playing or listening—and it meant the thrill of the libidinous prowl, and he rarely went home empty handed.

The front buzzer to the shop sounded. Larry hung his moss-green apron on a hook, went to the entrance and opened the door. "You must be the Westwood's," said Larry.

"Yes," said the man on the stoop, standing with his hand resting affectionately on the woman's shoulder. "I'm David Westwood and this is my wife, Samantha." For the role-play, Duncan had donned his one decent suit. Unfortunately, although it was made of tropical weight wool, he could feel the perspiration beginning to seep out of his armpits and under his collar, cinched snugly with the silk tie that Simone bought the night before. When he had shown her the tie he planned to wear, she insisted on a more fashionable replacement. He envied Simone, who, besides looking beautiful with her raven hair tied back, could appear well heeled without donning heavy armor. She wore a cream-colored skirt and sleeveless, azure blouse.

"Welcome to Allegro Antiquities," said Larry. "Please come in." He led them into the main gallery where James had numerous instruments on display. Larry offered the visitors refreshments. Simone, as Samantha Westwood, declined, but David Westwood gladly accepted a chilled glass of Perrier. The three took seats among the baroque style furnishings. "As we discussed on the phone, my partner, James Dickerson is away today. In the event that you have any questions that I can't answer, I'll make sure to discuss them with James and get back to you."

Samantha spoke first. "I know we kind of popped in on the spur of the moment. We're just in town for the weekend. Most weekends, daddy let's us have the Gulfstream, so here we are in Boston to visit friends."

Larry laughed affably. "Well, we're glad you stopped in. How did you hear about us?"

"To be perfectly honest, I found you in the Yellow Pages," said Samantha. "Usually when we come to Boston, I drag David out antiquing." She gave a coy nod to her partner who responded with an appropriately forbearing shrug. "We decided we would do this trip a little differently. Instead of finding pieces to go in one of our houses, I thought perhaps we could look into musical instruments."

"I see," said Larry. "Are you musicians or collectors, or both?"

"Musicians," said Samantha. "That is David is a musician. He has just been awarded a seat in the National Symphony in DC." Now she glowed with pride. David shifted in his seat. He could not decide whether to lean back or continue perched, stiff-spined, on the edge of the silk covered chair. "To celebrate, I've been wanting to get him a viola that reflects his talents and his new position. Unfortunately, this is easier said than done I've found out. There aren't that many violas floating around that are up to the standard we are looking for."

"I see," said Larry. "What in particular do you have in mind?"

"Well, it would have to be something a few cuts above what he's playing now." Samantha turned to David, who was beginning to feel like a small child in a shoe store, sitting between his mom and the salesman. "What is your current viola again?"

"It's a Georges Chanot, 1827." He had been repeating these details in his head since learning them on the taxi ride over. Samantha had handed him a page photocopied out of a reference book. The page now sat folded in his breast pocket. "Uh... It actually has a beautiful sound. I've played it for ten years. I paid around twenty-five for it. I have no complaints, but... Well, I've always wondered what it might be like to own a real Italian masterpiece."

"Honey, you're moving up," said Samantha. "We've got to make sure your instrument keeps up with you. I saw the way that Anja Mironov turned up her nose when you told her about your viola. She thinks she's better than you because she plays a Grancino that's a hundred year's older than yours. Well, I'm not having that. We're going to show her. When we find what we're looking for, it will be daddy's and my present to you."

"We have two violas in our in-house collection," said Larry, suppressing amusement at Samantha's determination to dominate her social milieu, taking no prisoners. He stood and walked to a glass display case on the wall. He read the calligraphy on the small white cards propped in front of each instrument. "This is a Tommaso Eberle from 1780 and here we have a... Ferdinando Gagliano from 1778. These are very fine instruments. Their sound is magnificent. You'll likely find that their Neapolitan origins give them a different tone than the French viola you've been playing."

"How much are they?" asked Samantha without awaiting her husband's reaction.

"The Eberle is offered at nine thousand five hundred. The Gagliano is available for thirty-four thousand six hundred."

Samantha frowned in disappointment. "Oh," she said. "You don't have anything that is more... *upscale*?"

"I'm afraid not at the moment," said Larry. "But let me check my files in the back to see if we have any clients who are in the market to sell an upscale viola. I'm not aware of any, but I'll have a look in case James has added something that slipped by me. Feel free to look around."

While Larry disappeared into the rear of the shop for several minutes, Samantha and David browsed the inventory on display. Samantha drifted over to the luthier's workshop area and nodded in appreciation of the enviable collection of expert tools and finely crafted works-in-progress. The two visitors had the feeling that it would be unwise to break character and risk exposure as pretenders, even though the visit did not seem to be yielding any useful insights. Thus, they simply wandered the well-appointed space, like silent strangers in a museum.

When Larry returned, he was shaking his head with regret. "I had hoped I might find something in the client files, but I just don't have anything at the moment. I would be delighted to take down your contact information in order to reach you in the event something comes in, which is entirely possible." Larry held out a pencil and small note pad.

Samantha and David stared at one another, momentarily dumbstruck by the simple request. For once, it was David who took the initiative. "Right. We'd appreciate that. I'll give you my email address." He made a quick scribble on the pad and returned it to Larry who gave it a perfunctory glance and then read it again.

"Puffmeister?" said Larry.

Simone stared at the floor and David grinned sheepishly. "That's the best way to reach me," was all he said.

"Okay, then," said Larry. "Otherwise, is there anything else I can show you while you are here?"

"No thank you, Mr. Giles," said Samantha. "We appreciate you taking the time."

"One other thing," said Larry. "I don't know if it will lead anywhere, but a dealer called on us recently. We had never dealt with him before. He was apparently in town beating the bushes. I wouldn't even mention it except that he made reference to representing a client on some high dollar instruments that he planned to place at Sotheby's in the fall. I believe he said there was a viola in the lot. He left a card. If he has something of interest, you may be able to get a jump on the auction." Larry extracted a business card from his shirt pocket and extended it to Simone.

She glanced at the card and nodded her head in appreciation. "Yes. Thank you. We'll have to give Mr. Overby a call."

Duncan and Simone left Allegro Antiquities and walked briskly down toward the river. The taxi driver had said that Charles Street was only a few minutes down the hill and had lots of shops and restaurants. They headed in that direction automatically since they had agreed beforehand to do so, but sightseeing was not foremost in their minds. After a block or so, Duncan slipped off his jacket and glanced behind him. The cool atmosphere of Allegro had not prevented dark patches of moisture from expanding beneath his arms and between the shoulders of his starched, white dress shirt. The two had not spoken since leaving, and they continued, oblivious to the quaint, historic surroundings. They seemed to be concentrating on the worn, red brick sidewalk baking beneath their feet. The card Larry handed over provided them with the missing piece of the puzzle, and neither quite knew what to say.

Finally, Simone handed the card to Duncan. He examined it as they walked, now slowing their pace to a more leisurely stroll. "I'd say now we have what we need to go to the police," she said.

Duncan did not respond. He was preoccupied with Dale Overby's business card.

"We now have evidence to connect Alex and his strange behavior to Nils's purchase of the Amati," she said. "He was obviously working with James Dickerson. He made calls to Dickerson around the time your viola was stolen. Then somebody named Overby sells Nils a viola identical to yours— probably fabricated in that workshop we saw back there. This card proves that Overby is connected to Dickerson. Who knows, they may be the same guy. Or maybe Larry Giles is Overby. In any case, the chain is complete."

Duncan just kept walking in silence.

"This is all good, right?" she said, looking at Duncan quizzically. "We learned what we came to find out. We have enough to let the police sort out the rest. Now we can just be plain old tourists."

"What about my viola?" Duncan said. "Where's my viola?"

Simone stopped and peered up at Duncan, who paused as well. She wiped her wet forehead with the back of her wet hand. "Dickerson has it somewhere. You saw their workshop. They obviously made the fake that Nils bought and they've got yours under wraps. Don't tell me you're interested in trying to find it ourselves, because *that* would get *sticky*."

Duncan laughed. He was more himself now, he seemed to have shaken the cobwebs from his mind. "A couple of things bother me," he said. "It bothers me that we didn't get to see Dickerson, unless he's like the Wizard of Oz and Larry Giles is really Dickerson. But it mostly bothers me that my viola is still missing. To be honest, until back there, I didn't expect this trip would get us anything other than maybe embarrassment for being exposed as imposters. Now, I see that you were right all along and we've got proof of everything except the whereabouts of my viola, which is ostensibly the point of the whole exercise."

"But that's where the police come in," she said. "We give them all the evidence and they track down your viola."

"Or we have Samantha and David track it down."

Twenty minutes later, they ducked into a little bistro and ordered a couple of sodas while they sat at a small corner table considering the options on the laminated menus. It was a good half an hour before noon, and the place was still making cool, unhurried preparations for the lunchtime rush.

"So, what do you want to do?" said Simone.

"I'm not really that hungry," said Duncan. "I'll probably go with the gazpacho. What about you?"

"I mean what do you want to do about the viola?"

"Larry suggested we call Overby. That's exactly what I think we should do."

"I'm not sure where this bravado has come from," said Simone, shaking her head and breaking off a piece of bread from the basket the waiter delivered with their sodas. "You said you didn't want any confrontations. Calling Overby feels like it could only lead to a confrontation."

"I'm not looking for a confrontation," he said. "But I've decided that I do want to track down the viola. I'm worried that if we get the police involved asking questions, these guys will dispose of it somehow and it will be gone." He laid Overby's business card on the wooden table and poked it firmly with his index finger. "Or we can RSVP to this engraved invitation and see where it leads."

"What have you done with the Duncan that I flew up here with?" she said with a laugh. "He didn't even like the thought of making phone calls that might ruffle feathers."

"Okay, I know this is a complete reversal for me," he said. "It's just that I had written off the viola as done and gone. I've been trying to turn over a new leaf and to let go of old baggage. I guess I considered the viola as a symbol of what I was letting go of, so I wasn't interested in hearing about resurrecting it. But you know what? I'm realizing how very special it is to me. I still remember that awestruck feeling I had when my Pappy told me he was passing along a sacred trust. I remember how proud I felt when I played for him and my parents, and how proud they were of me. I've decided it's worth some effort on behalf of my Pappy's sacred trust. And if I hold in my hand the key to get his viola back, damn it, I owe it to him and to myself to use it."

Simone just gazed back at him for a moment. She leaned forward and placed her elbows on the table, resting her chin in her upturned palms. "Well, then," she said. "There's no time like the present."

"My thoughts exactly," he replied.

A moment later a voice was speaking out of Duncan's cell phone. "Overby International. This is Dale Overby."

"Mr. Overby, my name is David Westwood..."

The two spoke for several minutes during which Mr. Overby informed David Westwood that indeed he had a rare masterpiece viola, made in 1661 by Nicolò Amati. Overby was visiting the east coast having just transferred his client's collection to Sotheby's in New York. At the moment, Overby was in Boston on various business engagements, including giving a private showing of the Amati. So, as luck would have it, he had the Amati with him. David expressed a keen desire to see the rare viola, given that he was avidly in the market for just such an instrument.

"So, it's settled," said David Westwood. "We'll see you in our suite at the InterContinental at seven o'clock."

Duncan flipped shut the phone and placed it on the table. Simone sat across from him, motionless, her mouth slightly agape. Her trance broke when the waiter appeared at their table for the second time to take their order. Duncan promised they would be ready in two minutes. "We're meeting with Overby tonight?" she said. "Since when did we have a suite at the InterContinental? Where did you pull that from?"

"I saw a spread on it in the airline magazine," he said. "It was the only ritzy hotel I could think of. I sure hope they have a suite available. I suppose it will cost a bit more than our two rooms at the Best Western."

With a nominal discount thanks to Simone's automobile club membership, a night in a junior suite at the InterContinental still cost over six hundred dollars. Duncan paid all of it himself since it was his idea. He expected expensive, but he had to swallow a gasp when the hotel clerk announced the rate.

"Junior suite. You'd think for that price, they could come up with a name that didn't sound like you're getting something from the kids menu," he said as he and Simone rode the elevator up to their floor. Duncan had declined the offer of assistance with their hand luggage.

Despite its diminutive name, the suite did not disappoint. Its opulent furnishings and panoramic view of the waterfront district would certainly match the expensive tastes of Samantha and David Westwood, having ostensibly just whizzed into town in the family's private jet for a weekend of affluent merry-making. It had taken some extra discussion at check-in for Duncan to arrange with the clerk for the suite to appear in the guest directory under David Westwood and not the name on the credit card that paid for it.

A few minutes after seven, Overby phoned the Westwoods from the lobby. David gave him the suite number and invited him to come up.

"Are you sure about this?" said Simone. "If he walks in with your viola, what are you going to do? If we're right about this guy, he's a criminal. Who knows what he's capable of."

Duncan rubbed the back of his neck and bit his lip as he reflected on this thought. He had prepared himself for a verbal confrontation, but the possibility of physical danger had not occurred to him. "I don't intend to start a fight with the guy," he said. "But maybe it would be a good idea if you stepped out. Nothing's going to happen, but there's no need for you to get tangled up in some kind of argument."

"Wouldn't it be better to have two of us?" she said. "Safety in numbers."

Before Duncan could reply there was a wrap at the door. "Shit," he hissed. "Go hide in the bedroom." He made a frantic underhanded wave toward the other room to shoo her out.

Simone smirked. "That's absurd. I'm not going to do that."

"Okay. We're fine. Just relax." He straightened his already-straight tie, tugged down on his jacket lapels and went to the door.

Dale Overby glided into the room, the picture of confident sophistication in his double-breasted Savile Row suit. On this occasion, given the season, he had dispensed with the bowler hat. He carried at his side an oblong aluminum case, apparently identical to the one that Nils had brought to Duval Violins when he was making his purchase from Overby.

After brief introductions, David Westwood invited Overby into the suite's elegant seating area, arranged before a granite-lined hearth. Overby laid the case gently on the ornate mahogany coffee table at the center of the seating area. "It is such a coincidence that we should cross paths here in Boston," said Overby. "I understand you are in town just for a few days. I'm passing through as well, departing tomorrow to reunite the Amati viola with the remainder of my client's collection at Sotheby's in New York, and then it's back to LA."

In contrast to the morning's encounter at Allegro Antiquities, it was David Westwood who seemed inclined to speak for the couple's interests. "Truly a stroke of luck," said David. He glanced optimistically at his partner, who, like himself, hoped her nervousness was not evident. David rubbed his hands together. "So, can we take a look at what you've brought?"

"I would be delighted," said Overby. He had a pair of cotton gloves at the ready in his jacket pocket. As with the Nilsson transaction, he took great care that he should touch nothing on the case or the instrument other than the handle of the case, and this he would inconspicuously wipe clean with the gloves themselves. He did not expect to leave the viola behind this evening, but it never hurt to be prudent. Overby explained his client's insistence about the gloves and he went on to provide a brief review of Nicolò Amati and the particular hallmarks that he imparted to the viola he was about to show them.

Now Overby had all the latches raised and his white-gloved hands rested lightly on the exterior of the still-closed case. "Mr. and Mrs. Westwood, you are about to see a rare treasure of baroque instrument-making, crafted by a master of masters." He lifted the lid proudly and rotated the case to give full view to the Westwood's. The two clients inhaled in nervous unison, reasonably interpreted by Overby as the result of his careful build-up.

With soft cotton hands and earnest eyes, David and Samantha examined the viola with Overby's gracious encouragement. They nodded their heads and expressed certainty that this was indeed exactly what they had in mind. Samantha rubbed her gloved finger on the top of the scroll. "This is quite a scratch," she said. "I'll bet there's a story there."

"I'm sure there is," said Overby. "Alas, it is lost to history. Unfortunately, while there is complete paperwork to authenticate the origins of this viola, we'll never know its full, no doubt colorful, three and a half century saga."

Samantha cast an amused glance at David, but he did not seem to be reflecting on the colorful saga that unfolded the day Beethoven's head inflicted the scratch on the scroll. Instead he maintained a straight business face. "And we are to understand that your client is willing to entertain offers before the auction in September?" said David.

"Absolutely," said Overby. "The thing about auctions is they are highly unpredictable. For every case where a bidding war erupts, there is at least one case where the reserve is not met. If an interesting offer appears before the auction, my client will be happy to consider it."

"And what would your client consider to be a reasonable offer?" said David.

Overby did not hesitate. "I am authorized to accept an offer of three hundred thousand to avoid that the piece goes on the auction block."

Duncan stood and walked to the cold fireplace, placing one foot up on the raised hearth. He held the viola by the neck and propped the elbow of the same arm onto the mantelpiece. "I don't know, Mr. Overby," he said. "I have a lower number in mind."

Overby smiled deferentially. "Although I do not have the authority to accept a lower number, I am always happy to relay any reasonable proposal to my client. What did you have in mind?"

"Zero."

A brief flash of white appeared in Overby's eyes and was gone. "I'm sorry," he said. "Did you say 'zero?' I don't understand."

"Let me explain," said Duncan. He was trying to look nonchalant in his pose by the hearth, but he suddenly felt the urgent need to move his bowels. "This viola is stolen property. It belongs to me."

Overby leapt to his feet. "This is outrageous! If you are not a serious buyer then I will ask you to return the instrument or face the serious consequences."

Now Simone was on her feet, moving behind the chair in which she had been seated. She glanced skittishly between the two men. Duncan did not move. "You can save the drama, James," he said. "James Dickerson, right? We know you're not Dale Overby. If it will make you feel any better, we're not the Westwoods."

Overby, unmasked as Dickerson, stood paralyzed, his mind racing though a variety of unpalatable options. With conscious effort, Duncan kept cool. At least the threat of explosive diarrhea seemed to have past. "If you think about it," he said. "My offer is a generous one. You hand over the viola and walk out of here. We'll just forgive and forget. Based on what Nilsson paid for that fake you sold him, I suspect you'd be coming out way ahead."

The antiquities dealer did not respond immediately. His expression was that of a petulant chess player frantically scanning the board in search of a move that would defy his opponent's declaration of checkmate. After a moment he murmured, "How do I know I can trust you?"

Duncan sensed the sigh of relief that Simone quietly breathed. He too felt a swell of confidence in his chest at the recognition that the match was over. "You don't know that you can trust me," said Duncan. "But, frankly, I don't care about you. You're not the one who stole my viola. Just leave me my instrument, along with its fancy new case, and our business is done."

Dickerson sniffed and raised his chin. His neck had gone crimson. He turned crisply and departed the room without another word.

The door clicked shut behind Dickerson, leaving the room in silence. For a moment, the two he left behind remained frozen in their poses, eyes fixed on the heavy oak door as if it might burst open anew. They soon relaxed and turned to one another in expressions of amazement that were soon overcome by laughter, a giddy sort of mirth that one might experience after surviving a first sky dive.

"Oh, my God," cried Simone. "I had no idea you were going to just swipe it back from him."

"I didn't know what I was going to do either, but as soon as I saw my viola, it all became clear."

"You don't think he'll be back?"

"Are you kidding?" Duncan collapsed onto the nearby loveseat, still holding the viola by the neck. "He got a very nice payday out of Nils. Coming back after us can only have downside for him. And by the way, we haven't done anything wrong."

Simone moved from behind her chair and slid into the place next to Duncan. "So, what do you plan to do next?"

Duncan smiled philosophically. He leaned forward and placed the viola back in its case. "First, I'm going to take off these ridiculous white gloves. If I had a top hat, I'd be perfectly dressed to extract a rabbit from it." He flung the gloves behind his head.

Simone gave Duncan's shoulder a playful shove. "I mean what do you plan to do when we get back—about Alex and Nils?"

"Ms. Duval, you mustn't trouble me with these matters of business. Can't you appreciate that we're on vacation?"

"Well, I do hate to be a trouble," she said. She reached over and pinched the knot of his necktie and glided her hand down its length giving it a tug when she reached the end. "But I do feel obligated to point out that we *have* done something wrong."

"And what might that be?"

"There's only one bed. It looks like we're going to have to share."

CHAPTER TWENTY-TWO ───────────────────────

Back in town after the eventful weekend in Boston, Simone bustled about her shop with her feather duster, flicking away the fine layer of particles that had begun to accumulate on the inventory during her absence. As she hummed contentedly, Alex's still-gleaming Lexus sped to a stop in front of the shop. He popped out quickly and jogged up the walk. He was soon standing inside with the door tinkling to a close at his back. Having seen through the window that it was Alex arriving, Simone continued her dusting for a few more strokes.

"Hey, baby," he said with a confident grin as he slid his aviator glasses onto the top of his head. Simone noticed that these shades were a new addition to Alex's summertime ensemble of work boots, blue jeans and a t-shirt. "I was glad you called. Have you been missing me like I have been missing you?"

"Probably," she said. Her smile was neither warm nor cold. She came to the front and moved deftly behind the counter lest Alex attempt some affectionate grope. "But that's not why I called, Alex." She raised her voice half a notch when she spoke his name."

Following that cue, Duncan emerged from the workshop, where he had been applying a coat of paint over the obscenities on the two doors. "Hi, Alex," said Duncan. "I thought I heard you out here."

Alex pressed his lips together and glared from Duncan to Simone. To her he said, "So I guess your old boy friend is all moved in now. Did you call me over here to show off your new living arrangements? Well, news flash, I don't give a shit." Alex turned to leave.

"Hold up, Alex," said Duncan. "I'm the one who wanted to talk to you. Not Simone. It has nothing to do with anybody's living arrangements, although that is none of your business." He took the opportunity to slip his arm around Simone's waist. "I actually wanted to let you know that I got my old viola back."

Alex froze. He turned slowly and squared to face Duncan. At first Alex only squinted suspiciously at his erstwhile victim. Somehow Duncan must have located the burnt viola carcass in the dumpster behind The Cavern. KG probably blabbed or, more likely, was tricked into blabbing. "Well... good for you. It was worthless. Those vandals were bound to chuck it somewhere."

"You don't understand. I got my viola back. I'm not talking about that piece of junk you burned up with my car."

Alex crossed his arms and inflated his chest, taking on what he estimated to be an imposing attitude, but his jittery eyelids defeated his intent. For the first time, it occurred to Simone that Alex did not resemble her father at all. Alex was more like a troll. "I don't know what you're talking about," said Alex defiantly.

"I'm talking about you destroying my car and selling my viola to your friend James Dickerson," said Duncan. "I'm talking about you trashing this shop in order to get rid of the substitute viola that wasn't supposed to survive the car fire." Duncan would not mention his knowledge of the fraudulent sale to Nils. "To get my viola back from Dickerson, Simone and I had to fly all the way up to Boston."

Alex took a step back. He looked cornered. He looked like he might run out the door.

"Settle down, Alex," said Duncan. "There's no need for this to end badly. I've got my viola back. If you will just compensate me for my other losses, I think we can all just walk away."

"What is it you want?"

"Well, mainly I think it's only fair that you should replace my car," said Duncan. "I've already got one all picked out."

"That old Honda of yours was not worth much. I hope you don't think you should get a brand new car for it."

"Not at all. I'll be happy with a used car. I'll settle for your Lexus, parked right out front."

"There is no way you are getting my Lexus." Alex took two aggressive steps toward the counter. Having had the experience of Dickerson's impotent outburst only three nights before, neither Duncan nor Simone felt particularly threatened. "I spent all the money I had on that, plus trading in my truck. You are dreaming if you think that old Honda of yours is a fair trade for my Lexus."

"I'm afraid I just have my heart set on it," said Duncan. "No other car will do. I can see how you wouldn't want to part with it, but honestly, I doubt they'll let you drive it while you are serving time for grand theft auto and arson and destruction of property. On the upside, you may finally be recognized as a gifted and prolific painter of penises."

"Okay, I think we will call it a night. Good work everyone." said Theo van Winkle from the podium beneath one of the basketball goals in the Holy Trinity Lutheran Church gymnasium. The musicians of the Church Hill Philharmonic began to rustle like students when the bell is about to ring at the end of a class. Before the scene melted into complete disarray, Theo raised his voice for a few parting comments. "We've all gotten a little rusty over the summer. I need you working on your parts so when we come in here next time, we can really role up our sleeves and unpack the passion. I'm excited about our new season. The fall concert will be here before we know it so, please, *practice, practice, practice.*"

The atmosphere in the gymnasium shifted to the restrained chaos of post rehearsal as the musicians jockeyed like ants to reunite their instruments with the respective carrying cases in the bleachers and along the walls. Each player was also expected to deliver at least one chair to the seven-high stacks along the south wall. Mr. Hanes, as usual, oversaw this effort. His punctilious philosophy was that each musician sat in a chair and each musician should stack that chair, but he had long ago reluctantly accepted the distasteful reality that some musicians stacked multiple chairs, and some stacked none at all.

One of the musicians, who had never stacked a single chair during many seasons of membership in the Philharmonic, came over to Duncan as he stood up from snapping shut the latches on his brushed aluminum viola case. "Duncan Flowers," said Nils Nilsson. "What a pleasant surprise to have you back in the fold."

"Hi, Nils," said Duncan as the two shook hands. "It's nice to be back."

"Did you notice that we're scheduled to play a Gershwin piece in the spring. I imagine you'll be looking forward to that given your penchant for Broadway tunes."

Duncan laughed as if he thought Nils were genuinely funny. "I can't wait," he said. "So, will you be playing the Strad or the del Gesù this season?"

"Neither. Those instruments should be played by virtuosos. I had my little show. I'm just happy to be associated with them and the quartet collection. We hope to complete auditions for the Nilsson Quartet over the next several months. We expect they will tour and record beginning next year."

"That reminds me," said Duncan. "I planned to chat with you anyway about some amazing news I just got about my viola. I don't know if you recall my old viola. I got it from my grandfather. I've played it all my life."

"What about your viola?" Nils had no more interest in whatever viola Duncan played than he had in stacking chairs after rehearsal.

"My grandfather told me that the viola he gave me was an old Italian masterpiece," said Duncan. "But nobody in the family ever believed him because he tended to tell tall tales, plus at the time he was pretty senile. Anyway, just for the heck of it, I finally took it up to the Smithsonian to get their opinion on it. It turns out that my viola is an authentic Nicolò Amati from 1661. Unbelievable!"

Nils cocked his head and raised an eyebrow. He seemed to be considering the purpose of Duncan's absurd claim. "You mean to tell me that you just happened to be walking around with an original Amati viola?"

"Apparently my grandfather's story was accurate," said Duncan. "He told of receiving it as a gift from a dying old man who had been a collector. The man had no remaining family and offered the viola to my grandfather, who had become like a son to the man. According to the Smithsonian, my viola perfectly matches the description of one that had once belonged to a wealthy collector named Gutmann. It was the only catalogued surviving Amati viola whose whereabouts were unaccounted for."

Nils still appeared uncertain of what to make of Duncan's story.

"I told the curator at the Smithsonian that this was such a huge coincidence because my former quartet partner had just purchased a *1664* Amati viola," Duncan continued. "He found this intriguing since, according to him, that would represent a new, uncatalogued Amati entering the scene, which would be very exciting. I'm sure you have your resources you work with, but if you ever want the curator's name, just let me know. He'd love to have a look at your viola."

Now Nils's expression sagged. He looked as if he might be working up the courage to swallow a freshly administered spoonful of cod liver oil. "I must say that among my collection, the Amati seems to have gotten the most attention." Having swallowed the medicine, he flashed into annoyance at the person feeding it to him. "Frankly, the viola was an afterthought. They usually are. I've gotten numerous calls from so-called experts who have learned about my purchase and want to get a close look at the Amati. But having put the collection together based on impeccable documentation, I'm no longer interested in appraisals. I'm interested in letting the instruments do what they were designed to do, *play.*"

"Sounds good to me," said Duncan lifting up his case, which Nils noticed for the first time as identical to the one he got from Overby. "See you at the next rehearsal." Duncan patted Nils on the upper arm as he strode by to grab a chair and tote it with his free hand across the room to the nearly completed formation of little chair towers. Nils dropped into a nearby unclaimed chair and sat motionless and distracted. Duncan Flowers and all the other musicians had departed when a harsh voice jolted him back into the moment. It was Mr. Hanes.

"Up and at 'em. I've got to lock up. Get your chair stacked."

The River Road Ravens won their homecoming game against cross-town rivals, the Tuckahoe Tigers. Duncan took Simone to the game, arriving during half time since the shop was open half-day on Saturday's. She was still breaking in her new assistant, a severely nearsighted young woman who had just finished a two-year degree at Patrick Henry Community College.

Now they had returned to Duncan's house and were spending the mellowing hours of the ripe, cloudless fall day working in Duncan's shabby yard. "I feel terrible having you spend your Saturday afternoon doing tedious manual labor," said Duncan. The two were squatting on the crumbling sidewalk pulling weeds from between the ubiquitous cracks.

"Are you kidding," said Simone. Her tanned face glowed with a misty sheen of perspiration. "I adore the outdoors and getting my hands dirty. This is just what I need after spending all week in the shop."

"Well, over the past couple of months your odd taste in recreation has gotten my place looking downright stylish, both inside and out"

Simone smiled and continued her relentless grooming of the concrete jumble beneath her. A placid, baritone voice emerged from around the side of the house. "*Miss* Duval and *Mister* Flowers," said Willie Hamilton. "How are my favorite neighbors? I just had to come say hello on this fine afternoon."

Duncan and Simone uncoiled from their crouches, feeling stiff and grateful for a pause. Simone felt a small twitter of pride in her chest at being considered a full-fledged neighbor. Duncan arched himself backward and grimaced as he worked to reassume normal posture. "Willie, you have arrived not a moment too soon," said Duncan. "We got so distracted that we almost worked straight through the cocktail hour. It's time for me to have a beer. I hope you're thirsty."

"Well, I suppose it is getting to be about that time," said Willie. "Why not."

"Simone, what can I get you?" said Duncan as he trotted up the nearly denuded walkway. "I'll have what you boys are having."

The three sat on the stoop, with Simone in the middle. Willie took up half the available space. Seated, he had roughly the dimensions of a washing machine. After swallowing his first zestful slurp of beer, he motioned with his can out toward the street. "How are you liking that Lexus?"

"I love it," said Duncan. "I just had it in for its fifteen thousand mile check-up."

"That's my man."

"Yep. I've taken your advice to heart. Better overall care and maintenance."